Richard Malcolm Johnston

# Widow Guthrie

A novel

Richard Malcolm Johnston

**Widow Guthrie**
*A novel*

ISBN/EAN: 9783337000486

Printed in Europe, USA, Canada, Australia, Japan

Cover: Foto ©Andreas Hilbeck / pixelio.de

More available books at **www.hansebooks.com**

# WIDOW GUTHRIE

*A NOVEL*

BY

RICHARD MALCOLM JOHNSTON

ILLUSTRATED BY E. W. KEMBLE

NEW YORK
D. APPLETON AND COMPANY
1890

TO THOSE

SURVIVORS AMONG THE ASSOCIATES OF MY YOUTH

TO WHOM, AS TO ME,

THE OLD GEORGIA SEEMS TO HAVE BEEN

MORE HAPPY THAN THE NEW,

THIS VOLUME IS AFFECTIONATELY DEDICATED.

# CONTENTS.

# ILLUSTRATIONS.

# WIDOW GUTHRIE.

## CHAPTER I.

### CLARKE.

Among those Virginians who, some before, others after the War of Independence, settled upon the fertile lands bordering on Broad River, in the State of Georgia, were the Guthries, Macfarlanes, and Ludwells. With considerable properties at their coming, they had availed themselves of abundant opportunities, and become what was then regarded wealthy. Dennis Macfarlane, when about thirty-five, married Louisa Pollard, whose people had come into the settlement later. Alan Guthrie, considerably his senior, five or six years after, being a childless widower of fifty, took to wife Hester Pollard, who was ten years older than her sister. Some time prior to the incidents hereinafter narrated, the brothers-in-law, while holding and continuing to work their plantations, removed a day's journey south to Clarke, a village of about five hundred inhabitants, situated on an elevated plain sixty miles west of Augusta. Mr. Macfarlane built a large handsome two-story frame dwelling in a spacious grove of red oak and hickory at the west end; and Mr. Guthrie did the like at the east, his wide piazza contrasting well with the deep portico and lofty

Doric pillars of Mr. Macfarlane's. Of the three Macfarlane children, only Charlotte, lately come to womanhood, remained with her parents, her older brothers, James and Malcolm, both married, dwelling upon their plantations, which had been assigned to them by their father off the large tract owned by himself. Ten years back Alan Guthrie deceased, leaving his widow and his two minor children, Caroline and Duncan. Caroline was now wife to John Stapleton, a planter of moderate means, living near Little River, ten miles below the village. Her brother, somewhat more than a year back, had married Alice Ludwell, who, with Charlotte Macfarlane, had but lately returned from Mrs. Willard's school at Troy, New York. These were living in a red brick house with white piazza about two hundred yards from the street extending north, at half a mile's distance from the court house square.

A church building, commodious and reasonably tasteful, had been erected by each of the religious denominations, Baptist, Methodist, and Presbyterian, and, chiefly through the enterprise of Mr. Macfarlane and Mr. Guthrie, a large sightly academy for girls. This institution, after a varied experience, had lately risen into much reputation under the management of Mr. Wendell, a Boston man—large, erect, of light complexion, thoroughly educated in books, manners, and discipline —and now it had near a hundred and twenty pupils, more than half of whom were boarders. The head master dwelt in a roomy, irregular mansion opposite that of Mrs. Alan Guthrie. Boarding with his family, ·besides a dozen girls, was Miss Sarah Jewell, his cousin, who had lately come to be, with Anna Wendell, his daughter—a rather *petite* brunette—an assistant in the school, particularly in music, drawing, and painting. Entirely faithful to her school engagements, for which she was known to be more than competent, she was much more gay than Anna Wendell, and more fond of being in society, with the best of which she soon became familiar. Until her coming Charlotte Macfarlane had been regarded as perhaps the best musician and the beauty of the village, although if Alice Guthrie had not been a married woman judgment on neither of these accomplishments might have been unanimous. Yet Charlotte, of similar make to the New Englander, blonde like her, though less tall, from the beginning seemed willing to accord to her all that was due.

Duncan Guthrie was a graduate of Yale. A lawyer, he gave promise of making a good professional career if he should rid himself of some drawbacks which were attributed to the well-known fact of being his mother's favorite, expectant of a large fortune from her and another from his father-in-law. About five feet ten, fair, excellently rounded in shape, always tasteful in dress, fascinating in speech, he had won Alice Ludwell more easily perhaps because the seriousness in her being had need to be joined with what it felt to be wanting. Of medium height, not a blonde, yet not quite a brunette, her smooth white face that lit up sometimes, not very often, with redness, harmonized with her brown hair and browner eyes. Her voice was sweet, and when she smiled, whether while talking or listening, people regarded her as beautiful as she was lovely.

Sixty years ago the controlling tone of society in Clarke and three or four neighboring county seats was high.  Not avowedly or conventionally aristocratic, it could not fail to be so to a degree natural and fit from the easy superiority of a few families of wealth and culture whose forbears in the old State were known to have been among the best.  It had not to be aggressive or supercilious in order to support natural and necessary leadership.  It was somewhat more exclusive in the villages than in rural districts as will be seen farther on, yet even here its ascendency was as well marked.  Mr. Macfarlane, now sixty-five, would not have owned that he regarded himself better than any other honest born, honorable man ; yet many a one of this sort, after calling upon him at his residence about a matter of business, feeling for the time being sufficiently at his ease, when the business was over, chose to leave rather than remain, with a consciousness that his company could add little to that gentleman's enjoyment. Yet that very man looked up to him with affection as well as respect, and would elect him over any of his own likes to offices of public trust.  Mrs. Macfarlane once small, dainty of shape, had taken on a fleshiness not uncomely.  She had a gentle disposition that always had yielded cheerful assent to her husband's rule, yet kept her individuality and the loyal love and admiration that she had won from him.  Between her and her sister, intercourse, never very affectionate, had been less so since her marriage, still less since the latter's widowhood.  Mrs. Guthrie, much taller and stouter, was of imperious temper, and had always seemed to regard her junior as much below herself in other respects as she was in physical structure.  They visited each other at intervals decent enough considering that

the elder seldom went abroad, and, if for no other reason than that Mrs. Macfarlane could not have been
drawn into disputes, they never had them. Indeed,
Mrs. Guthrie during her widowhood had grown to
doubt if in business matters Mr. Macfarlane, despite
his reputation in that line, was fully her equal, and this
thought had added to her reconciliation to an old disappointment. The estate left by her husband, at his
death about equal to that of Mr. Macfarlane, through
the management of herself as executrix, had grown to
be at least twenty per cent larger than his, a fact of
which she was not sure that he was not rather ashamed.
In her the feeling of class was more pronounced than in
any other in that whole region, not even excepting her
son Duncan. Proud of the ancient connection of her
family and its set with the English Church, she despised
the sects which were overrunning that region to the
bane, as she believed, of honest religion and good society. She attended with some regularity public religious services, mainly in the Presbyterian Church, but
her demeanor even then, cold and rigid, indicated that
she was there because of no opportunity of attending
a more decent worship elsewhere. Untiring in energy,
exacting of service from subordinates, a lender of moneys at the highest interest possible and a shaver of notes
at the lowest, eager to restlessness for the accumulation
of property, yet she kept the most costly establishment
in town, her servants were most devoted to her, and
although she never went to a party of pleasure, she
occasionally gave one as if to let people see that she
could get up such a thing and conduct it better than
any other woman of their acquaintance.

Between such a woman and her daughter-in-law
relations could not be very closely affectionate, although
the former was well pleased at her son's marriage. As
if in foresight of this, she provided a residence for
them to occupy and everything needed for their living
in comfortable, even luxurious style, and she hoped,
even to anxiety, that the bride would never subtract
from the affection of Duncan for herself, a possession
prized above all others. Of her relations toward her
daughter I will tell later.

----

## CHAPTER II.

### THOMAS TOLLY.

Among other native families of proximate if not
quite equal social rank with the two aforementioned were
the Jamisons, whose home was picturesquely situated
between the court house square and the Macfarlanes.
Arthur Jamison, never an eloquent advocate, but always
a reliable counselor, when at seventy would have liked
to retire on the sufficient fortune gathered in a long
professional career, and now, three years later, he regretted that he had not done so. One day he said to
Alfred, his son and partner, for whose sake he had been
lingering this while in what he had hoped would be, or
at least appear, a merely nominal connection:

"Alfred, I'm going to do at Christmas what I see
now that I ought to have done when you came to the

bar. I made the same mistake as many old lawyers who think to bring on their sons faster by hanging on to their offices after it has got to be time for them to retire. I find that I've been doing you more harm than good, to say nothing of failing of the rest to which I think that an old man who has worked as hard as I have is entitled. Not only our clients depend upon me, but you also. That must stop at the end of this year. If you are ever to be a lawyer you've got to lean only on yourself."

The young man did not complain. There was too much of acquired prosperity in the family for that. Amiable, gentlemanlike in all his ways, he did not neglect business, and went along as if satisfied with what progress he was making.

Much faster was the rise of Thomas Tolly, son of a plain farmer on Little River. After graduating at the State College and studying law in the office of the Jamisons, he had rented one in the court house, and, although only two years at the bar, had made several good hits by his management of cases which, not very important as to the amount of money in litigation, required talent, learning, and skill to conduct to successful issues. He was not quick to part from country manners and especially country speech, for the latter of which many men of highest eminence in the rural region used to have much fondness. Rather tall, bushy haired, stalwart, not unhandsome, he moved with satisfactory ease in the best company to which his acknowledged abilities gave him access, and he did not seem to feel it worth while to be in a hurry to obtain the position, professional or social, to which his hopes pointed. The one there least cordial toward him was Guthrie. He seemed to like not that an awkward youth fresh from the country, about whose ancestors not even any of the family had anything special to say, the property of whose father, although respectable, in comparison with the Guthrie and other like estates was scant, who had never been further from home than Athens, the seat of the State College, fifty miles distant, should demean as if he felt himself to be anybody's equal.

"I think I have about sized Tolly," he said one day at his home to Charlotte Macfarlane. "He has a right good education and some talent, which, if he wasn't so well satisfied already, might lead to—to a reasonable height. But the luck he has had in a few petty cases, and the praise he has got from Judge Ansley, who compliments every young lawyer at the start, have turned his head and even kept him from trying to get rid of his country manners. He believes his standing at the bar and in society to be good enough already. He won a case from me last court because the judge ruled plainly against the law; and it put him into such glee that but for the presence of the Court I should have said to him that he was making much of a very small matter."

"I think he is handsome and right interesting, don't you, Alice?" said Charlotte.

"Yes, rather good-looking. I've not seen very much of him; but he impressed me as an uncommonly intelligent, simple-minded, earnest, upright young man. I think he's handsomer than when I first knew him."

"Oh, yes," said Guthrie, "let a young man have moderately good looks, be tolerably smart, known to be ambitious, and single withal—these are enough to win the admiration of young women, married or unmarried.''

"And that speech," retorted Charlotte, "was made by a married man—married to the finest woman in town —who, more than any unmarried man that I have heard, praises the beauty and vivacity of Miss Jewell."

Guthrie glanced at his wife, whose downward look showed that these words were not pleasing to her car. The girl hastened to qualify them by saying:

"I was exaggerating there, Cousin Duncan; but, indeed, I can't see how anybody, man or woman, can help admiring Miss Jewell. I regard her as rather the most variously gifted woman that I ever knew."

He waited for his wife to reply.

"Miss Jewell is beautiful," said the latter, "very, and an excellent pianist. I should admire her more but for what seemed to me the few times I have met her rather too much consciousness of her gifts; for instance, at Mrs. Jamison's that evening last week, I thought she was somewhat patronizing toward Anna Wendell, who, quite accomplished herself, is very modest. Then, candidly, though I would not think of saying such a thing to anybody except you and Duncan and perhaps Sister Caroline, she acts, at least to my view, as if she had a greater preference for men's over women's society than to me seems quite becoming."

"O Alice!" said Charlotte, "I don't think you do her full justice. She and Anna love each other dearly, and Anna bears as she ought, to my notion, her cousin's efforts to make her put herself at more ease in company. Miss Jewell does like men's society, when they are bright like Cousin Duncan, and—yes I'll say like

Mr. Tolly, and I have frequently heard her express much admiration for both. Her freedom from constraint is simply the outcome of usage in good city society, which allows a woman, of course within just limits, to feel as much at ease, and have as much enjoyment in men's company as in that of women. *I* like the society of nice men myself; that I do."

"I am glad you hold such a good opinion of her," said Alice. "I am sure I would not do her wanton injustice. Indeed, it troubles me to feel that I may have done it, even unintentionally."

At this period she was not quite well. The death of a child on the day of its birth three months before was a sore distress. With no suspiciousness in her nature, yet about this young woman, whom she had met less often than her husband, she felt an indefinite apprehension, which it would have been better if he had respected.

---

## CHAPTER III.

### THE WENDELLS GIVE A PARTY.

In acknowledgment of the attentions paid to their cousin, the Wendells gave a party about two months after her arrival. Though not expensive, everything was in good taste. Miss Jewell showed to much advantage. Her dressing and the arrangement of her hair were in perfect taste, giving the best possible expression to her fine head and almost matchless figure.

Guthrie's admiration, notwithstanding the presence of his wife, was apparently without bounds. As often as he could he put himself between her and Tolly or Alfred Jamison, or other beaus, and did his best to attract her special attention throughout the evening, except when she was in conversation with his wife. At such times upon his face appeared some shadow of impatience. Alice, as I shall speak of her hereafter to distinguish from her mother-in-law, was exquisitely dressed in a gray silk gown modestly decked with laces and flowers. Though not quite well, and sitting in a corner of the parlor during most of the evening, she accepted with accustomed politeness attentions from all, men and women, who came where she was, and she seemed as if she was enjoying everything more than she had expected. Miss Jewell several times lingered while passing to one and another of the guests, and seemed as if she would like to be specially considerate of her. Alice received her as the rest of the company, but what she had to say in praise of the entertainment she said to the members of the family. Occasionally a pained expression, but only of momentary duration, was upon her face while looking at her husband; but she instantly addressed some person near her a remark, playful as conscientious politeness could make. Perhaps only Charlotte guessed at the reason for this. If Miss Jewell did, she behaved as though she did not. Yet it was from regard for others rather than for herself that Alice tried thus to conceal what she felt when from her husband's looks toward Miss Jewell, with an occasional alteration of them toward her own pale face, she was obliged to suspect him of making inwardly a comparison between herself and the splendid woman so full of health, beauty, and vivacity. Yet accustomed to society as was Miss Jewell, who must have learned to observe some of the things that do not always come up to the surface in such a company, she showed once that she felt it to be worth while to make a special effort to re-assure this young wife if herself was felt to be cause of any degree of anxiety to her.

The occasion was this : Charlotte had played several waltzes. As, in answer to universal solicitation, she began with another, Miss Jewell, her hands upon the piano moving their fingers in harmony, suddenly ex-claimed :

"O Charlotte, that is exquisite!   I *wish* I could waltz!"   Instantly Guthrie, who was standing by, ex-tending both hands, proposed to lead her forth.   Her impulse was to accept, but, looking first at Alice, then at Mr. Wendell, who at that moment was moving toward her, smiling slightly and shaking his head, she seized Anna, and with her made a few rounds.

"Ah, Miss Jewell," said Guthrie, when it was over, "you should have had a man to help you show off as it deserved that perfection of movement."

"Oh, thank you for the compliment, Mr. Guthrie. Yes, one needs strong arms in waltzing; so I played the man to Anna.   She waltzes well, doesn't she?"

"Yes, but not—"

At that moment she looked at Alice, whose eyes were upon Guthrie.   She went to her and addressed some cordially hospitable words.   Alice looked up, gave a brief, simple answer, as if in parenthesis, then turned her face away.   Miss Jewell slightly reddened, turned, went back to the piano, and did the best playing of the evening.

"How did you like that last piece, Mr. Guthrie?"

"Nothing could have been finer. Indeed, I have never been so entertained as to night."

"Mrs. Guthrie does not seem quite well," she said lowly, as her fingers ran up and down upon the keys.

"Oh, she's well enough. Mrs. Guthrie, you may know—" But she rose instantly, and went moving among the rest.

Tolly took Charlotte home.

"A very pleasant party," he said, when they had passed through the gate.

"Yes, the Wendells are nice people, and know thoroughly how to entertain, even without the help of Miss Jewell. Wasn't she fine, though? Taking her all in all, she's the finest woman I ever knew."

"I've never seen her show to quite such advantage as this evening. But I could not say with you that she's the very finest woman *I* have known. I do admire her very much, however, in every particular."

"She likes you, Mr. Tolly."

"I am delighted to hear that from such authority! Yet I have been trusting that she was one of my friends, feeling that she could not but know what high esteem I have for herself. The waltzing of hers to me seemed perfect, although I've had little acquaintance with that sport, or even with ordinary dancing. Miss Wendell's part was done well also, I thought, in spite, perhaps, of what I suspected her consciousness of inferiority to her magnificent cousin."

"Yes, it was perfectly done. Anna is a girl of much

gracefulness when she feels entirely at ease; but every woman must suffer somewhat in comparison with that exquisite creature. It was amusing to me to see how delighted Cousin Duncan was. He whispered to me that he was dying to waltz with her; but I'm rather glad that she wouldn't let him—under the circumstances. Cousin Duncan, I think, for a married man, is rather more fond of young women's society than seems quite proper. I've told him so, and so has father. But he says that he doesn't see why because a man is married he mayn't have fun like others. He has about the best wife in this whole world, and he knows it, but I wish he'd be a little more regardful of her. He is as good to her as he can be; but he's not quite as considerate as he ought to be—at least in some companies."

"Mrs. Guthrie looked to-night as if she were not quite well. Indeed, she told me she was not; but that she had come because she felt that she ought to do what she could to 'show her appreciation of the Wendells' civility."

"Yes; still she would not have come but for the insistence of Cousin Duncan. She's not *ill;* only a little out of sorts, and will soon be all right again. I'm not sure but that he'd have gone there alone, except that he knew that such a thing would not have looked well."

"To me that is strange. It seems to me that if I were a married man I should feel like giving up society except to the degree that my wife might claim my escort."

"That would be gallant, Mr. Tolly, even knightly!"

"No, it wouldn't seem any thing of the kind to

me. It would be only that I regarded her society sufficient."

"But women, married and single, you know, must
have, or they feel that they must have, other society
than domestic sometimes, if for no other reason, to gossip and listen to gossiping."

"For other reasons quite above that. What I mean
is that I should wish for my wife to regulate such vis-
itations by her own feelings and her sense of the duties
which she and I owed to society."

"But suppose you should find that she carried that
liberty to excess?"

"I could not suppose such a case. I should trust
that in such matters her judgment was better than mine,
and I am very sure that I should feel much embarrassed
in any company of gentlemen or ladies to which my
wife would decline to go, or would go reluctantly and
only for my sake."

"Then, if you had been in Cousin Duncan's place,
you would not have gone to the Wendells'."

"I certainly would not."

"Not even to meet Miss Jewell?"

"Not even to meet anybody. Though, of course,"
he added, as if he supposed that he ought, "I do not
judge Mr. Guthrie, who doubtless feels that he entirely
understands his own case."

"You've seen Alice at her home, haven't you, Mr.
Tolly?"

"No, Miss Charlotte."

She suspected that he had never been there, and it occurred to her thus to intimate her disapproval of Duncan's neglect of inviting to his house a professional brother.

"Ah! Cousin Duncan has been more careless than I would have thought, priding himself as he does in knowing all about society manners and duties. But he seems to think that Alice doesn't care about young men's society other than his own. I have sometimes berated him for never introducing a gentleman to her. It's ridiculous; he ought to know better, and he does know better. Well, if you ever *are* in that house, you will see, if there is such a person in the world, a perfect lady. As a wife, as a mistress over servants, as an arranger and manager of house matters, and as a hostess, there's never a place for an objection to her."

When he had seen her home and bidden good-night, he turned, and on his way to the tavern where he boarded ruminated on the incidents of the evening. Country-born as he was, loyal to his origin and his family, he had a head as cool as his spirit was aspiring. Charlotte was a prize above the reach of any present endeavors on his part. He knew that well enough, and, indeed, he regarded it as most probable that she always would be. Yet the rise and growth in his heart of a strong affection served to make no alteration in his habits—not even in his bi-monthly visits to his native place from Saturday night until Monday morning. In town he visited in moderation at houses to which he had been invited and knew himself to be welcome. Courteous to everybody, frank in speech and bearing, considerate toward women of every degree of property and culture, yet, when waiting upon Charlotte Macfarlane, in his manner was something which told that the interest felt for her was different from that indulged for any other. Well aware of the feeling of Guthrie, who looked upon

him at first as an audacious country upstart, and latterly
as a formidable professional rival, he was of a sort that
such hostility stiffens rather than discourages. After
conflicts at the bar, in which successes outnumbered
defeats, he felt himself stimulated to yet more determined purpose in the silent pursuit of one dear object
by thoughts of an opponent to whom he had proved a
full match elsewhere.

The courtship of a man in such circumstances is
necessarily slow. That of Thomas Tolly was too much
so for the movements of the other persons in this tale,
in which he is to take a subordinate and not sentimental
part; and so, with good wishes for his ultimate success,
I must leave out that portion of his career.

## CHAPTER IV.

### WIDOW GUTHRIE.

ANOTHER talk more or less confidential was had that
same night and at the same hour.

"Alice, I think you might have exhibited less de-
mureness to-night, and I don't well see how you can
easily excuse yourself for—what I should call rudeness
to Miss Jewell."

"I was not rude to Miss Jewell, Duncan; at least,
I did not mean to be. Her compassion of me, as I
regarded her occasional gushing cordiality, was not as
agreeable as the chat I was having with Mrs. Wendell

at the time she came to me last, and I merely wanted
to let her know it, and that I was satisfied with the hospitality I received from the family without need of her
special assurances."

"I can't divine what you mean by the use of the
word *compassion*."

"She looked as if she was rather sorry for me, I
thought."

"I'd like to know for what. For God Almighty's
sake, do tell me."

"You need not have used such an adjuration about
so small a matter as Miss Jewell's pity for me. I suppose she guessed that I was feeling bad, and thought
she might extend at least temporary relief, and decided
to do so."

"Oh, Alice, Alice! What is the use of tormenting
yourself and me also by indulging in suspicions that are
wholly without. foundation? You hurt the woman
keenly by your conduct."

"Yet she went back to the piano, and, smiling gra-
ciously upon you the while, played in a way the most
elaborate of the evening."

"Yes. And it was done in answer to your treatment of her."

"So, I regarded it, and—"

It was on her tongue to say that it was not quite
loyal of him to be so complacent at an understood instance of resentment toward his wife. But she was
weary, and so held her peace.

"Oh, well, well," he said with sudden affectionate-
ness, "I was wrong to urge you to go there against your
feelings, and I ought-not to have said what I did just

now.  You know, Alice, that I not only love you with all my heart, but admire you above all women."

And in the shadow of the cedars lining the avenue to his house, putting his hand under her chin, he lifted her face and kissed her.

It all seemed so natural that as she wept thankful and regretful tears, encircling her with his arm, he bore her within.

The next morning at the breakfast-table, Mr. Macfarlane asked his daughter:

"How did you get home last night, Charlotte?  Alfred Jamison bring you?"

"No, father, Mr. Tolly."

"Aye?  Young Tolly visits a good deal, doesn't he?"

"About the same as other young men, I think."

"How does he hold with the rest, including Duncan?  for they say *he's* as fond of going about as any of the unmarried ones, though Alice, sensible woman, isn't much on that line.  How does Tolly get along?"

"Very well, father, as far as I know.  He hasn't Cousin Duncan's polish, but he doesn't seem to care much about acquiring it, and therefore appears to be at sufficient ease.  He is certainly very courteous, and to all women alike."

"That shows sense, and principle too.  They are an independent sort of people, the Tollys, and entirely respectable; plain about like their neighbors, the Stapletons, whose coming into the family your Aunt Hester thinks such a disgrace that she won't do what she ought for Caroline.  Tolly is rising at the bar very fast, and in time, if he lives and persists on the line he's been pursuing, is bound to become a leading lawyer.  Does the fellow seem to have a fancy for any young woman in particular?"

"How should I know, father?" she answered, laughing. "I have never heard of any pronounced movement that he has made in that direction."

"That looks sensible, too; the longer a young man in his circumstances waits—that is, in reason—the better are his chances to marry to advantage. If he is not in too great a hurry, he'll get a wife if he wants one such as I suspect he couldn't get just now. If Miss Jewell had money, that might suit, provided he could get her, as I suppose he could. She and the Wendells came of good old New England stock. We made that a condition in our inquiry for a teacher. What a magnificent young woman she is! If she had been here when I was a young man, and your mother hadn't been about, there's no telling what might have happened."

He smiled as if thinking what a destiny had been missed by Miss Jewell's coming on so late.

"If you had seen her waltz last night, father, you would have thought her magnificent, indeed."

"Waltz? I didn't know that Mr. Wendell allowed waltzing in his house."

"It wasn't on a scale that would hurt, husband," said Mrs. Macfarlane. "Charlotte tells me that only Miss Jewell and Anna Wendell engaged in it. Duncan wanted to, but Mr. Wendell said no."

"Duncan! Yes, I'll be bound for Duncan getting into such as that when he can. Mr. Wendell was right. Does Tolly ever allude to John Stapleton, Charlotte?"

"Often, very often; he says that Cousin John is the best man he is acquainted with."

"Yes? Everybody thinks well of Mr. Stapleton except Hester—and Duncan, of course. Ah, me! trouble is to come of it, some time, I fear."

Indeed, here was a case which had given to the Macfarlanes much anxiety. Mrs. Guthrie, now in the sixties, in spite of her snow-white hair and furrowed face, was handsome. The original ruddiness of her complexion had been saved by energetic work and generous living. Married to a man much older than herself, after she had borne to him two children, he went into a decline. It was not a difficult matter for such a woman to obtain ascendency over a husband whose understanding dwindled faster than his physical being. Availing herself of this opportunity, assured that she was doing what was her full right to do, she induced him to execute a last will and testament in which she was nominated executrix and sole legatee. She had managed the estate well. The first child, Caroline, on coming of age, against her mother's most hostile opposition, married John Stapleton. A happy marriage it had proved, although the husband had added little to his own small patrimony and the dowry of half a dozen negroes given reluctantly and against her previous threatenings by Mrs. Guthrie. A sturdy, handsome, rather gigantic countryman, he attended with reasonable diligence to the business of his little plantation, had his hounds and his pointer, lived well, but kept himself out of debt. He worshiped his wife, and, whenever he met with her mother, treated her courteously as other elderly ladies. This was not often. He never went to her house, except to carry thither or bring away his wife, or, at the latter's request, to inquire,

when in town, about her health. Once or twice a
year Mrs. Guthrie went down in her carriage to see
her daughter, declaring every time that it was as much
as her own life was worth, to say nothing of the carriage, to travel over that awful road. Her son-in-law
listened to such complainings with polite sympathy
but never had a word to say in agreement with her de-
nunciation of the county authorities, two of whom
were his neighbors, and the other three well-known
good men. If she tarried the night he was not made
extremely unhappy by her saying she had had hardly
a wink of sleep, and he expressed neither surprise nor
gratification at her relish of the good breakfast which
his wife had provided. When she was leaving he bade
good-by as he would have done with any respectable
parting guest, and perhaps for the rest of that day was
more demonstrative than usual in words and caresses
bestowed upon his wife. The latter, a tall blonde of
much beauty, loved him with all her heart, and believed
in him as the very best of mankind.

The difference in the manner of living of her children led Mrs. Guthrie to prefer that at least her kins-
folk and her few familiar acquaintances should understand her feelings and the motives for her treatment.

"I like the creature well enough, and I'd try to
like him better if he had some manners, and if he'd show
some sort of respect for me, knowing that even if I did
think Caroline threw herself away when she married him,
still, I'm her mother and I'm entitled to be treated decently, especially as I've got the property all in my hands.
But John Stapleton is one of that kind that he don't
appear to have any more respect for property than he

has for me; and sometimes I'm not quite certain in my mind if he's got right good sense. Not that he's *dis-*respectful; because, even if Duncan was out of the case, he ought to know, I suppose, that I'm not the woman to stand such as that from him nor anybody like him; but it's his unconcern that after I've laid down my work and my business, and taken the trouble to make Moses stop his work in the garden and about the lot, and hitch the horses to the carriage, and run the risk of my life over those roads that are a shame to the whole county, he meets me and he treats me as if I was nobody but any other common country-woman; and he never says here nor there about me nor about my peace of mind except what everybody is bound to say the whole time I'm there, and not even when I come away. And every time I go there I wonder what it is in him that makes Caroline so wrapped up in him. It seems to me that she gets worse instead of better, and she won't even listen to my making over to her another family of negroes which Mr. Macfarlane kept on hinting I ought to do. She says she wants no property to come there that don't belong to John Stapleton. I'm not denying but what he's a great, tall, healthy, good-natured, and reasonably good-looking sort of a fellow; but when I was a girl such as that never moved me, and I kept myself from marrying any of them until one came that had something to back it, and was of good old Virginia stock in the bargain. Mr. Guthrie was a man that had the sense and the judgment to see he had a wife that looked into things before she plunged head-foremost into them, and that made him leave the will he did. Never mind; they'll both find out who they're

fooling with, and that to their sorrow. Now, there's
Duncan. I don't say Duncan Guthrie is any saint, nor
he doesn't set up for one. But he has never forgot
who he came from. Caroline never—not from the
time she was a child—she never appeared to feel that
her business was to help keep up the family name.
Now, Alice may think that she has some fault to find
with Duncan as a husband; but my experience of men
is that the most of them are going to do pretty much as
they please about some things, and if I was in Alice's
place, I shouldn't be bothering myself too much about
what I couldn't help. Duncan is not a quarrelsome
person, and, with me to help him, is a splendid pro-
vider. His wife had family, and she had property;
and still that boy treats me with the very same respect
he always did, notwithstanding Alice—this is in confidence just between us—she did it at first; but she
don't now; she tried to make me divide out with Caroline as far as I had with Duncan. For Alice is a
woman that, though an excellent good woman to my
belief, yet she's not had experience, living all of her life
away up there on the other side of Broad River, where
society is entirely too much mixed up to suit my notions. But I nipped that in the bud, and I gave her to
understand that I'd rather not hear her express any
opinion about the way I was managing my own business. I tell Alice she ought to be satisfied with how
much better she did marrying than Caroline, although
Caroline thinks no more of me than to tell me to my
very face that she believes she has the very best husband in this world, sickening as she knows it is to me
to hear such foolishness. But, after all, I'm glad Alice

isn't ashamed of them and likes them as well as she does, because it saves talk and looks better in a community."

Alice, at her coming into the family, had conceived for her sister-in-law a warm affection, and, in her simpleness of heart, expressed her surprise at the dissatisfaction with John Stapleton, who, as she said with native frankness, was a man much to be admired. Feeling it her duty to try to effect a reconciliation, knowing little of the inner natures of those with whom she was to deal, she went to her task with the directness in which she had been reared. Pained and ashamed to find her efforts wholly unavailing with both her mother-in-law and her husband, she ceased to interfere. It was a great disappointment, the first she had ever had, and it served to bring upon her heart a dread that was to grow darker. No quarrel had ever been between Duncan and his sister or her husband. He had never been at their house, and although Alice and Caroline visited occasionally, John Stapleton had never been at Guthrie's except on the occasion when with his wife he had called upon the bride. Whenever the men happened to meet, they spoke as any other two acquaintances between whom was no familiarity. The decisive answer given by her husband to Alice's remonstrances regarding the state of the family relations was in these words:

"Alice, my advice to you is to let that business alone. You don't know mother. I do. If she were to try not to make a difference between me and Caroline, she couldn't. She always would have favorites. In this case it is myself, and it isn't every man's wife that would object to such as that. If it wasn't I, it would be Caroline. That's just my luck. Mother, as I think you must have seen, is not pleased with your interference, and if it does anything, it will do no good, to Caroline certainly. I've tried, and so has Uncle Dennis, to get her to let them have at least another family of negroes and a little money to add to their plantation; but it served only to anger her, and she said at last that I stood in my own light by asking such a thing of her. Still, she did offer to make over to Caroline some negroes; but she would not accept them on those terms. Stapleton, no doubt, had put her up to it."

"He is a noble gentleman, that's what Mr. Stapleton is; and his wife, who is as fine a woman as I ever saw, knows it!"

"High!" said he, smiling with good-humored irony, "that tall chevalier seems to have struck your fancy, my dear, as well as Caroline's."

"Duncan," she answered, "fancy has nothing to do with it. If father had proposed to make over to my separate use the property he gave you at our marriage I shouldn't have been willing to accept it. Would you have wished me to?"

"No; that I wouldn't. The cases are very different."

Stung with shame for his selfishness, she became silent, and for a long time did not allude to the subject again.

In those times, curious as it may seem to us, a man at marriage became by law entitled to all the property then held by his wife or afterward devolved upon her by purchase or inheritance, unless by antenuptial settlement or other paper by which it was acquired it was made free from marital control. Even as to property not reduced into possession during the wife's life-time, the husband, by becoming her administrator, was exempted from making to the Ordinary returns of his management, and thus made sole owner of that also. As for such precontracts, they were seldom made. The public mind, almost universally, was opposed to them, as degrading to the husband's manhood and prolific of domestic unhappiness. Marriage was regarded as merging of a woman's being in that of her husband. There are persons yet living who remember the first libel for divorce in that whole region, and the surprise and awe when its news was spread abroad. Women grew up to have the same views as men upon this subject, and in the few cases where such settlements were suggested by parents, their daughters cordially ratified refusals by their husbands to accept property upon such terms. In this case the community, without exception, justified Caroline Stapleton, who did not even wait to consult the feelings and wishes of her husband.

Affection and confidence between these two young women grew in tenderness as they came to know each other better. Along with compassion in the one who seemed far more fortunate, there was in her heart gratulation for the other whose husband had shown himself full worthy of all the affection and trust and reliance that were bestowed upon him. Mr. Ludwell had given Duncan a handsome portion of his large estate. The young wife, like Portia, wished for his sake that she had been ten thousand times more rich, and she joyed in the feeling that herself and what was hers to him and his had been converted. He could have had much happiness

3

with such a wife if he had been one to appreciate the gifts for which she was to be loved more than for the beauty and wealth which she had brought. Her mother had warned her against being exacting of corresponding returns for what she was giving so freely, and she had tried to school herself to make allowance for faults which, to a degree apparent to herself, more so to her parents, before the marriage, were found to be more pronounced and reckless than she could have been made to believe. Rumors of some of his habits had reached her father, and although indefinite had disturbed him, yet less than those of the treatment of Mrs. Stapleton by his mother, a thing which Mr. Ludwell believed that he ought to have prevented. Duncan, during his courtship, had alluded to this, but, seeing his mistake, afterward spoke of his sister in very affectionate terms, and said that his mother was in some respects a rather peculiar woman, and that it was his own intention to see that Caroline should get a just portion of the estate left by their father. To Alice it was some consolation, poor of its kind, but better than none, to blame Mrs. Guthrie for never having curbed but, instead, striven to intensify a selfishness and exacerbate a temper inherited from herself. Yet she behaved toward her with as much consideration as was consistent with the absence of filial affection that was impossible. A loyal wife, made more loyal, if possible, by fears of being driven to prize her husband lower than she had counted upon, she strove to persuade herself that it was her duty to be happier than she felt herself to be. The return of physical health made her stronger in heart, and people were gratified when she seemed to take on some gayety which contrasted prettily with her native seriousness. Always having loved Charlotte Macfarlane, she grew to have much affection for her parents, especially her mother, upon whom, as it must go somewhere, she bestowed the feeling that she acknowledged in her heart to be due but could not be paid to her mother-in-law. Seeing that her husband cared not that she should have much of the society of young men, married or unmarried, she treated these with simple civility, and let her social cordiality go to ladies and elderly gentlemen. Lately, and notably since the evening at the Wendells', Guthrie had been uncommonly affectionate, and she was beginning to hope that after all she might come to be as happy a wife as most married women with whom she had acquaintance. Perhaps the standard she had lifted was too lofty. Her husband felt that he knew well enough how to conciliate when conciliation was important for the compassing of a desired end. Conscious of this gift, he seemed not to be afraid of losing it, but it is one whose security against abuse requires cautiousness that he had not well learned. Indeed, he never had opportunities to learn it. Nurtured from his very infancy in exorbitant selfishness which he believed himself entitled to indulge notwithstanding every risk, along with the blame for much of his deportment there was in thoughtful minds some compassion. Not irascible like his mother, instead, affable in his address and liberal with his money, he could never attain popularity, which he anxiously desired, because it was impossible for him to conceal, or even try to conceal his sense of superiority over a large majority of people which had been imparted by his birth, education, and fortune.

The path in which he had been trained to walk must lead to misfortune, and good people pitied that he had never seen the need of divergence.

----

## CHAPTER V.

### PETERSON BRADDY.

THE tavern in Clarke, kept by Lewis Junkin, was better than it looked. A lumbering building, begun in the infancy of the village with a two-story house whose piazza opened upon a corner of the public square, facing the street that led southward, it had grown irregularly back and sideways, one addition opening with its plain but threatening piazza upon the back yard and looking into a garden in which Mrs. Junkin raised vegetables more than enough. It kept an inexpensive but uncommonly nice table. Tolly was one of the regular boarders. Almost every day one or more men from the country, and even in the village, came there to dinner. Guthrie did this sometimes rather than walk to his residence, half a mile distant. After dinner the guests usually sat for an hour in a large chamber, called in that time the bar-room, and chatted before going back to their business. Guthrie was there on the day after the party at the Wendells'. The subject of interest, both at the table and in the bar-room, was a duel that had taken place a few days before between two South Carolinians, news of which had just come. The occasion was an alleged wrong done to a man's sister; the result was the escape of the injurer and the dangerous wounding of the other. Guthrie was quite pronounced in his opinions. After dinner, the rest, except Tolly and the landlord, having had as much discussion as they cared for, went away, leaving these in the bar room.

"Yes, Tolly," said Guthrie, after lighting a cigar, "I say, good for Gregory! General Frierson could not consent to a connection so far below the standing of his family, and the girl might have known that he wasn't going to marry her."

"But they say that he was actually engaged to her."

"So they say, I know. But must a man who is a gentleman born, whose ancestors before him were gentlemen, lose his life for flirting with a pretty girl who enjoyed the fun as much as he did, and then fire up because she was disappointed of making it a lifetime piece of business?"

"Well, Mr. Guthrie," said Junkin, "I shouldn't want no man, no matter who he was, nor what sort of folks he come from, to be projeckin in that kind o' style with a girl that was anything to me."

"O Junkin," he answered, as if kindly to assure him of his entire security from such an injury, "I've no idea that *you'll* ever be bothered in that way."

The only Miss Junkin, though an excellent daughter and help to her mother, was rather lank and plain faced to be in great danger from such a man as General Frierson.

"I should much ruther hope not, Mr. Guthrie."

"But, Junkin, suppose your fatherly feelings should

be wrought up in that way; what would you do?
Would you challenge the fellow?"

"I couldn't say what I'd do, Mr. Guthrie.  But I'd
do somethin' that would be a caution, without he killed
me before I done it."

"Ah! there, you see, is the difficulty, Junkin."  And
he seemed quite amused at the possible category into
which Junkin would be thrown by a temporary infatuation for his daughter on the part of some young man
of high family.

"Yes," was the humble reply, "but, Mr. Guthrie, a
man, no matter how poor he is nor how little some
people may think of *his* people, if he's a man at all,
he's bound to take the resk of his family sometimes.
And then, you know, Mr. Tolly, that if a man ain't
what the other think is his equil he won't fight a juel
with him, even if he was to channelge him; so they
ain't nothing to do, seem to me, but to pick up somethin', and haul off and knock his brains out."

The words stung Guthrie somewhat, but, as they
were addressed to Tolly, he said nothing in reply.

"I agree with you, Mr. Junkin," said Tolly, "that
a man in such a case would be apt to feel as if he must
do something, no matter how far inferior in some respects he might be regarded by the assailant of the
peace and honor of his family."

"Among gentlemen, equal or approximating equal-
ity, or for the nonce admitted to be equal, you know,
Tolly," said Guthrie, "the *code duello* is regarded sufficient for providing for the redress of grievances, real
or imaginary.  As for unequals, they have their resort
to the courts for pecuniary damages."

At this moment Junkin was called away.

"Aye; but, Mr. Guthrie, there are few so poor and so humble who would not feel that the acceptance of money for an injury done to one's honor would add to the first disgrace rather than condone it. Such cases, fortunately rare in our society, must be settled each according to its circumstances. They would be more rare if the public laws and society would make punishment, one felony and the other social ostracism."

"Impracticable, both, Tolly. The mistake with the friends of such a girl is in making too much ado."

"Better let her suffer in silence, eh?"

"Well, yes, unless she can be content with redresses that are provided. The best way to simplify such matters is for the different ranks of society to keep apart from anything like serious connection, and let it be understood generally that mere gallantries must take care of themselves. Then, you know, Tolly—ah! good day, Peter."

The person who had just entered the room, rather diminutive in stature, black eyed and black haired, his high hat worn jauntily on a side of his head, neatly dressed in home-made clothes, moved and looked as if he felt entirely competent to take care of himself on any sort of occasion.

"Do, sir," he answered stiffly to Guthrie's salutation. Passing on to Tolly and extending his small hand, he said:

"Howdye, Tom. What's all the good news with you?"

"Well, Tolly," said Guthrie. "I've stayed here over my time, and forgot an appointment with a client." Saying which, he went out. The new-comer looked at him as he was departing, and said:

"That great man is so condescendin' that he can fall in here sometimes and chat with common folks?"

"Oh, yes, Peter, Guthrie stops in right often, and we have a little chat while smoking our cigars. How are you all?"

"Ma's not quite as well as I'd like for her to be. Sister Patsy is all right. So I believe they are over at Emily's. As for me, I'm straight as a shingle, like I always am, thank God. You look well, Tom. I expect I know more about your folks than you do. I was down to Jack Stapleton's yisterday. He said everybody over at your pa's was alive and kickin'."

"How is Jack? and how are Mrs. Stapleton and Alan?"

"Missis Stapleton is simple splendid, splendidest woman in the State. Alan grows like a pig, and Jack's fine, a heap finer than any such triflin' fellow had ought to be. I go down occasional and have a fox hunt with him, and give him a little cussin' out for his no-accountness. I love him so much I can't cuss him hard enough to do any good. But yit I ain't without hopes, as the preachers says."

"What are you cursing Jack about?"

"Oh, you know, Tom Tolly. It's for lettin' hisself and his wife be run over by Dunk Guthrie and his old mother, and be kept out of prop'ty that they're as much entitled to as you are to that coat you got on your back—and more too if you hain't paid for it, which I doubt, livin' in town, frolickin' around at parties, and dressin' every day same as Sunday. Take a pile o' law practice to keep up with such as that. I been doin' my best to git you a case, and I will some day if Jack'll ever live to be any account."

"I thank you for your solicitude, Peter," Tolly said good-humoredly, "but" he added with some seriousness, "I'd rather you would not suggest my name as a lawyer to Jack. If he should ever conclude that any of his rights are withheld, and then should decide to try to obtain them by resort to legal proceedings, I would not like for any friend of mine, especially one as near to him and me as you are, to even suggest my name to him as counsel."

"Oh, I'm not goin' to hurt you with Jack, Tom Tolly. I couldn't, if I was to try. He knows you too well for that. I've only tried to git him for the sake of his wife and child, and another he's goin' to have soon, and the Lord knows how many more, to wake up and git some lawyer—makes no odds who, if he's got the sense—and go to court and knock the old man Guthrie's will sky high, which it ought to have been done long ago. Anybody else but Jack would have done it, because everybody that knowed Alan Guthrie knowed that his daughter Calline was his favorite child if he had any favorite, and he knowed his wife was predijiced in favor of Dunk; and so when he broke down in his head as well as his body, and didn't hardly have sense enough to git out of a shower o' rain, much less make a will, she got that fellow Suttle to write one, and then made Mr. Guthrie sign it, givin' the whole kit and bilin' of it to her a even includin' the appurt'nances. But I don't want to talk about that to-day, so soon after haulin' Jack over the coals. I come in on a little business, and as I was about to go back home, I thought I'd step in and see how you was a thrivin'. The sight of Dunk Guthrie made me think of Jack, and the mad come over me not expected. What's on top of his big mind to-day? I heerd him a-ex'cisin' his woice time I put my foot on the tavern step."

"We were discussing the question of dueling that was suggested by the late rencounter between Gregory and General Frierson."

The little man laughed.

"Yes; he's a nice fellow to talk about julin! Well, I got to go back. Take care o' yourself, Tom. You know I can't be always with you to keep you out of destruction. Good-day."

As this gentleman is to take a part in a few of the scenes in this story, I must give some account of him and his surroundings.

Two miles south of town, near the road leading to Philips's Bridge on Little River, in a humble story-and-a-half house, surrounded by a few large red oaks, dwelt the Widow Braddy and her two children, Martha Simkins, now a widow, and Peterson, whom we have just seen. They owned a small farm of very good land, adjoining a larger estate of William Pruitt, who was Mrs. Simkins's son-in-law. They had a few negroes, whom they worked with moderation. Not ambitious to be rich, they lived freely and so hospitably that they made but slow reductions of a debt left by their late head as surety for one of his neighbors. There was much family affection among them, especially on the part of all the rest for Peterson, who, notwithstanding his fondness for society of various sorts, was never neglectful of home duties, for the sake of which he had remained unmarried. At home, simple and deferential to his mother and his widowed sister, abroad, the announcement of his views was in inverse ratio to the size of his body and the extent of his information. Yet the full trust that everybody had in his integrity and courage kept him from being made a butt of any more ridicule than he seemed willing to endure. His sleeping chamber, detached from the main dwelling, was a sufficiently comfortable hewed log structure of sixteen feet square, situated in a corner of the yard near the garden gate; for he was fond of being considered and called a little wild, and his hours did not always suit those of the ladies whose wont was to retire to bed of nights at nine o'clock. In these bachelor quarters he usually did likewise when he had no companions. Young men from the neighborhood and from town, after being out there to supper, which they knew before was to be as square a meal as any reasonable body would conscientiously look for, afterward delayed for a little game of " poker " or " old. sledge." The stake was always inconsiderable ; but it was pleasant among his companions to hear him curse the cards whenever he was loser and lift up his laugh when he had an extra dollar or two at the end. It was not that he cared so much for the money, although in money matters calculating and economical, but he delighted in victory even more than he raged at defeat. In business matters he was thoroughly reliable. In reports of what he had done he was always pardoned for suspected exaggerations. The principal field of his autobiographical narrations was the State of Florida, where, when he was about grown, he served with General Floyd during the military operations under General Jackson in the late war with Great Britain. It was the pride of his life that he had been with that illustrious hero and known him personally. In his eyes dueling had been consecrated ever since the meeting of Jackson with Dickinson. Personal courage he regarded as the highest attribute of a man, and he was one of those, not numerous, who, while fond of talking about fighting, was intrepid to the last degree. Not quarrelsome, a taker as freely as a giver of practical jokes, yet on public occasions, as election days, muster days, days of court sessions, and sometimes unmarked days, besides a heavy walking-stick heavily loaded with an iron point, he carried a small single-barreled pistol. This last he had never been known to draw but once, and that was on an election day, when, having given his cane to a small man whom he did not know, but who was backing from the assault of one his superior in size and strength, he made himself ready to defend his own interference.

"The fact of the business is," he said sometimes, "I'm most ashamed to ever put a pistol in my pocket; but, as everybody knows, I'm not a very large man, and I have my opinions, and I don't exactly like the idea of bein' run over when I'm a expressin' of 'em; and fightin' these days, I mean honor'ble fightin', has got to that, if you channelge a man, he'll aggervate you worse by pleadin' he aint your equil, and in that way crawfish out of it."

Some there were, not many, who knew that in these last words he alluded to Duncan Guthrie, with whom only a few weeks before the latter's marriage he and his family had had a rather trying experience. Emily Simkins, his sister's daughter, at fifteen was almost a beauty. Already at the village school she had got more education than had fallen to the lot of the rest of the family, when William Pruitt, a sturdy well-to-do young bachelor near by, made her an offer of marriage. The girl, knowing what a good opportunity it was, and seeing that her family were much in favor of it, accepted on condition that she should have another year's schooling. In the following fall it was noticed that she began to talk about her lover and to him with less cordiality than theretofore. His patient nature and his great love for her made him endure without complaint. In this while she was more vivacious than usual, and took uncommon pains in her dressing and such adornings as she could command. She usually went forth and back with some other children whose parents dwelt a little further on from town. Latterly on the return she often loitered behind them, getting home alone. One evening her mother having expressed her disapproval of such behavior, she answered fretfully :

"Ma, I wish you wouldn't pester yourself about me. I know how to take care of myself."

This answer, uttered at the back door, was overheard by her uncle, who was sitting under a fig-tree before his door.

"Why 'high!" he exclaimed, to her surprise and alarm; for, with all her fond affection for him, she dreaded his displeasure more than that of both mother and grandmother. Inquiring the occasion of such petulance, he learned that for several evenings Duncan Guthrie had 'joined' her at the edge of town as she lingered behind her companions, and had accompanied her a part of the way home.  Alarmed and incensed, he questioned the girl closely enough to find out that Guthrie, deny-, ing the reports of his engagement to Miss Ludwell, had been making pretense of love to her.  She was stopped from school at once, and this fact was made known to Guthrie the next day by the children, of whom he had inquired the cause of her absence.  William Pruitt, forgiving her temporary disloyalty, took her to wife a few weeks afterward, and since they had been living in contentment.  But one morning, some days after hearing of the connection with Guthrie, Braddy rode leisurely to town, hitched his horse to a rack on the court house square, and seeing Guthrie among others before the door of the post-office, where the weekly mail from Augusta was being distributed, he sauntered thither. Cordially greeted by all, after returning their friendly assurances, he rested his eyes with apparent complacency upon Guthrie.

"What's all the news with you, Pete?" said the latter.

"Oh, nothin' so very interestin'.  Country folks have to come to town to git news.  They tell me there's a weddin' on hand.  That's always good news."

"Aye! what's up now?"

"I'm told that you're to go through the preliminaries before long somewheres t'other side of Broad River."

"But, Pete, you know that is nobody's business but mine."

"Oh, that's so, I expect, Mr. Guthrie; still, that kind

"I got a little business with you, Mr. Guthrie."

o' news is always in gener'l interestin' in a community where such high and interestin' people lives."

Guthrie looked at him darkly, and his look was met with a steadiness that seemed as if its giver was amused. After a moment the countryman said:

"I got a little business with you, Mr. Guthrie, when it suit you."

"All right, Pete," he answered, dismissing the feeling that had risen momentarily at what he considered a rather insolent liberty. "Come to my office in half an hour."

When he entered the office, Guthrie, from an arm-chair by his desk, said:

"Take a seat, Pete."

"I don't care about settin', Mr. Guthrie. It ain't a business of *law* I wanted to see you about, because, in a event of that kind, there's other people I should call on. I just wanted to say that your waylayin' of my sister's daughter, that she's not old enough to know the worth of any sort of attentions from a man like you, weren't what a honor'ble man, and one promised to a honor'ble woman, it weren't what he ought to have done."

Guthrie rose, took from the mantel a box of cigars, chose one, bit it, and, partially extending the box, said:

"Smoke?"

"I do, but not now."

"Mr. Braddy," said Duncan, shifting his cigar about in his mouth, "I declare I don't exactly know what you mean by such talk. As for the few little playful chats with your niece, which I thought she understood, I—of course, if she says so—I'll not repeat them."

"It ain't her that has anything to say to you about it, sir; it's *me*."

"O Braddy," waving his hand testily, "I've no time to be discussing such a trifling affair with you, and I've got no more to say about it."

"All right, sir; I just wanted to tell you that if it wasn't for fetchin' out my sister's child's name, I'd channelge you to fight a juel, sir."

A hearty laugh was the answer to this threatening speech. A quivering hand was thrown by Braddy behind him, and grasped the weapon in his coat pocket. An instant afterward he smiled and said:

"No, it wouldn't be right. There's no more danger in him nohow. But, lookee here, my Lord Guthrie, as old Gen'al Jackson used to call people he had a perfect contemp' for, I give you warnin' not to cross my path any more. If you do, and then is above fightin' a juel with such as me, I'll shoot you the same as I'd shoot a dog after one of my lambs."

Then he turned and slowly went out.

Few men were more brave than Guthrie, and few more apt to recognize the necessity of curbing resentment. In any circumstances it would have seemed to him ridiculous to have to accord to such a man the satisfaction then usual among gentlemen; but, except for his approaching marriage, he would have attempted to chastise him. As it was, he congratulated himself upon his composure. Yet on the next day he rode up to the Ludwell's and succeeded in hastening his marriage, which took place soon thereafter. There was some talk about the affair, but the girl's marriage put an end to it.   From that time, whenever Braddy spoke of Guthrie, and this was seldom, it was with disgust.

---

## CHAPTER VI.

### MISS JEWELL AT DUNCAN GUTHRIE'S.

ONE outcome of the restoration of Alice to health and confidence, and from these to cheerfulness, was the following :

"Duncan," she said one morning when breakfast was over, "if it will suit your convenience and your wishes, I am going to invite Miss Jewell to tea and to spend this evening with us."

"All right, darling," he answered, "if you feel like it. I don't know but what we would be expected to show her some little civility for the sake of the school if nothing else.   But I want you to do just as you feel like doing."

Kissing her good-by, he left at once and proceeded to his office.   An hour afterward Miss Jewell received a note of invitation for that same evening, Alice adding that she would provide for her an escort home afterward.

It was a good supper and a dainty.   The hostess, in a pale gown with flowing drapery which set off modestly her fine figure, was cordially hospitable.   As if she would make manifest her entire confidence in her husband and her guest, she remained longer than was

4

necessary in the dining-room, to have the table cleared
and the china and silver put away.  Afterward she did
her best to make her entertainment pleasant to both.
Her husband, well experienced in society, made himself
agreeable to both ladies, and seemed by his well-timed
remarks to wish them to be well pleased with each
other.  Once while standing near his wife, placing an
arm behind her back, he said :

"Miss Jewell, I had heard of a rare flower that was
in bloom near the bank of Dove Creek beyond Broad
River, and I went up there to look for it.  When I saw
it I plucked it with all possible speed, fearing that if its
existence should become known to other men it might
be lost to me."

"It was a thing to do, Mr. Guthrie," said Miss Jewell, "as happy as it was prompt."

Alice accepted their compliments as things more
than she expected, and set herself to other entertainment.  Miss Jewell brightened more and more, and
when at the piano played with noticeable preference
the pieces that Alice had asked for.  In their intervals
she addressed herself mainly to her, and praised, but
not too much, the arrangement of her furniture and the
flowers in the vases.  A true man would have been
pleased by what he knew to have been done at some
sacrifice.  As it was, after making his one speech, he
smiled feebly at the efforts of these ladies to entertain
each other, and seemed to be waiting with commendable patience for the evening to come to an end.  All
except Miss Jewell were surprised at ten o'clock by a
knock at the door.

"Aye," said she in a business-like tone, rising from

the sofa, "there is Mr. Tolly, whom I asked to come
for me."

"What!" exclaimed Alice. "Why, Miss Jewell,
Duncan has been expecting to take you home."

"Ah ha!" answered the guest, raising a finger,
"but that was a trouble that I meant to spare this
house, and so I put it upon one whom I knew it would
not very much discomfit."

Tolly, admitted by a servant, entered the drawing-
room, hat in hand. It was his first appearance there;
for, although Alice had suggested it once, and only
once, he had never been invited to the house. She
met him with both hands extended.

"Hello, Tolly!" cried Guthrie, with enforced cordiality, "I'm glad to see you; rather, I'm sorry, considering the errand on which you have come," taking his hat
and putting it on the rack. Then he added with polite
complaining: "As this is the first time that you have
honored this house with a visit, you shall sit down and
take of such refection as Mrs. Guthrie may have to
offer to so distinguished a guest."

Tolly took a chair and accepted easily what was
brought in. In his own house Guthrie had no difficulty in covering his disappointment. The rights
and duties of hospitality in that generation had kept
much of their old-time sacredness, and, a man of
brave instincts, he could not but feel some pleasure in
having under his roof such a man as Tom Tolly, and
some regret that he had not been there sooner. Alice
behaved toward the guest with a simple graciousness
that was delightful, and in the brief while that he was
there seemed to him, while chatting and looking at

Miss Jewell, sometimes as if she would appeal to her not to molest her in the possession of what undeniably was her own. When they were about to leave she said :

"Mr. Tolly, here are some flowers that I gathered for Miss Jewell this evening, and have been keeping in water that they might remain fresh. Now, sir, you are to carry them for her with much carefulness. In advance, as part of your reward, I pin this rosebud and this little white jessamine on your coat. The rest you are to have in the pleasure of escorting her home."

When they had gone, Guthrie said :

"You did nicely, Alice, very nicely." Then lighting a cigar, he went out into the piazza and sat and smoked until long after she had gone to bed. She had expected a more hearty indorsement. Now she felt disappointed and humiliated. Yet she tried not to complain even to her own heart, and, after saying her prayers, went to bed and in time found sleep.

"How well Mrs. Guthrie shows in her own house?" Miss Jewell said to Tolly; "her tastefulness and her ladylike hospitality impressed me much."

"Yes. Guthrie, if he could know it—that is, if he could know it constantly—has for wife an uncommonly fine woman."

"Of course he knows it, Mr. Tolly. He seemed to-night particularly fond of her."

"I'm glad to hear it; yet he could not hide from me at least his disappointment at my coming for you."

"That must have been only in your imagination. I only wished to save them inconvenience—begging your pardon for preferring to put it upon you. I would have asked Cousin William to call for me, but he was busy looking over the girls' compositions.  Then I knew, at least I decided, that you had no very troublesome incumbrances on hand, since it was only last night that you were at the Macfarlanes."  Then she slightly shook his arm and laughed merrily.

"How did you know that?"

"Charlotte came to see me this morning and mentioned that as one of the incidents in recent village history."

"Aye?  You know, Miss Jewell, that you may always command my service, the same as if I were—your brother."

"Oh, that dash, Mr. Tolly!"

Then they both laughed heartily, and Tolly said: "If Guthrie suspected that I had ambition to be any nearer than that, and besides had any even remote chance of sucsess, he would have looked longer than momentarily dark at my unexpected entrance to-night."

"What do you mean by that?  You are a goose, Tom Tolly, as the men folks call you."

"But even a goose may be of value sometimes besides the humble uses which are generally made of him. Recall, if you please, the happy consequence of his cackling in the Roman citadel."  He looked smiling toward her, as if this bit of pedantry was meant for mere pleasant badinage.  She so understood it, but presently said:

"Do you know, Mr. Tolly, that lately, and until I received an invitation to sup there to-night, I have had an idea that Mrs. Guthrie disliked me?  Why, that night at our house, when I was doing my best to entertain her, she kept herself as cool as a cucumber, as you people say.  I do think you all have some of the funniest phrases!  I never did anything to her that she should be a cucumber to me.  But I concluded that perhaps she was not quite well.  Indeed, Charlotte told me afterward that she was not.  To-night she was as cordial as could be.  She'd be weak to let herself be fretted by her husband's attentions to other women."

"I am confident that she does not, in general; though perhaps sometimes she may think that they're more pointed than those of a married man should be."

"Well, well!  You know, Mr. Tolly, that that's one objection I have to country society?  It is so in New England, and, if anything, more so here.  Married people are expected to be always on their *p's* and *q's* with unmarried.  If I ever get married, I am going to let my husband know from the start that I don't consider him the only interesting man in the world or among my acquaintance, and that I expect to admire other men that are to be admired, just as I do now, and that I shall be rather tired of him if he does not feel the same about other women, instead of tagging on to me all the time as if he were afraid of both of us otherwise going to destruction.  Now, the truth is I wanted to waltz with Mr. Guthrie that night; because there's little enjoyment in waltzing without a woman has a man to support her.  But Cousin William must shake his head, though he acknowledged afterward that he didn't think there was a particle of harm in it, but that some of his patrons might not have liked it, as I was one of the teachers, and he added that he doubted if Mrs. Guthrie would.  I had just to laugh about *that*, and I believe, from her treatment of me to-night, that Cousin William was mistaken, and that she acted so only because she was not quite well. For surely the woman has more sense than to be fretted by such a trifling matter."

"I was glad you rejected Guthrie's proposal to waltz."

"Why so? Because the sight of us might have made you sorry that you couldn't have similar fun with Charlotte? She's a beautiful waltzer." She tapped his arm with her fan.

"Oh, no; first, I've never learned to waltz; but if I had, I rather think I should never ask a woman in this society, as it has become now, to join me in that amusement, especially before the faces of elderly persons, who, I would be sure, would rather that it were not done. About such things Guthrie is defiant and audacious. He knew that he ought not to have proposed to you to waltz with him—at least on that occasion, for your sake, if no other's; because here you are comparatively a stranger."

"I hope I know how to take care of myself, Mr. Tolly. Now, I'll just say this, that I think all such as that is nonsensical despotism, and I don't propose to submit to it any more than I'm obliged to. Why, it is *too* ridiculous." She laughed outright, and thus proceeded: "I suppose if it becomes known in this burgh that I asked you to come for me to-night, it will ruin me. But, then, I can deny it, you know. You're a sort of Puritan, yourself, young man, a species of the animal creation that I did not expect to find in this warm, sweet latitude. To tell you the truth, that's the only objection I'd have to you if you were a richer and

more distinguished man.   You *seem* so moral and good
that I'm almost afraid you are deceitful."   Then she
laughed aloud.   "Oh, law me!" she continued, "how
imprudent I am in running on thus with a young man
on the street at this time of night!   But I told Charlotte that very thing about you, not that you were deceitful, but that you were too good; and I told her so
because I knew you were in love with her.   But I didn't
tell her *that*.   You want to know the reason why?   Because I didn't think it was just the thing for her to
know certainly that you *did* love her.   I'm talking to
you as if we were confidants, as I'm sure we will be
some day, unless I should get to be too bad or you too
good, both which extremes, in my opinion, people ought
to avoid.   You are right in not courting Charlotte yet.
She likes you better than she thinks she does.   But
you've got to do something much greater than you have
done yet before you can be bold to advantage in that
suit.   The Macfarlanes, however, I think, could be won
out of any prejudices they may have sooner than the
Guthries; but that's because mainly of your professional rivalry to Mr. Duncan.   I mean to see if I can't
do something with him in your interest."

"My dear Miss Jewell, I'd much rather you would
not."   Again she laughed aloud.

"I knew you'd say that; at least I thought so, and I
talked so to try you.   Still, if I should get to knowing
Mr. Guthrie better, and *I* don't see why I should not, I
mean at least to hint to him that a man as prosperous
in every way as he is ought to feel that he could 'tote
far,' as the negroes here say, with others who are not
so fortunately settled.   Do you know, my fair youth,

that but for one thing, poor as I am, and poor as they say you are, I might have set cap for you myself?"

"And what barrier so dire got between me and such consummate felicity?"

"Oh, la! I doubt if even Mr. Guthrie could have made such a gallant speech. Well, sir, one reason is, that I'm not yet in the humor to be tied to one who, in spite of what I can do or say, I suppose must be my head. Then, I think, I can do better." She shook his arm in the exuberance of the gayety of this last reason.

"The last is sufficient," said Tolly humbly. "You *ought* to do better, Miss Jewell, a great deal better. I suppose you have already such a one in your mind."

"Well—no; not exactly. What I want now mostly is, not a beau, that is, a lover—and, if I did, Charlotte has got ahead of me; but I want a—a sort of cousin. Won't you be a poor Yankee girl's cousin? You understand? No? Well, well, you will in time. I want a fellow that I can call cousin and talk with confidentially and—and—do you know a lawyer in Augusta named Bond?"

"Christopher Bond?"

"Yes, a good pious name, isn't it?"

"I've seen him at Columbia County Court once. They say he is quite promising. What about him?"

"Oh, nothing much. It has occurred to me several times to ask if you knew him. He's a good friend of Mr. Dunbar and my sister. She wrote me that he might come to your spring court, as Mr. Dunbar has a little business here. If he does, you must be good to him, for her sake and mine, my very dear cousin. Hear?"

"I hear, and will attend to the gentleman as well as I know how, for all sakes."

"That's a good cousin. La La! Here we are home! Let me see. Yes; you've brought securely my flowers and me. Good-night; don't get into any mischief on the way home."

Then she ran up the steps.

Tolly debated with himself that night whether he ought not to have given her more distinct warning, particularly regarding Guthrie. He believed her entirely honorable, and so did the whole community, strict as was the common law of its society, and her accomplishments, with her faithful, laborious attention to her school engagements, had made her very popular. Yet some of the more elderly ladies occasionally had expressed the wish that Miss Jewell, being a new comer and a teacher, would not be quite so free in young men's society, for the sake of example to the school-girls, you know, mistress so-and-so, or sister so-and-so. So Tolly debated, but to the time of going to sleep, he had not quite decided. The next morning, Guthrie, while passing him on the street, lingered to say:

"You cut me out last night, Tolly. Isn't she a splendid, voluptuous looking creature?"

"Voluptuous, Mr. Guthrie?"

"Oh, I don't mean anything bad."

Then he went on his way.

"You *do* mean bad," muttered Tolly, and afterward he wished that he had gone at once to Miss Jewell and given her warning.

# CHAPTER VII.

### CHRISTOPHER BOND.

On Greene Street, in the city of Augusta, near the intersection of McIntosh, was a large brick mansion in which dwelt the Dunbars. George Dunbar, six years back a student at Harvard University, had left that seat of learning without taking a degree, having made up his mind to follow the business of his lately deceased father, a hardware merchant. But this was not done until after he had contracted with Miss Jewell, an older sister of Sarah, for a marriage which came off a year afterward. He became heir (besides the business) to this house and another three miles out of town on the Sand Hills, by some called Summerville. It was while on a visit to her sister that Sarah had been prevailed upon by Mr. Wendell to be one of his assistants. During her sojourn of several months, among other acquaintances made by her, was that of Christopher Bond, a young lawyer who had moved there from the county of Jefferson and was believed to be making his way in the profession with some rapidity. Very tall, slender, dark complexioned, his deportment in society effected, perhaps, an earlier favorable impression because of a sort of gravity which, while it kept him from making much merriment, did not hinder a quiet enjoyment of it when made by others. Too devoted to study to have very much to do with society, yet he visited sufficiently often, particularly at the Dunbars, with whom he had been on terms of rather intimate friendship before the coming of their sister. Between her and himself grew relations more cordial perhaps because of the difference of their temperaments. The heartiest laughs he could give were at the sallies of her vivacious humor, sometimes when made at his own expense, as when she merrily criticised an awkwardness for which he seemed not to care, yet was often promising to amend; but when he was in serious mood, to no other man's conversation did she listen with more pleased attention. People used to jest with her about the impression which seemed to be made upon her by a character so different from her own, whose chief interest came from subjects pertaining to the bar or others as serious; but she answered lightly, as if no two persons were more likely to keep apart than Bond and herself.

In those times lawyers at Augusta habitually attended court sessions in the county towns of that judicial district, and occasionally one or two on the eastern border of the northern, in one of which Clarke was the county seat. It used to be an interesting sight, the judge with a dozen or so of his bar, traveling, every one in his sulky, from court to court. Some of as good things as a man fond of humor would wish to hear were uttered along the highway, in tones loud enough to be heard all along the line, followed by laughter that was echoed far on either side. Many a pious country-woman, knitting or sewing on the porch of her cottage, looking and listening to the cavalcade, would reflect what an ungodly set they must all be, from the judge down.

Bond, with intent to extend his acquaintance and

with hope to better his practice, was beginning to attend a few of these courts, and he was well pleased when employed in one which, but for Miss Jewell being there, was not of importance enough to warrant the expense of going to Clarke.

Except during Christmas-tide, court week was the gayest of all in the year; but of the parties at this March term Mrs. Guthrie's was most notable. She not often gave one, but when she did it lacked nothing to make it successful. Guests always put on the best they had when going to a party at her house. Ladies wore—what we see in portraits of those times, so strange looking now, then thought to be so becoming—gowns with short waists, *bouffant* sleeves, and a modest train, silk stockings, satin slippers fastened with ribbons crossing the ankles and upward, hair, except two or three ringlets on either temple, wound in a lofty knot behind and fastened with elaborate combs of tortoise-shell. The men were in blue dress-coats with brass buttons, buff vest and trousers, and high white satin neck stocks. They wore also silk stockings and slippers. Mrs. Guthrie shone in a long gray silk gown that seemed more becoming and interesting for being of a fashion of a quarter of a century past that was both more elaborate and more expensive than any of that time. The numerous syllabub stands, some three feet high, holding near a hundred tumblers, with curiously cut paper hangings on the circumferences of the several stories, helped to set off tables heavy laden with viands. The graciousness of her manners and her taste in everything were subjects of general comment. She accepted congratulations of parting guests with mild satisfaction, as if it

had cost little trouble to cater to people's tastes and en-
joyments whenever she felt like it.

In accordance with his promise, Tolly was particularly polite to Bond, and he was well pleased when
Guthrie, after several essays to get Miss Jewell into a
corner for a special chat, failed, because she was intent
on putting her friend at ease and helping him to make
acquaintances.

At the tavern, late that night, Seaborn Torrance, a
lawyer from the county next below, said to Tolly:

"Tom, the old lady Guthrie—isn't she royal?  I
declare she looked as queenly as old Elizabeth in her
silks and flounces and laces, and I don't know what.  I
told Guthrie I couldn't go there to-night, not having
with me any party clothes, which I always despise to
put on anyhow, especially pumps.  They made a mistake when they threw away fair-top boots and came
down to pumps.  I'll swear they make me feel as if I
was barefooted.  However, Guthrie told me that his
mother said I *had* to go, if she had to send a special
deputation to take me in her carriage.  So I went, and
I was glad of it.  She impressed me deeply.  Why, sir,
that woman has sense like a man ; and, don't you know?
She told me that if she ever should have a law case of
importance she would want me, and her big fiery eyes
showed that she was in earnest.  Sensible woman, isn't
she?  Ah! ha!  And that's a blamed fine-looking
woman, that Boston schoolmistress.  Guthrie, a rogue,
tried to get her to himself, and looked at her as if he'd
like to eat her up.  He'd better mind ; married man, and
with such an elegant wife.  I'm not sure that she wasn't
the most interesting-looking woman there, of course ex-

cepting the hostess. *She*—oh, my Lord!—she was head and shoulders above them all. I think she knew it, too, but didn't think it worth while to be proud of it."

Bond's case was not tried, yet he lingered several days after adjournment of the court with prospect of a settlement, which was effected through Tolly. In this while these two formed somewhat of a friendship. The night before Bond was to leave, he said:

"I like this village, Tolly, and am glad that business, unimportant as it was, brought me here. There's quite a city-like air about it. I have met several, men as well as women, who in what people call society are as *au fait* as any in Augusta. My! what the collecting of four or five families with good manners and taste can make of even a small village! What a fine woman is Miss Macfarlane! But it is easy to see that you found that out long ago. So has young Jamison; but I, who am a poor judge of such things, thought that I could see that she didn't take much interest in his small talk. I suspect he's been running too mainly on his father's success to be much anywhere. Yes, she's a fine young woman, isn't she?"

"Yes, indeed; it takes only a brief acquaintance to find out that. And Miss Jewell; what do you say to her?"

"Oh, she and I have been acquainted for some time, you know. Her sister, Mrs. Dunbar, and her husband are about the closest friends I have in Augusta. They wanted Miss Jewell to live with them, her parents being both dead, and Dunbar has plenty of money besides a good business. But she said she meant to maintain herself, and so she accepted her cousin's offer to take a place in his school.  A girl full of life—good-looking, too, isn't she?—and I don't know a brighter.  She's going to spend her summer vacation with the Dunbars on the Sand Hills.  She likes you, she says, first rate, and says she calls you 'cousin.'  I suppose Miss Mac farlane can console you for the temporary absence of such an interesting relative, eh?"

"If anybody could, it would be she, provided she'd be kind enough to undertake it."

"I thought so.  By the way, I was particularly im pressed by Mrs. Guthrie, young Mrs. Guthrie.  The elder is a striking woman herself, vast and magisterial; but her daughter-in-law struck me as a woman filled with the best sorts of character, and I'm not sure but that she was as good looking as any at the party.  I was glad to make her acquaintance.  The elder Jamison did me that service.  Guthrie, so it seemed, didn't care to do it himself, at which piece of neglect, as in part he was host, I was rather surprised.  Between us, I'm inclined to suspect that Guthrie forms his manners more with reference to women than men.  It's a mistake to do that, I think.  A man who is fair and courteous with other men can get along well enough when he gets to where women are.  Of all your bar he has been least cordial in extending welcome to me, and I noticed that he showed some fretfulness whenever the court made a ruling against him.  But with women, particularly Miss Jewell, he's as mannerish as a Frenchman.  I had a good time with his wife.  She's devoted to him; I could see that from the way her eyes followed him.  She's a serious woman, I take it.  She smiled only once while I was talking with her, and, bless me, how it did light her up!  May be my small talk wasn't of the proper sort.  It's deuced inconvenient to a fellow, isn't it, not to have at command fit words for everybody he meets in a promiscuous company?  Sometimes I almost envy such a man as Guthrie—that is, in that particular.  However, such as that is only for a moment.  When a fellow means well and does the best he can he ought to try to be reconciled to himself. Eh, Tolly?"

"That's my hand, Bond, the only one I've got."

"I'm told Guthrie is rich.  He dresses, looks, and behaves like a man that had money.  He has talent enough to make a capital lawyer if he'd study his cases better.  I suppose he practices mainly to keep himself before the public."

"That's about his case.  Yes, Guthrie is rich; born so, married a rich man's daughter, and, unless something is done to hinder, is destined to get all, or nearly all, of the estate left by his father, to the exclusion of his sister."

"Was she at the party that night?"

"No; she does not go out now, and, even if she did, I hardly think she would have been there; I know her husband would not, and I rather suspect that the mother gave her party at this particular time because of her knowing that people would not expect to meet the rest of the family."

"Aye?  What's the matter with the son-in-law?"

"Nothing, except that he had no fortune, and his family can't run back to the very oldest bloods of Virginia, that is, not that they know of.  But he's a prince of a man himself.  Yes, Bond, between ourselves, Guth-

ric is as selfish as a bull terrier, to whom, not inaptly,
Mr. Torrance compared him that night after the party
while speaking of him in another attitude. He can't
help being proud of that wife of his, whom I regard,
if not the very finest woman I know, the equal of any.
But she's not enough for him, and I'm inclined to suspect that already she has been suffering somewhat from
his attentions to other women."

"Miss Jewell tells me she likes him very much. I
don't think she understands him well. I believe I'll—
no, people know best how to take care of themselves."

These words were said rather gravely. He turned
away from the subject, and said :

"But, Tolly, how is it that Guthrie is to get the
lion's share of his father's estate? Did the old man
leave it all to him and his mother?"

Tolly related what he had heard and what he had
been told of the Guthrie history, and then said :

"Bond, would you regard as entirely on the line of
professional duty to give information to a man who had
not made himself a client touching rights which, if not
for his own, for his family's sake, he ought to enforce?"

"If the man was a friend, I should say, emphati-
cally, *yes*. Even if he were not, I should rather regard
it as a lawyer's duty to see that such information got to
him in some way."

"He *is* a friend, and a dear one. He is the husband of Guthrie's sister."

"Then I should not hesitate."

"He already knows the facts as well as I do, but, of
of course, not all the legal principles on which redress
might depend. The difficulty is that he's rather indif-

ferent, and both he and his wife are averse to bringing family matters before the public. Lately, a friend whom he loves very much came to see me about the case, and since then has been plying him more earnestly to do something. If a suit is to be instituted, I've no doubt it will be represented by me. In that event, if you say so, I will join you with me."

"Thanky; you're as good as you can be, Tolly. But, my dear fellow, how would that affect the Macfarlane business?"

"Oh, every case must depend upon itself."

The next morning Bond left, making a brief parting call on Miss Jewell on his way.

"You'll be coming back again before long, you say, Mr. Bond?"

"Most probably. Tolly has a good case in prospect and wants me to join him. He's a cousin of yours, he also tells me."

"Oh, but isn't he? Well, by-by. My dear love to sister and Mr. Dunbar."

---

# CHAPTER VIII.

### A PICNIC.

On a Saturday early in May there was a picnic in Mrs. Guthrie's woods adjoining her residence on the east and south. This was an institution of Miss Jewell, nothing but fishing, chincapin-hunting, and like parties among the young of both sexes being known theretofore.   In these woods of a hundred acres and more was abundant growth of oak, hickory, poplar, intermixed with dogwood, maple, crab apple, etc.   Here among people were fond of strolling, and they did so without remonstrance from the owner, except in the case of boys with shot-guns, whom, if she could not always turn away, she reminded in threatening words of the law ; and so a few gray and flying squirrels and a goodly number of birds not fit for the frying-pan nor the griddle had their habitations there.   Through Guthrie permission to hold the festival was obtained.   It was a most fair day.   Boys had gone early among the deeper woods beyond to gather yellow jessamines, bubby blossoms, and other wild things, and had them ready to distribute among the girls and young women to weave and to wear in nosegays and garlands.   Baskets with good things were sent by every family, and, although this had not been foreseen, a floor of unplaned boards had been laid on a level not far from the spring branch, where Andy Nicol, a well-known fiddler, early in the afternoon made his appearance.

"I didn't expect this, Mr. Guthrie," said Miss Jewell.   "Will it be all right ? "

"Oh, yes.   I mentioned to several that I was going to get up a little dance, and nobody said anything against it."

Whether so appointed or not, he made himself leader in sports and exercises.   These, besides dancing, were walks beneath the trees on the rising grounds and along the bank of the little stream in the bottom, games among the younger lads and girls, and occasional duets and singings in chorus.   Alice was there and looked cheerful, showing or trying to show that she took pleasure in everything.

"There, Mrs. Guthrie," Miss Jewell said about noon, "is the best I can do in return for the sweet flowers you gave me the evening I was at your house." Then she handed her a wreath which she had woven of jessamines.

"Beautiful!" said Alice, "and I thank you cordially."

They could not prevail upon her to dance. She said that Charlotte and Miss Jewell must alternately take her place. Yet she looked on with interest and smiled at an occasional awkward figure made by one of the men. Tolly was not a practiced dancer, but he knew the figures and acquitted himself to the apparent satisfaction of his partners. Guthrie looked as if he felt that he was throwing away his agility on an arena so small. Yet he took out Miss Jewell as often as he could, and it was very interesting to note their perfect harmony of movement. She smiled at his whisperings, and occasionally, when she came within view of Alice, nodded to her.

Toward evening Peterson Braddy appeared, having come on Tolly's invitation. He would not have put foot there if he had known that Guthrie had had anything to do in getting up the party. Fond of dancing, yet he did not indulge until bantered by several of the younger girls. Always avowing the wish to marry, but known among his friends to have no sort of notion of the kind, on such occasions he was a beau devoted to any belle near whom he happened to be. Tolly made him acquainted with Miss Jewell, and she professed to be delighted with the gallant things he said to her. He

had no doubt that if he were to try, he could foot it
equal to Guthrie or any other man that ever stepped
into a ball-room; but he seemed to feel that this was no
occasion for the exercise of his best endeavors.  The
tips of his little partners' fingers he took between his
thumb and forefinger, smiled in condescension to their
level for their entertainment, and he just knew that it
was inimitable when, instead of turning one of them at
the word, he twirled her round like a top.

"Just look at old Pete Braddy!" said Guthrie to
Miss Jewell; "did anybody ever see such an awkward
conceited old fool?"

They were seated upon the roots of a large white
oak.  Guthrie's back was toward his wife.  He had
been, with much apparent earnestness, saying several
things which Miss Jewell, intent upon the cotillon did
not seem to be hearing, and she was not aware that
Alice was looking intently at both.  At the last words
of Guthrie she turned her face to him and said:

"Don't you speak in such terms of Mr. Braddy.
He's a dear friend of Cousin Tom Tolly."

"Your Cousin Tom Tolly?"

"Yes, didn't you know I had taken him for my
cousin?"

"No, indeed; but I am glad to hear it, because—"

"Because what?"

He bent closer toward her and whispered a few
words.

"Do you—"

Leaving the question unasked, reddening to her tem-
ples, she looked at Alice and noticed that the latter's
eyes were intently fixed upon her.  She rose and com-

menced to advance toward her. Alice, who had been talking with Alfred Jamison, rising, said :

" I feel chilly. Will you see me to my carriage, Mr. Jamison, as I don't like to interrupt Mr. Guthrie ? "

Leaving upon the bench the wreath that Miss Jewell had given her, she took Alfred's arm and walked away. A moment after, Guthrie, suddenly become pale, hurried after, reaching her as she was entering the carriage.

" Why, Alice, my dear child, what is the matter ? Thank you, Alfred. Drive on home Marcus," he said to the coachman as he entered and took the seat by her. Miss Jewell looked for a few seconds in that direction, then turned. Tolly had been called away by a client a few minutes before. Calling to Peterson Braddy, she said aloud :

" Mr. Braddy, you haven't asked me to dance a single set. I'm surprised at you. Mr. Tolly told me you were one of the gallantest of mankind."

" Madam ! Why, by the—why, madam, it was because I thought you wouldn't want to dance with an old rusty country blade like me. Will you be my partner for the next quitilion, madam ? "

" No, thank you, I'm tired. Girls, I think we'll break up now. Get up your things."

While they were busy with this order, she said to him playfully, although her face and the tremble of her words indicated excitement :

" Mr. Braddy, I wish I was a man, and could be as brave as you are. Would you fight for me if I were to need it and ask you ? "

" Madam, by blood *and* the eternal—which is the biggest oath I ever swears by—I would."

"Right or wrong?"

"Right or wrong."

Then she laughed again, almost hysterically. After a moment of uncertain pause, she said:

"Oh, I was joking, Mr. Braddy. You are not to repeat a word of what I said to you, not even, and especially not to our friend Mr. Tolly; hear?"

"I hear, madam, and to hear is to obey. May my tongue cleave to the roof of my mouth—"

"Oh, that is more than enough," and having seen that her girls were all ready, she bade him good-by and went her way.

When Duncan entered the carriage he felt a trepidation greater than any in his whole experience, and he never had had more pressing use of all of his gifts.

"My dearest Alice, what in this world is the matter?"

"I am sick," she answered coldly.

"Sick? From what?"

"Sick at heart, from the sight of perfidy!"

"I knew it as soon as I saw you moving toward the carriage. I am glad to know that it is only that, and that I can relieve you in half a dozen words." Then he laughed a laugh as artful as it was audacious.

She looked at him mournfully and compassionately.

"Alice" he said, withdrawing himself a little apart as if there were things owed to himself as well as to her, "I determined, for my own sake as well as yours, but particularly for Miss Jewell's, that I would this day test the character of the feeling she had for me. I have done so, and I have just now found that it is different from what I had supposed. So different that I have determined to withdraw from her society altogether."

It is not strange that the innocent are credulous to the denials of those whom they love. She turned and looked into his eyes that, clear as the cloudless heavens, let themselves be searched. A moment more and she was sobbing upon his breast, while he laughed the laugh of a physician who instantaneously had remedied what seemed a fatal malady.

"O Duncan, Duncan!" she said, when she could lift her head, "forgive me for a weakness which the love I have for you has made so uncontrollable. If I could believe that Miss Jewell was a woman with inordinate feeling for men, because they are men, and that you had been tempted by the knowledge of it and the sight of it, I think I could have borne. I know I would have tried to ignore what sometimes comes almost irresistibly in the way of a man who in other respects may be all that a wife would have him to be. God knows that *that* is hard enough. Or, if I believed that the poor woman's affections had become inevitably entangled, a thing I could understand, knowing you as I do, I could compassionate her as a sufferer for what surely is the keenest, because most irremediable and most humiliating of griefs. But, Duncan, to me Miss Jewell to-day did not look like a bad or even a weak person. That is, never until just now, when she rose from the foot of that tree and looked at me and began to approach. Then some powerful passion seemed raging in her breast. It looked as if it was fright at being detected, and I decided to retreat from her. I can now understand that expression from what you tell me, which, my husband—" then she looked him again in the eyes—"I believe because *you* tell me of it. Charlotte Macfarlane has talked with me much about Miss Jewell, and Charlotte has said often that, though an impulsive woman, she believes her to be as innocent as any. Would you know, then, what has been with me the source of the most painful feelings I have had about her? Not *jealousy*, Duncan!"

She paused a moment and uttered a low laugh in the mild scorn that the utterance of the poor word had raised in her heart. "No, I could no more indulge that feeling than I could have distrust in the Creator! If I were to feel that I had not the entire confidence of you to whom I have given myself and all of mine, I should conclude that you had nothing to give back or that I was not worth the giving. But I never should go out of my own experience to invent or to imagine any other cause, and I would try to live, until the time came for me to die, upon whatever nourishment could be got from my own poor resources. I hope you understand me, Duncan, and that you mark well what in my thoughts of this woman has given me most anxiety. It is, or it was the apprehension that, seeing her so fair to look upon, so gifted with all goodly gifts, you, attractive like her, instead of avoiding the temptings which you led her to extend—if she did extend them, and the good God knows that *I* don't accuse her— you were meeting them, forgetful, not so much of what was due to me, as of what was due from every man to young womanhood, especially when separated from its natural protectors. My action at the Wendell party was mainly to warn her, and *some* of it this afternoon was to make that warning so pronounced that repetition of her imprudence would seem to herself impossible without disgrace. I was acting less in my own behalf, much as I felt that I needed some defense, than for her safety—and my husband's honor."

"No, my dear Alice," he said, with a show of mildness which the simplest innocence could not have improved, "I was pleased with the woman's society, as any man of taste must be, and I confess that I had not enough objection to meeting her half-way in a little flirtation that would do no harm to me certainly, nor, as I could see, to her. When I found I was mistaken, and that her interest in me was of a kind dangerous to her reputation, I decided to do as I have told you."

She believed what he said, for she was one who, as she must give all or none, must accept or reject all. She sighed; but neither she nor her husband believed it to be a sigh of distrust. Yet each felt that as much had been put upon her as she could endure.

----

## CHAPTER IX.

### A NEW-COMER ON LITTLE RIVER.

THE next morning John Stapleton rode into the village, and going into Tolly's office, after the usual salutations, reported, in the tone of one telling of moderately interesting news, that a daughter had been born at his house three days before, and that he had come to town mainly to report to the doctor the condition of mother and child, which, he was glad to say, was as fair as could be desired. He was a good specimen of manly strength and beauty.  Over six feet in height, straight, muscular, with complexion somewhat this side of fair, easy, unstudied in manners, modest but satisfied looking, he was one to be noted in any crowd of men.

"Ah ha! congratulate you.  That sets you two, Jack, eh?"

"Yes, sir; a brace: doing pretty well for a little over three years, isn't it, Tom?"

"It is, indeed.  I like to hear of that sort of stock multiplying.  The way you've started out, you'll have to stir your stumps to raise and educate and settle aright."

"Oh, yes; but there's plenty of time.  I called in to tell you that Caroline wants Alice to know about it.  I didn't see Duncan on the street, and I don't care about going to his office just for that.  Won't you try to see the fellow some time to-day and let him know?  And if you can't, get the interesting news to Alice in some way?  That's a good boy."

"Certainly, Jack, I shall be delighted, proud indeed to hand about generally, and specially to Mrs. Duncan Guthrie, information so important.  Aren't you going to send word to the old lady Guthrie?"

"I think not; she'll hear of it in satisfactory time, I guess.  She doesn't have a great fancy for my stock, you know, and Duncan thinks he must follow her suit, although he has sense to not bother with me.  Alice, bless her heart, is made out of pure gold.  By the way, Tom, I hear some talk about Duncan and that Miss Jewell.  Peter says that people tell him Duncan on the street is everlastingly talking about what a magnificent piece of furniture she is—that's the way Pete puts it; and he says that they say he pays her more attention than looks well in a married man."

"Oh, you know how some people will talk, Jack. Guthrie may have been a little too pointed, as you know he is generally with fine-looking women; but it amounts to little."

"Well, it's no business of mine. I must go. Thanky, Tom. Good-by."

He went out, and as he was remounting his horse, "Hello, Jack!" called Guthrie, who was standing on a sidewalk some rods away.

"Hello!" he answered and rode away.

The sun had just set. Alice was in her flower garden that lay aside from the great oaks in front of the mansion. She was clad in a light-muslin gown, whose loose flowing sleeves were folded back upon her forearms to allow facile use of the pot with which she was watering. Upon her face there was, perhaps, some deeper shade of habitual seriousness, but this was lifting as she moved among her flowers. Occasionally she lingered before a bush and, plucking one of its blossoms, looked at it affectionately for a while, then putting it to her nostrils, closed her eyes. These and her piano had become companions more dear than during the period of maidenhood. The greater the disappointment in failing to hold as fast as she had expected the one great love of her being the more fondly she allied herself to these. To a woman of virtue, sensibility, and culture, these are resources of priceless value. Alas for the wife who, when she can not, or when she believes that she can not hold her husband to the marital obligations that are her dearest, has not learned to love music and flowers! Even if she have consolations of assured religious faith, there come seasons of dryness in the life of even the most devout, which next to prayer, wrestling prayer, there is nothing like music and flowers to comfort. Indeed, a sensitive, devout soul that suffers feels that these are the most fit accompaniments to the beseechings of an overflowing heart. When I was a little child, the sweet smells and the singing on Sundays in our country meeting-house were felt by me to be as religious and worshipful as anything that came down from the lofty pulpit.

Alice looked so beautiful and pure that her husband on approaching, stopped and watched her as she stood in one of the walks contemplating a white rose that she had just plucked; she kissed it several times, then placing a hand upon her eyes, stood there for several moments. Guthrie waited for her to move; then advancing, he called out:

"Good evening! I was just thinking how uncommonly pretty and sweet you are looking, Alice."

Startled somewhat, yet she smiled, and when he came up and took her in his arms, she looked up into his face, and he understood some, not all, of the longing that was in her heart. She was in that state wherein, along with confidence again restored after another violent assault, is a drop of indefinable apprehension. It is more hazardous than some suspect to trifle with the love and trustfulness of the meek. I have often thought of those words in Revelations about hiding from the wrath of the *Lamb*. Punishment from such a source, when it comes at last, after long trials and

numberless entreaties to beware of its coming, seems
more terrific than the swift sword of vengeance.   It is
terrible when the face of the injured is turned away
and the injurer is left to himself.

He had been home for an hour.   They were chatting on the piazza when he said:

"O Alice! I forgot a bit of news I have for you.
You looked so lovely there in the garden that you put
it out of my mind when it was on my tongue to tell
you.   Caroline has a girl baby!"

"Is that so?" she answered quickly.   "I didn't know
they were expecting it quite so soon.   How is she?
When was the child born?   How did you hear it?"

"Tolly told me, and he said that Stapleton informed
him of it.   I saw Jack as he was about to mount his
horse to return.   We merely exchanged salutations, as
he appeared to be in a hurry."

"And *he* said nothing to you about it, dear?"

"No; but Tolly said that Jack asked him to send
the news to you."

"Does mother know it?"

"I can't say.   I guess not, though, as Jack never
goes there, you know.   No, I don't think mother can
have heard it."

"When was the child born, did you say?"

"Three days ago, Tolly said."

"Three days ago!   I wonder Caroline didn't send
word sooner.   I told her that I would go down when it
happened for a day or so.   If you're willing, I'll drive
down there to-morrow and spend the night."

"Why, of course, my dear, though I shall be very
lonesome without you.   However, I can spend the even-

ing with mother, unless she goes with you, which I hardly expect she'll do."

The next morning, soon after breakfast, Alice took
the carriage and drove first to Mrs. Guthrie's. The latter, always professing to be glad to see her, exclaimed :

"Why, good morning, my child. I see you came in
the carriage; don't you feel quite well ? You haven't
been looking quite as bright as I want to see you."

"I'm as well as usual, mother. How are you ?
You always look well."

"Do I ? I'm glad to hear you say so. Isn't it a
pity that people, especially those who have a plenty to
live on and enjoy themselves, and help others to do the
same—when they deserve it—that they have to get old,
and can't get as much sleep of nights as they'd like, and
have to be troubled thinking how short life is and other
things that they didn't use to bother their minds about ?
You Judy, come here and get your Miss Alice's bonnet."

"Howdye, Judy," Alice said to the negro girl who
had come in. "No, mother, I'm on my way to Sister
Caroline's. Did you know she had another baby ?"

"No, I didn't," was the cold answer. "I didn't
know it had come. When was it, and how did you
hear it ?"

"Mr. Stapleton was in town yesterday, and sent
word that it was born three days before."

"Whom did he send word by ?"

"Mr. Tolly told Duncan that he had been so requested by him. I believe he came merely to report to
Dr. Poythress, and returned almost immediately."

"More expense. Dr. Poythress is the highest
charging doctor in town, and that's one reason that he

has the biggest practice of them all. It's just the way people are about lawyers and doctors—the higher they charge the more people think they're worth. In my time women never thought of sending for doctors at such times, rich or poor. But Caroline always was proud, except when she came to get married, which, of all times to *be* proud, is the main one. How did he say they both were?"

"Very well, very well, indeed."

"No, child, I hadn't heard a word of it, though, of course, I'm not surprised. I never asked Caroline anything about it, and she never opened her mouth to me. Poor child! she knew that-the prospect of adding another to John Stapleton's stock wouldn't be such an interesting piece of news as to make me get up and go to dancing around out of pure joy."

"You don't feel like going with me, mother?" asked Alice, suppressing as well as she could the pain she felt at these words.

"Well, no, my dear, not to-day. I'm not right well, though you tell me I look it, and am glad to hear it. And then I've got a heap of business to lay off and see that it's attended to. You know how negroes are when you ain't right behind 'em all the time. If Caroline was real *sick*, I'd go to her, of course. She knows that; and she knows that no matter how little respect she's always had for my wishes yet I can't but have the feelings of a mother, as I suppose there's few women that have children that don't."

"Why, my dear mother," Alice ventured to say, "Sister Caroline, I am sure, both respects and loves you very much, and would do whatever she could for

6

your happiness that she would believe consistent with her other duties."

"I know Caroline Stapleton, Alice," the red upon her face growing a trifle more fiery. "I know her better than you do or anybody else does. From a child she was of the kind that she is now—that she always would have her own opinions. I never was able to give her one single *jostle* about that John Stapleton, that he wasn't worth two thousand dollars to his name; and he acted like he didn't care whether he was worth even that much or not, except to dress as well— mighty nigh as well as Duncan Guthrie—and keep his dogs and hounds. And Caroline, marry him she would, spite of my telling her if she did the back of my hand to them both as to any property they'd get from me, though I let myself be overpersuaded by Dennis Macfarlane to let them have a family of negroes; and when their oldest child was born, and they named it after Mr. Guthrie, although *that* made me mad, still I offered to make over to Caroline another bunch of negroes and some money to add to their land. You think she'd take any of it? Why, she told me to my face that she didn't want any property that didn't belong to her husband. Dennis Macfarlane had to say that she was right; but it was none of his business, and I hinted so to him; and I made up my mind that I'd keep down my feelings, and I'd be firm with Caroline Stapleton. But, law me! I despise to have to talk about such a disagreeable subject. You haven't told me, Alice, if it was a boy or girl."

"It is a girl, mother."

"A girl! worse and worse! I was in hopes that

it was going to be a boy, and till you said to the contrary I've been supposing, if I supposed anything about it, that it *was* a boy. Boys can stand roughings and poor living, and blaze their way through. That's what boys can do; but girls are delicate, if they can only be kept so, and— You're coming back to-night, Alice, I suppose, of course."

"I rather think not, mother. Caroline may need me for some little service. Indeed, I'd like, and I think I ought, to spend two days and a night with her. Duncan says I may."

"Well, do it, then. Just like Duncan. When you come back you can fetch word how everything is. You may tell Caroline that, as she told me nothing about it, it was obliged to come on me unexpected, and specially a girl— No, don't tell her quite that; because I was *not* taken entirely by surprise, and I might have known it was going to be a girl, just from her bad luck ever since she married that man. But if she needs any thing that she knows she ought to have, and hasn't got it, and no way to get it, why, of course— Oh, the feelings, the feelings that a mother may feel like she ought to try to get out of her breast when she's badly treated and can't! You haven't had those feelings, Alice, and—"

"I think I'll go on, mother, as the morning is already quite advanced, and Sister Caroline will want a good dinner set for me, I've no doubt."

"Yes, yes, oh, yes," she said rising. "But just one thing more. Did you hear anything about what they were talking about naming it? Though of course I don't suppose you did. One thing is certain. I want none of John

Stapleton's stock to bear *my* name.   Well, good-by, my
child ; there's a plenty of trouble in this world any way
you take it ; but it seems to me, at my age, some things
are harder than *I* ought to be made to suffer, trying as
I always have tried to do my duty.   Duncan will come
and spend the evening with me, of course ? "

" He said he would do so, mother."

"I knew he would.   O Alice, you've got the *exception* of a husband, that was first good to his mother,
like he always has been from a child.   Good-by.   Make
Marcus drive careful over those awful roads."

<hr>

## CHAPTER X.

### ALICE VISITS THE STAPLETONS.

The way to Stapleton's, though subject to some complaint, was not as rough and perilous as, from Mrs.
Guthrie's words, one might apprehend.   It was not level
and smooth as that over which she traveled at least
once a week to her large plantation some miles west of
the village, yet intent sufficiently attractive, as a visit
to a daughter with a husband less objectionable than
John Stapleton would have been, ought to have made
her feel reasonably secure whenever she felt like making the journey.   Less than a third of the forests had
been cut away, but owing to the noted fecundity of the
soil and the healthfulness of the climate, they were beginning to disappear fast before the extending acquisitions
of the older settlers and the frequent incoming of new.

Even upon the sides and very summits of the hills, wherever inclosed by fences, the reed-cane grew out of the blood-red ground not very far below the height reached in the rich alluvium in the bottoms between. Dense woods, fairer to see and sweeter to be among than could well be found in any other region, lay all along. Amid many other kinds of growth, large and small, Nature had produced just enough of short leaf pine for supplying its own peculiar needs in building and kindling. To another person than Alice Guthrie the fast growing cotton and corn and oats and the yellowing wheat might have been most interesting. But she loved better the continuous sweet sounds and smells that came forth from the deep shades on the other side of the road she was traveling. Occasionally she bade Marcus, her black, sleek coachman, to let the horses slacken to a walk that she might linger a little while with some unwonted delicious thing that seemed as if it had come out of its thicket to gladden her senses and comfort her spirit.

On a high level, half a mile from the hither bank of Little River, a hundred yards or so from the road, was the modest mansion that was sought on that fair morning. There were two large single-storied rooms with a wide passage between. In front was a piazza extending the whole length, to the ends of which two other rooms with piazzas had been joined, facing each other. At the rear of the passage were the dining-room and pantry. Flowers, except some cape jessamines and vines that had been trained on a lattice between the posts of the piazza, found no place because of the oaks and hickories, but were in the large garden  •

at some distance aside.  The yard of four or five acres was fenced with poles of pine, known as old-field, from their coming up on the worn ground on which had stood the oak and its companions.  This wood, light and spongy, differing from both the short-leaf and the long, yet when peeled of its bark and fastened with chestnut posts, made enduring and not unsightly fences.  Along the front and a portion of the sides of the inclosure, the Cherokee rose grew in much profusion.  Everywhere about were evidences of neatness and tastefulness, to which the economy observed in their appointments gave an added interest.

Stapleton was sitting on the piazza near a window of the chamber behind him, looking backward occasionally and telling to his wife within how he was amused by their son Alan, astride of a large black-and-tan hound that lay stretched upon the sanded walk. Alan wanted to have a ride, and was seeking to enforce his commands by pulling at the dog's ears.  The good beast would like to take a nap.  He gave some whining growls meant for remonstrances, and once in a while raised his head and looked at his master as if to ascertain if such interruption was ratified by him.  Suddenly he rose upon his feet and gave a loud bark as of inquiry. Then Clarissy, a young negro woman who had just gone out to bring the child away, cried:

"Law, Mars Jack! yonder's a cayidge at de gate, en I do believe its Mars Duncan's.  Yes, dat's Markis, sho', en dar I see Miss Alice lookin' out de winder!  Git up off dat nasty dog, boy, befo' yer Aunt Alice see you dar."

Gathering him speedily, she bore him in.  As she was passing her mistress's door, she cried:

"Law, Miss Calline! I know you glad; me, too—come along here, mister—mister houn'-rider, and let me see if I can't git you in some sort o' fix for comp'ny. Which one o' his new frocks must I put on him, Miss Calline, his red streaked or his yaller striked."

"You're a goose, Clarissy!" said Mr. Stapleton in good-humored tone; "go and wash his face and hands and comb his hair, and bring him back. I thought she'd come soon, Caroline."

"I knew she would."

The dapple grays came up trotting gayly.

"Bless your heart for coming so promptly!" said the host while assisting the visitor to alight.

"Howdye, Mr. Stapleton!" she said joyously. "I congratulate you. How are Caroline and the baby?"

"First rate, and will be the better for your coming. Run along in, and you and they have over the Oh heavens part to yourselves while I attend to Marcus."

It was at home that John Stapleton showed to best advantage. Manlike, with unstudied manners midway between entire ease and a degree of awkwardness that was rather pleasing than not, he was one to be loved by men and women, old and young, equal and dependent.

"O Caroline, my dear sister!" said Alice.

She bent down and let the white round arms encircle her neck as she kissed the lips of the young second-time mother. In another corner of the chamber was a bed as nicely appointed, on which the husband was wont to lie. Upon the large round table was a vase of flowers, and two smaller upon the mantel.

"Why, who *did* arrange those flowers?" asked Alice. "Clarissy?"

"No, dear," answered Mrs. Stapleton, pointing to her husband. "That old fellow did it."

"*Mister* Stapleton!"

"Caroline told me how, Alice," he answered meekly.

"I did no such thing, except in trailing that spray of jessamine. Why, he can arrange flowers almost as well as any woman, Alice."

"Come, come, Caroline."

"O Mr. Stapleton, you needn't be ashamed of that one feminine accomplishment," said Alice.

"Oh dear, no; I'm delighted rather than ashamed when I can do anything that pleases Caroline's taste. I tried to remember how I had seen her handle them, and then I went to work."

"That is the very highest motive by which you could have been inspired, sir; and, thus inspired, I don't wonder at your doing perfectly."

"Thanky-do, ma'am. And now let me say that, hoping you've come to stay a day or two at least, I told Marcus to not put the horses in the stable until I could know your intentions. Say yes, if it is possible, and I'll give directions for them to be turned into my river-bottom pasture, where they can get some good green pickings, which I'm sure they'd like, and which will do them good."

"Yes, Caroline, I made up my mind to stay one night with you if you wanted me; Duncan said I might. But bless us all! where is the baby? I've been here full ten minutes and haven't seen her nor Alan, nor heard a word about either."

"Come out from under that pile of cover, Miss Callinc," said the father, "and show yourself to the company."

Laying the covering aside tenderly, he said:

"Now, Mistress Guthrie, I leave you to contemplate the next greatest picture in the world while I go out and attend to your team."

Upon another walnut table, covered by a cloth woven of homespun thread by a weaver of the neighborhood, was a dinner as good as could be got there, and good enough for any *bon vivant* who could be content for once to go without wine. Alice sat at the head of the table, Alan in his own chair by his father at the foot. His rattlings about the hounds and the new baby were interesting to both.

"And you've named the baby Caroline, Mr. Stapleton. I thought you would, and it is just as it should be."

"Of course. That would have been this fellow's name if he'd been a girl. You know what it would have been if not Caroline?"

"No; but I suppose the name of your mother or of Mother Guthrie."

"No; Mrs. Guthrie, I suppose, would not care to have her name continued in this branch of the family, and my mother always said that no granddaughter must ever be named for her, because she didn't want her to be ashamed of it when grown. *I* think Hannah is a very good old name, myself; but when I said no to Caroline's proposal, then she said Alice. But I said no again, and then I took the Bible and wrote it what it is."

"And you did exactly right; bless Caroline's dear heart for suggesting my name!"

"She loves you, Alice, loves you dearly."

Her eyes moistened as she spoke in return to this assurance, so needless to be given, yet so fond to hear.

After dinner, when Stapleton had gone to where the hands were at work, Alice, placing a rocker by the side of the bed, said:

"Mr. Stapleton is very proud of his baby, Sister Caroline, including the name."

"Oh, yes, dear Jack! I knew that he'd want to name it for me; I suggested that it should be Alice; he answered no, not this time; but said if we had had a Caroline, this one should have been Alice."

"It was very good of you both to think of me; but of course she should have had your name. I am delighted to see you looking so well."

"Why, I am so all the time, dear. I'm almost ashamed of myself sometimes for being always so well," she answered laughingly.

And she looked it, as she lay there rosy as the morning, her deep-blue eyes and her long, loose, yellow hair helping to make her the beauty that she was. If they had been born sisters there hardly could have been a warmer affection between them, nor greater confidence within limits which others with wrong purposes had marked. Each could not fail to know the other's thoughts of things beyond those limits, and one of them yearned for utterance of some of her own.

Of a family among whom domestic affection, the sense of justice, and fair dealing had been handed down from generations, Alice, from the time she became familiar with the relations among the Guthries, had suffered all the pain which an honorable woman can not but feel in such circumstances, a pain the more grievous because, being a woman, she not only could not right the wrong-doing, but for the same reason must even seem, by the silence expected of a wife, to be a partner in the continuance of its infliction. The ways in which such remonstrances as she had made had been parried added to her sense of the shame there was in it all, when she had come to know of what sort was the man on whose account such treatment had been inflicted. It was a pity for Guthrie that he had not yet come to know well this wife, and to understand that the sorrow he had put upon her on one line of his conduct was not very far below that which he suffered her to endure from his mother. Alice was better understood by the Stapletons, who, with delicacy corresponding with her own, kept themselves while in her presence from complainings of any sort, and in any mention of Mrs. Guthrie or of Duncan spoke in generalities in which an outsider could not have known but that all their family relations were such as were common among the best people in the community. Once, and once only, when Stapleton was not present, Alice thought she might venture to hint a hope for change in their property conditions. She spoke with embarrassment. Mrs. Stapleton answered quickly:

"I thank you, Alice, dear. I, and so does Jack, understand entirely your feelings and wishes about us. But, my little sister, you see how well we are doing; Jack says as well as he cares for us to do. We have a first-rate piece of land, and get a good living and something over to lay up for the children. I don't know that you know it, but when Alan was born, mother proposed to make over to me some more property.  But I told her without hesitation that Jack and I were one person, that that one fact was the foundation of my greatest happiness and hope for this life, and that nothing, by my consent, should come here which, being known as specially mine, might make me feel to any degree separate from him.  I told Jack afterward what I had said.  He laughed, kissed me, but said not a word."

" "You have a dear, good husband, sister."

" Alice, he is perfect.  Dear mother never could understand Jack; but, indeed, she never seemed to quite understand me, and somehow always had a notion that I didn't love her as I ought; but she was mistaken.  Jack says that it will all come out right in time.  He understands you, Alice, as well as I do, and, I believe, loves you as well."

Alice looked at her, and big tears were in her eyes. " O Sister Caroline," she said, " ever since I have come to know well you and Mr. Stapleton, I have felt that you were to be praised and congratulated rather than blamed and compassionated."

Seldom since her marriage had Alice passed a night alone in a chamber of a country-house; never in this. They put her in a wing facing the south.  The night sounds imparted soothings to which, if she could, she would have kept awake in order to indulge at length. But, as a baby, she fell asleep in the midst of the singing of a mocking-bird that from a plum tree near the garden gate was serenading his mate reposing upon her nest in a vine before the chamber in which she lay. Whoever has not heard the night music of the mocking-bird has failed to find at least one thing not to be forgotten throughout life. Beloved as he is in the day, as sometimes from the top of a peach tree he becomes so transported with exultation that he 'can not but spring and soar high upward, as if some of his exuberant gladness he must send up into heaven, yet he is sweeter in the night season. Sing he must, by night and by day; but at night his joy takes on serenity. Away from the sight of his love, whose rest and whose ponderings in hope of maternity he must not disturb, he subsides into quiet melancholy, whose low, painless, tender moanings the listener feels to be the sweetest of all sweet sounds. On the morrow, at sunrise, Alice was awakened by the same bird, as from a nearer tree he poured his throat in salutation of the new day.

## CHAPTER XI.

### MR. BRADDY'S EXPOSTULATIONS.

MARCUS, as most of his race were usually, was an ardent admirer and partisan of his master. He well knew his sentiments and feelings toward the Stapletons. Besides, being a genuine negro, he had for poor white people a contempt that was graded by the degree of their poverty. He had laughed inwardly at the idea of driving his fine team ten miles just to see a baby newly born to those who, compared with his own people, although of the same blood, were poor folks. Yet he was a skillful coachman and in every respect trustworthy in his business. He said to the other servants at home, and to others that, of course, it would be hard, but he hoped to be able, to stand it for one night, and neither get snake-bit nor come back with loss of all town manners. In the afternoon he walked about the premises, taking a lofty vague interest in what was to be seen. The dinner he had eaten was far more satisfactory than he had counted upon, and, upon the whole, things were not as bad as had been expected. At night the male negroes, very few in number, tired · from the day's work, not long after supper left off listening to his talk, and went to their beds. But Clarissy, who, notwithstanding her having come from the Stapleton side, had looks and manners for no town negro, male or female, to pretend to despise, politely lingered in the kitchen until her services would be needed in the house. Marcus thought he would make an impression upon her-and Ritter, the cook, her mother, and thus he began :

"Must be monstrous lonesome livin' down here, Miss Clarissy, so fur away from town."

"*Miss* Clarsy!   Umph!" muttered the mother, whose back was turned, as she was kneading her dough for to-morrow's breakfast rolls.  She shifted her work so that she could face the guest, and, as if it was her special task to try to maintain the conversation with one so distinguished, said :

"Lonesome!  What 'bout?  We all gits a plenty, jes as much as dem dat lives in town en think dey got to think more o' deyself den what we country niggers does."

Marcus had hoped rather to engage Clarissy in the conversation ; still, he knew that he could more than

In the afternoon Marcus walked about the premises.

hold his own with any one of a people so benighted, and so he blandly replied:

"Yes'm, Ann' Ritter; but people does natchul love to see somebody besides home folks sometimes, ef fur nothin' else, fur to enjoy deyself."

"Yes; ah ha! now I understands you, Markis, en dat is jes what we does down here, when its conwenant, en we wants ter, white folks *en* niggers."

"Yes'm, but den in town, you know, Aun' Ritter, dey is some fun."

"What sort o' fun, man? Don't you en dem tother niggers dar have no work to do dat you has all your time exceptin' when you eat'n en sleep'en to have your fun?"

"Oh, yes'm, we has our work; but when it through wid en night come, a body ken step out en git some fresh ar, en have a little talk along wid 'quaint'ces en—en females, en dat make whut we calls town siscicty."

She grabbed her dough as if she would squeeze every breath out of it, but did not delay in her words.

"Town 'siety! Markis, does you want to try to make me b'lieve white folks lets you niggers go trompin' about all over dat town uv a night, havin' your 'siety, as you call it, long o' your 'quaint'ces en—en—whut wus dem tother folks you said?"

"I said females."

"Does you mean women, Markis? Beca'se ef you does, en we all lived dar, I wouldn't let Clarsy have nothin' to do wid it. Dat I wouldn't! 'Quain'ces en females! My Lord! Whut will niggers come ter when dey gits togedder in swarms dat way, and ain' got white folks follerin' 'em 'bout all de time!"

"Oh, laws o' me, Aun' Ritter, no ma'am," said Marcus, deprecatingly, "we don't do no *trompin'*, because we has de manners to not do sich *as* dat. But we walks out, en may be, en may be not, jes as it happen, we draps in en has convisation wid genelmen en ladies."

"Umph, umph! but, Markis, in dat town does dee call nigger women—does dee call 'em females en ladies?" Then she paused in her work for a moment and looked at him searchingly.

"Yes'm, course we calls 'em females en ladies, des like dee does ev'ywhar." ˜

"No, *sir*, none o' dem big words out here. We calls niggers here jes whut dee is, ef its men, er ef its women, er ef its boys en gals, includin' childern. En whut time does you break up wid your con'gations you're talkin' 'bout, Markis?"

"We, in gen'l, Aun' Ritter, we manages to be home by nine o'clock, en may be leetle befo'; beca'se den de bell ring, when its agin de law for colored people to not to be at dey home."

"En s'posen you ain' notice de time 'mong dem females, en you git berlated, den whut? You has ter dodge en cut dirt, don't yer?"

"Oh, in dat case, we does de bes' we ken, Aun' Ritter; but we in gen'l always knows de time, en its monsous sildom anybody git took up."

By this time Ritter's work was over, and she said:

"Clarsy, time you goin' in de house."

The daughter obeyed instantly, then going out for a few moments her mother found and brought in a young man and said:

"Markis, I hope you ken try to put up for one

night with sich as dis place can 'ford. 'Pears like your Miss Alice kin."

"Oh, Aun' Ritter, law me, ma'am! I been perfec' delighted down here. I jes run on jes to spen' de evenin' wid you en Miss Clarsy."

"*Miss* Clarsy!" She laughed heartily, then said to the young man:

"Lias, take Markis 'long wid you for de res' o' de night. You kin give him dat cot in your house, er you can give him your bed en you take de cot, whichever you en him moughtn't to do betwix' you. You kin bofe go now."

Marcus, on his return, reported having had quite a lively time of it, especially, as he described, "wid ole Aun' Ritter, a high ole case."

The visitors left next morning in time to reach home at dinner. It had been a happy meeting for all.

"What a lovely woman Alice is!" said Stapleton.

"Indeed, she is! I wish in my heart that brother knew and valued her more."

"Oh, well, my dear, he'll find her out in good time, I suppose."

He was always an apologist for the infirmities of his wife's people.

They had not long been gone when Peterson Braddy made his appearance.

"Caroline," said her husband, "yonder is Peter. Coming, I suppose, to congratulate us about the baby."

"The dear old fellow! I'd been thinking he'd come soon. I'm glad he has."

Having alighted and tied his horse to a tree, he

7

came on up the walk, slowly and as if hesitating, Stapleton meeting him.

"Is sich a thing lawful, Jack?"

"What thing, Peter? Howdye. Delighted to see you; Caroline said she thought you'd be coming soon."

"Well, I didn't know as it would be lawful to come at sich a crootical and eventiful time."

"Yes, indeed, the very time *of* times. You heard the news?"

"Yes, I heard 'em. Curious how when babies are mighty nigh as common as blackberries how news of a fresh one will travel. Ma heard it the very next morning. The Davises told it to Emily Pruitt, and she made Billy carry it over to ma. All's well, I hope, and a doin' well? Girl, they said."

"Yes; just what I wanted."

A brief visit to the chamber and a brief inspection of the new-comer were allowed. Mr. Braddy made the speech that he had prepared while on the way.

"Well, madam, I congrateyulate you, and special that the baby is a healthy, and, as fur as I can judge from the way you've got it enweloped, a extremely nice and bootiful one for its age. But, madam, what I congrateyulate you specialler about is that, instid of bein' alike Jack Stapleton, it's the very image and pictur' of it's mother, as by good rights, a-bein' of a girl baby, it ought."

"O Mr. Braddy, it is exactly like Jack. Look at those eyes."

"Predijice, madam; nothin', not a thing, in this blessed world but predijice; and, if I might congrateyulate again and some more, it is to the effeck that I'm glad it's so for your sake and his'n to boot, for because, madam, when a married man have no great shakes to run on as to looks and, I may say, nothin' else, it's ruther to the advantage of both sections of the family when his wife think she can afford to take up a predijice for him."

He smiled the more because his "congratcyulations," as he termed them, turning inward, persuaded him that these extemporaneous remarks were nearly as good as his set speech. After more of such affectionate rallying there and on the piazza, the gentlemen went out for a stroll. Braddy gave a graphic account of the picnic, dwelling much upon the manifold charms of Miss Jewell.

"But, Jack, somethin' was ruther wrong I should say to-wards the last betwixt her and Dunk's wife. I don't suppose she said anything about it here—Missis Guthrie, I mean—and if she did it ain't any of my business."

"No, Peter, Alice made no reference to Miss Jewell that I heard of."

"Oh, well, mayby they ain't much in it; but if I ain't easier fooled than what I take myself to be, there's something. Dunk stuck to her close as he could git, and all the time, except when she'd just call up some other feller. Everybody saw how he were neglectin' of his wife, and I'll be dad fetch it if I wasn't sorry for her; but you know what sort of a bull-head feller Dunk Guthrie is, and it looked like he done forgot all about he had a wife, albe she was as handsome a woman. as was on the ground, to my opinion. I notice her a-lookin' at 'em sometimes, and then turnin' herself away,

like the sight wasn't exactly the thing she ruther see;
and final Dunk and the woman sot down by a tree and
Dunk begun to whisper, when all of a suddent that
Miss Jewell she ris like she was skeered, and she looked
at Missis Guthrie and she started to go to-wards her;
but, bless your soul, Missis Guthrie she ris too, and she
turned her back, and she went for her carriage, and
Dunk arfter her, like he had got to his senses at last,
and they went for home in short order. Miss Jewell
she looked non-plushed for a while. Still, she rattled
on with me while her school-girls were gitting up their
things. I hope they isn't anything serious. I jes
thought I'd tell you about it. I'm not going to open
my mouth about it to anybody else." .

Stapleton, after some rather grave reflection, said:

"I've been told that Duncan is sometimes imprudent in the society of young women. His wife, who
is the soul of honor and delicacy, may feel hurt occasionally by his thoughtless deportment; but I hope no
harm will come of what you tell me, Peter."

"I do, too, but I wouldn't swear it. I know Dunk
Guthrie better than you do, Jack."

"Perhaps you do."

"Jack Stapleton, you know, sir, that a good deal of
my time that I might put to better use is took up
a-thinkin' about you; and special these last three days
and nights, sence you've got another baby, and no tellin'
when sich as that is to stop, that my mind a heap of the
time I jes can't keep it off o' your wife and children?
You are the doggona-mightiest, doggonedest feller I
ever knowed in all my life that's got the wife you has
and keers nothin' for her intrusts nor her children's;

them that's done come already, and leavin' out them in rapid sequession that's *to* come, and if that's cussin' you'll have to excuse it ; that's all I got to say."

"My sakes ! I don't think I understand all your oaths, Peter ; but they sound awful."

" That's the way I want 'em to sound to a man that's a-letting Dunk Guthrie and his mother cut his wife and children out o' their rights, and he hain't the enigy nor not the sperrit to try to stop it. And I want you to know that I ain't the ouliest man nor woman that talks that way, not by a jugful."

Others of the neighbors, with more or less directness, had hinted to Stapleton their opinions that he was too submissive to a state of things that it was worth while to protest against if not endeavor to alter, and even-tempered as he was, the subject was disagreeable to think about, more so to discuss. He answered with some impatience.

" Why, Peter, what am I to do ? In the first place, the property belongs to Mrs. Guthrie by Mr. Guthrie's will. In the next place, neither Caroline nor I care enough about the matter to make any public ado. We've got as much as we need now, and we are in-creasing it as fast as we care to. Then we both know that complaining will have no result but set people to talking more, and put Caroline on hostile terms with the family, a thing she wants to avoid."

Braddy, looking at him with a grin that tried to be as savage as possible, asked :

" What about your children, sir, male and female, female and male, special, female. What about *them* ? "

"O Pete ! You talk as if the children were bound

to perish. Rather than that, I suppose Mrs. Guthrie will do something for them in her will; and if she doesn't, I'm not disturbed by fear of not being able to make as much for them as they'll need. I won't deny that sometimes I feel a little stung, and so does Caroline, by such undeserved treatment; but I don't see any way to remedy it, at least in Mrs. Guthrie's lifetime, and not much, if any, afterward."

"I should say so! In the first place, the old lady ain't a-goin' to die before you're an old man. She's a-goin' to live tell every tooth—"

"Come, Peter! Such talk is not right, nor like you."

"Doggone it all, no! It ain't, about anybody. I take it every word back. I forgot myself for the minute. But it's because I git so mad sometimes about this whole business that I can't always keep in the p's and q's like a man ought when he's a talkin' about females of all kind. But, Jack, die when she will, she's goin' to do nothin', or what's next to nothin', for anybody that's got your name stuck on to the end, and you know Dunk Guthrie well enough to not doubt in your mind that he'll take every blessed thing his mother will palm off on him *before* she die and *when* she die, and then it'll be too late, and Tom Tolly say it ain't fur from being too late now."

"That so?"

"Yes; it *is* so, and nothin' else *but* so. *I've* talked to Tom, if *you* wouldn't, and when I told him what my father used to tell me about old man Guthrie's will, which he was one o' the witnesses, and what the old man said about it, at the signin' and after the signin',

Tom said the will wasn't worth the paper it was writ
on. But now let me tell you. The children was nothin' but children, and everybody thought Missis Guthrie
was goin' to do right, like she had ought to and like
she promised the old•man. But what's closer to the
p'int, Tom asked me if your wife was of age when you
married her, and I told him yes; because you and her
waited a purpose till she were twenty-one, so she
couldn't be called disobedient to her mother. Then
what you reckon Tom said? Why he up, he did, and
he went on to talk about the law of the case, and he
say, Tom did, that the Statchit o' Limitations—you
know what that is better than I do—but it potects
orphans and minor children tell they git of age, and
after that, she don't bother with their business, but
lets 'em root for theirselves, that is providin' the female portions of 'em don't marry before twenty-one
and so git flung in the power o' their husbands, and in
that case the Statchit keep on hangin' to 'em. But
you see how it is in your case. That ar Statchit begun
a-runnin' ag'inst your wife soon in the mornin' the day
you got married, and Tom say that when she once
starts on a run, they ain't anything on top o' the ground
can head her or stop her, and he say, Tom do, that in
less than another year she'll be gone for good, because
the law give you four years, and you've used up three
of 'em. Now, Jack, I have brung in Tom's name
ruther aginst his consent, because Tom Tolly ain't one
to want *nobody* to think that he is after gittin' a law
case by meddlin' in other people's business. He jes
answered my questions as I asked 'em, and he answered
'em pine blank."

"Tom ought to know that I couldn't misjudge him, Peter, but don't you see that an attack upon the will would be imputing fraud to Mrs. Guthrie."

"No, it wouldn't. Or, if so be, it would be taken it off of *Mister* Guthrie. Why, sir, one thing made pa suspicion about the thing was because the old man Guthrie was so fond of his daughter. It was Calline this, and Calline that; and he proved everything he said about how good and smart she was by her own mother, and he got her promise to take keer of her, and after all that, lo! and behold! Oh, my Lord! If I can't sometimes think I can see little Alan Stapleton a growed up man, with his grandpa's name exceptin' of that tag a comin' on behind, and what's worse a awful sight, Calline Stapleton, the very pictur of her mother, bootiful as a pink, sharp as a brier, smart as a steel-trap, and both of 'em poor as Job's coffin, or his turkey, either. I'll be dogamighty doggoned to dognation, by the eternal, if it don't hurt my feelings sometimes to that I have to go off somewhar and mighty nigh cry!"

He rose from the log on which they were seated, strode around within a moderate circle, kicked violently several stumps and tender young trees, and thus having discharged some of his exuberant passion, raised his coat-tails, thrust them backward with disdain, and resumed his seat. After some further discussion in a calmer tone, they returned to the house. A little more of gallant badinage with Mrs. Stapleton, and the visitor took his leave.

———

# CHAPTER XII.

## MOTHER AND SON.

Guthrie had spent the evening with his mother. It was thus that she preferred to have him with her-self. Heartily as she had favored his marriage with Alice Ludwell, because it was in accord with her notions regarding property and family connections, yet she could never subdue the jealousy always indulged at the thought of his becoming attached to anybody else more fondly than to herself. This feeling was in her breast, distinctly asserting itself when for the first time she took into her arms his bride. When she discovered the infirmity, Alice partly compassionated and partly excused such devotion to one whom she herself worshiped, and she hoped and endeavored to become as much a daughter to her as Duncan was her son. The futility of such endeavor was soon made manifest, and the refusal to join in ignoring Mrs. Stapleton increased the distance between them. Mrs. Guthrie's jealous eyes noted not only without alarm, but with pleasure the failure of Alice to make Duncan less ready to accept her undue partialities. He did not appear to object to the growth of attachment between his sister and his wife, perhaps because they served in a degree to palliate public sentiment, which, as he must know, condemned the treatment of the former. So the relations between her son and her daughter-in-law had become about as Mrs. Guthrie would have planned.

At a massive mahogany table covered with red dam-

ask mother and son sat.  Thereon were two branched
silver candlesticks and a service of silver none or little
the worse from having been through several generations.  A variety of good things were served ; for Mrs.
Guthrie often said that the only difference between her
meals when alone and when having company was the
length of her table and the quantity of eatables put
upon it.

"I'll lay Alice, nor her mother before her, can't beat
that cup of coffee, Duncan."

"No, indeed ; but Alice tries to learn all the arts
about coffee, and she would succeed faster but that she
herself prefers it weak, having some sort of notion that
when strong it is not good for her."

"Yes ; that's just the notion of some young married
women and housekeepers these days.  They think they
must study about their nerves.  I'm thankful that wasn't
the case with me.  To tell the truth, I was married—and
not married young at that—and had children before I
knew that I *had* any nerves, and my suspicion is that
doctors encourage the idea of 'em to make people send
for them oftener, when my opinion is that often what's
the principal matter with complaining people is the
need of sticking closer to work, meddling as little as
they can help in other folks' business, and keeping up
an appetite for their victuals."

After supper they repaired to the piazza, Mrs. Guthrie taking with her a vast turkey-tail fan in defense of
the heat which her generous supper had encouraged,
and now she was ready for a chat of the sort she liked.

"So Alice thought she must go down to Caroline's.
Well, I'm glad she went.  If there's anybody *I am*

sorry for, it's poor Caroline. She was a beautiful girl, and could have done *so* much better. Yet, as far as I can see, she's never showed the first sign that she thought she'd made a mistake. Of course she can't help herself now; but I do think when she's in my presence and I happen to mention that man's name, she needn't take me up before I've said anything like what I started out to say, and then go to running on about what a great man he is, and how devoted to her and she to him. At my time of life, and knowing how violently I was opposed to her marrying him, such as that seems to me ungrateful. But I don't object to Alice going there occasionally, because it looks better before the community for some of the family to fall in there once in a while— Yes, light your cigar, my son. I don't mind it out here. Indeed, I love for *you* to smoke, although I despise the thing in the house when it's got cold. But I'd rather *you'd* smoke than not, because you love it, and because when other people are having you to themselves and I'm here all by myself, even the cold scent of your cigar, if nothing else, is some comfort to me, because it minds me of the times before anybody came between us; not that I don't think you married very well, and as well as any mother ought to expect, Duncan, and I think a heap of Alice; you know I do."

"Certainly, mother, and I am very glad to know it. Alice is a good woman and a good wife. She knows by this time that nobody can ever get entirely between you and me. She is sorry for Caroline, just as you are, and feeling that she ought to go there sometimes, I never object when she proposes it."

"I'm glad you don't, and it's very good in you to

be indulgent with her under the circumstances. Yes, smoke your cigar. I like to smell it when you are smoking. Nobody else. I hope Caroline, no matter how much *he* may want it done, will not name Jack Stapleton's child after me. I suppose Alice will tell me or send me word how Caroline is when she gets back. Ah me! It's hard at my time of life. But, Duncan, I've had so much trouble, one kind and another, do you know I've learned better how to fight it off than I used to? For fighting is the only way to meet it. I wonder if they'd take a few more negroes now since another mouth has come to be fed. That creature hooted at it when Alan was born, or made Caroline do it, having her under his thumb as he's always had her, because I wanted to settle them so he couldn't put his paws on them to sell them for his debts."

"I doubt if they would take them, mother, in the way you would propose. Of course, you will do as you think best; but, if I were in your place, I think I'd send them a few negroes and a little money, and say nothing about any settlement. Jack is not a money-making fellow; but he's not a spendthrift. Like other men, he's naturally opposed to his wife having any estate separate from his own."

To do Guthrie justice, his greed for fortune was far from being as eager as his mother's, and, while he was willing to have the lion's part of what she had to bestow, he really wished that his sister's should be larger than it was. This was as well from some sense of justice and natural affection as for the sake of mitigating public opinion, which he well knew to be against himself, though not to the same degree as against his mother. He had a desire for the Legislature, to which, during a period long before and several years after, the counties generally used to send their ablest men; but those closest to him had kept him from making a canvass, assured that he would be defeated. He made that suggestion to his mother sincerely, knowing that it would at least do himself no harm, if he had little hope of its doing Mrs. Stapleton any good.

"I shall do no such a thing! Whatever I may give, I mean to give to those children. I can't bear the very *thought* of Jack Stapleton owning any more of my property, dead or alive; and one thing I had on my mind to tell you to-night was I wanted you to make out a will for me. Not that I'm not as healthy and feel as healthy and strong as I ever felt in my life; and a will is a solemn sort of thing to keep about a body, or even to put their name to it, that they know is one thing to outlast them, and give every blessed thing away except the clothing they're buried in!"

She rose, fanning herself rapidly, and instantly sat down again.

"But," she continued, "all such as that is notions, of course, and means nothing here nor there, and I feel like it wouldn't be right to you to keep putting it off. I can sign the thing without looking at it, and you can keep it, as I wouldn't feel comfortable having it here in the house. So, when I get ready for it, I'll tell you how I want it."

The law, as Guthrie well knew, has always been suspicious of wills in the handwriting of favored legatees whose claims by natural right are not superior to those of some others. He informed her of this, and she caught instantly the need of making everything entirely secure.

"Well, who had I better get to write it, then? Mr. Jamison used to attend to what law business your father had; but I don't want him for *that*, and I have my reasons. Your father sent for him to write *his* will, when at last I got him to see he ought to make one, and he wouldn't do it, because he said your father wasn't strong enough at the time—like *he* knew anything about it, or that it was any of *his* lookout—and he went away saying he'd attend to it some other time; and so I got your father to let me send for Mr. Suttle, and he wrote it. The fact is, I knew it was a thing it wouldn't do to put off, because your father he got to going into some sort of decline. He could go about as well as ever, and had as good an appetite as he ever had; but he got to having some sort of headaches, and they made him fretful and rather suspicious, and it took a heap of pains sometimes to keep him down from being against everybody except Caroline! He was right in his mind except fretful and making more of Caroline than me and you both, and more than he always had been doing. But, by the closest attention and all of old Job's patience, I got him out of that long enough to get him to consent to make his will; and I told him he knew I was a business woman, and to will the property to me to manage the best I could, and he told me to have it made just as I wanted it. And so that was the will Mr. Suttle wrote, and he witnessed it, and so did Jimmy Butcher, that lived in that little house on the Augusta road just out of town, who used to do any little carpenter jobs we wanted about the lot. And Mr. Suttle said we had to have three witnesses, and at that very minute old Mr. Braddy, that Pete Braddy's father, was riding by, and Mr. Suttle went out and called *him* in. I was sorry he done it at first, because he seemed like *he* must be very particular, like Mr. Jamison. But I was glad of it afterward, because when he asked your father point-blank if that was his will he was signing, your father said yes promptly and squarely."

During this narration her fan was doing its best work.

"Have you ever mentioned those circumstances to any person, mother?"

"No, not until now, when I'm telling them to you. The main reason I never did it was because it was nobody else's business. It was all right, wasn't it, Duncan? You ask the question solemn-like—like *you* had some suspicions, too."

"No, no, mother. I could have no sort of suspicion of you doing anything except what you believed to be right. I merely thought I'd ask the question. I had no particular reason. What became of Butcher? Do you happen to remember? Mr. Suttle, I know, moved to Louisiana some years back."

"*I* don't know what became of Butcher. They moved away somewhere a year or so afterward, where, I don't know, and never asked. Such people are always moving and vibrating about. What makes you ask *that?*"

"Nothing very particular, mother. As you've told me of the will, I was just thinking I'd get all the information about it that I could. It is very interesting to me."

"Duncan," she said after a thoughtful silence of a

minute or more, "as I have told you that much I've concluded to tell you some more."

She rose, walked into the hall and called to Judy, who, answering from the rear part of the mansion, came quickly.

"You may go out to the kitchen, or one of the houses, and stay till I want you.  Don't you come till I ring the bell."

"Yes'm, mistess."

"Go on."

Returning to her seat, she then continued:

"Duncan, if what was done hadn't been done, something a heap worse would have happened.  The property you see me with, and the property you've got, except what you married into, instead of being where it is, would, a long way the biggest part of it, be on Little River, with Jack Stapleton a-lording over it; and you'd have been poor, and me—dead, I reckon, and that of a broken heart.  Your father always thought I was partial to you, and that made him more partial to Caroline; and the fact is, I had to do something to keep me and you from being cut off, as he came near threatening to do more than once after his headaches came upon him.  Caroline loved her father, and was always hugging and flattering whenever she was about him; but you was rather shy of him, and you held mostly to your mother, as, bless your heart, you have always done.  If it was to do over again, I'd do it a thousand times."

"You did as you thought best, mother, there can be no doubt about that.  Did father refer much to his will after it was executed?"

"What do you mean by 'executed'?"

" I mean the signing."

" No, not one single time ; not to me he didn't.   I think he forgot all about it, and I was glad he did.   If he hadn't, and had taken into his head to make another, woe be to me and you ; for he used to cry and go on, and say nobody cared anything for him except Caroline. But after he signed the will he calmed down out of all that, and never spoke a cross word till he died three months after.   But he never took to his bed till a week before that.   What makes you ask so many questions, Duncan ?   You actually worry me."

" I only wanted to get at all the facts, mother, so as to be sure of the ground we stand on.   Did he give you any directions or any advice about the management of the property ? "

" Not one word.   Your father knew, of course, that I had sense enough to do what was best with my own children, and I have done it, and I mean to keep on doing it ; but I'm going to do it in my own way, because I've been through too much for Caroline Stapleton, as she chooses to call herself, in disobedience to my wishes, to do according to her way, and specially the way of that creature."

" Well, mother," he said, rising, " it is getting time for us both to sleep.   You think about it, and when you have decided as to what you want let me know. I'd be as liberal with Caroline as I could.   There's nothing to hinder your giving what you please to the children."

" That's what I shall do with what I *do* do.   But don't go quite yet.   Sit down.   I haven't told all I wanted.   Sit down, sit down."

8

Her voice, which had been low, sank lower, and its tone was one of sadness with some bitterness.

"Old as I am, and young as I have been, my son, I've never had nigh the comfort that I think I ought. It's always been my nature to want to love and be loved, and I always knew how to give, but never how to get—that is, until you were born.  I can't tell you, nor I won't tell you many of the things I've been through, even with your father about Caroline.  But although I longed for it, the child never cared for me from the time even before she was weaned ; but her father was all, all, everything to her even then ; and when she'd get enough nourishment from me, if her father was by, she'd hold out her hands to him and cry if he didn't take her that very minute, and all I could do I couldn't get her to care anything for me except to be fed.  Your father, he'd laugh and say to not mind it, because she was too young to know any better, and she'd come all right in time.  But I tell you, Duncan, it rankled through my very blood to think after all I'd been through in my life, and what I had been through for her, that she was the most beautiful thing I ever laid my eyes on, and then for her to not have any love for me !  Why, it makes me wretched now, sometimes, here by myself to think of how miserable it used to make me when I'd be suckling her and she'd look up in my face, let go the breast, and go to screaming till I'd have to turn her over to her father or her nurse, and wished to God she'd never been born !  The child could see at that very *time*—she could see the misery she was giving me, and I declare sometimes if she didn't look like she was sorry she couldn't love me.  And when you came I said to myself, have I got to go through such as that again and have children to love other people and not *me?* and I could'nt tell the times before you were born, and after it, I got down on my knees and I *told* God Almighty that I thought any mother was *entitled* to the love of at least one of her own offspring, and then—come here a minute, Duncan."

When he came she embraced him, shedding hot tears the while ; but a moment afterward, releasing him, and drying her eyes, she said :

"That'll do ; go back to your seat. Only the Lord knows what a comfort he sent to me in you !

"But I never mistreated Caroline. Of course no mother could do that with her own child. I just let her alone, except to work for her and do for her the same as I worked and done for you. I never laid my hand on her to strike her in all her life. And when you showed so different, I said to myself, Mr. Guthrie had one to himself, now I've got one to *myself*. But a man's a man, and he wants all, and he tried to make you love him like you did me; but I swore you shouldn't. And when at last he began to fail, and go on so with his threats—" She rose, looked round, then advancing with one arm high lifted, whispered : "Duncan Guthrie, before that should have been done, *I'd* have done things which you lawyers, and you judges think you must send people that do 'em to your peni-*tentiary!* but I'd have killed the one that first laid hands on me to take me there ! Now," turning away, "you may go on home. I'll let you know when I want anything done. Don't name it to me till I tell you. I won't be fit in some time to talk about it, and I don't expect to get hardly a wink of sleep this night."

She let him press her cheek with his lips, then turned into the house. Her maid came running to the sound of the bell.

"Judy, put your mattress on the floor at the foot of my bed, and when you've washed your hands, sprinkle some cologne water over both my pillows; then, after I get to bed, do you go to rubbing me till I get to sleep or tell you to stop."

Guthrie pondered the revelations made by his mother, and they gave him some anxiety. Mr. Macfarlane, in his efforts through him to induce her to do a more liberal part by Mrs. Stapleton, had spoken with some earnestness of what was generally known to be the state of his father's mind about the time when the will purported to have been executed, and hinted that some trouble might come if efforts should ever be made to set it aside. Guthrie did not expect that such action would ever be begun, and he never had feared that if begun it could succeed. But his mother's case, he saw, was not as strong as he had always been supposing, and the bare possibility of public investigation gave him some apprehension. He wished now more earnestly than ever that she had done, or that she would do what at least would tend to satisfy the public, and he resolved that he would urge such action upon her as soon as he could find her in fit mood. He lay awake much longer than usual, but the night's rest reinvigorated his spirits, and he doubted not that he could manage the business with satisfactory results.

## CHAPTER XIII.

### ALICE INTERPOSES FOR THE STAPLETONS.

The sight of a peaceful home like that in which she had been reared, wherein domestic love and trustfulness far more than made amends for scant property and injustice endured, touched Alice with tenderness and sympathy. Her mind dwelt much upon the conjugal love and happiness which no outside assaults nor neglects could molest. Exquisitely painful was the sight of the care with which the Stapletons had to economize in their living so as to keep within their income and lay up a trifle yearly for future added needs. The home-made clothes of Stapleton and Alan contrasted with her own costly apparel and some she had wrought for the child just born, Alan's admiring embarrassed gaze at these, and many other such things, inflicted pain that was intensified by the thought that, although against her will, she in some degree was party to the wrong that had made these conditions exist. She shuddered to think that if not already, there was danger of her becoming an unhappy woman. She dared not admit to herself, as she rode alone in silence, regret that she had ever left the home of her childhood. For she had given to her husband her whole self, and she could not but continue to yearn for some at least of the returns to which she regarded herself, thus freely and entirely, given, to be entitled. Only one time had she remonstrated, and that with delicate mildness, with her mother-in-law about a state of things that she had never thought to be possible in a family claiming to be even respectable, and seen with grief and shame that the only result of such interference was diminution of her own value and influence in the family. Yet she felt herself bound by common honesty and common humanity not to give up all efforts in that behalf with her husband. He met her on her return with real pleasure.

"I've been as lonesome as a ghost without you, Alice. I spent the evening with mother; but I can't tell you how I missed you afterward."

He spoke sincerely. During her absence, her value, as it is with selfish people generally, seemed higher than when she was with him all the time. She was pleased by the many questions asked by him with more than usual interest concerning his sister and her children and the general aspect of things about them. Encouraged by his words, she said:

"Duncan, my dear, contented, even happy, as Sister Caroline and Mr. Stapleton are, I could not keep myself from wishing, all the time I was there, that they could be put upon a higher plane of living."

He had hoped that she would not mention that subject again, although he had thought to allude to it himself, but on his own motion and at his own leisure. He answered, dryly:

"I'm sure I wish so too."

She noticed his tone, but decided to proceed.

"Then why not urge mother to do more for them?"

"Because, Alice, it is simply useless. Mother has her own notions about Jack Stapleton, in which, to some extent, I agree with her. He has never made the least effort to conciliate her opposition, nor mine

either.   Poor as he is, and without hereditary name
and family importance, his bearing is, or tries to be,
like that of an owner of an inherited barony.   I'll admit that he's an attractive man—rather so—to women
particularly, and Caroline, poor thing, thinks she is
fully blessed in having such a fellow all to herself.   He
never comes to see mother, Caroline seldom, and when
she does, her deportment is constrained and unaffection-
ate.   Still, both I and Uncle Dennis Macfarlane have
urged mother to do something more for them in spite
of their treatment of her, and she offered to do so, and
only last night she assured me of her intention (as Caroline refuses the offer of any separate estate) to make over
to the children something—she did not say how much."

"As for Caroline's refusal, offered with such conditions," Alice replied in a low voice, wishing to restrain her feelings, "I would have done the same, and I
can not call to my mind a woman among my acquaintance, at least among my friends, who would have acted
otherwise."

"I don't see the aptness of comparing the action of
the wife of such a man as Jack Stapleton with what *my*
wife's might be in possible similar contingencies."

"The aptness is in this: Caroline, like every wife
who is thoroughly loyal, feels that she and her husband
are one, and that not a single item should be allowed
to come in that would tend in the faintest degree
toward their separate existence or any apprehension of
it.   You say Mr. Stapleton never comes in expressly to
see mother.   Has she ever deported herself toward him
so that he could infer that she accepted him as a member of her family ?"

"No; that she has not; nor have I. I'd see Jack Stapleton at the bottom of Little River before I'd call him brother; and rather than call him son, mother, I suspect, would see him farther than that."

"Such as that has surprised me more than anything that has ever come within my experience; for to me Mr. Stapleton has always seemed not only a good man, but gentle and gentlemanlike. I don't wonder that such a man could win Caroline's affections, and that she would abstain from everything that might imperil the perfect harmony that is between him and herself. What I do wonder at is that such a man is not justly appreciated where just appreciation is most needed, and where it would produce abundant blessing. Caroline is devoted to him, as any woman must be to such a husband; she has identified herself with him in everything —property, hopes of every kind—and a happier wife I do not, and never did know. But it looked wrong for a sister-in-law to be the first and only one of her immediate family to go to her with congratulations and proffers of aid on such an occasion as now. In spite of the peace and contentment to which I was witness, I was deeply pained by thoughts of the neglect in which they are suffered to live. What the end of such discrimination is to be God only knows. But I notice that you want me to stop talking about it, and I will. I owed it to—to myself, among others, to say what I have. That is said now, and you need not apprehend that I shall refer to the subject again."

He was not despotic, nor even petulant. Her words had little influence in the direction most desired; but, to some extent, he sympathized with her trouble,

Alice.

unreasonable though it seemed, and so, appearing to have been impressed by her appeals, he declared his intention to consider more carefully the case of his sister and her family, and he gave his promise that before very long he would confer with Mr. Macfarlane, and jointly with him move for whatever further advance his mother could be induced to make. After that they had other talk and some music.

Alice, when she went to bed, hoped that her visit and the report made concerning it had not been in vain. Upon the mind of her husband, fixed within the last few days firmly as unexpectedly, was the conviction that it was to cost more pains than he had counted upon to hold respect where so easily he had conquered affection. The promise just given he intended to fulfill, particularly as it was in the line of the resolution made the night before. But he felt no need to be in haste, and so he delayed and kept delaying until it became too late.

---

## CHAPTER XIV.

### AT THE MACFARLANES.

Mrs. Macfarlane, rather small in youth, now rounded by time, good-living, and good temper, differed from her sister in disposition as much as in stature and general appearance. As good a housekeeper, she was quiet and kindly in her domestic rule. They were no wider apart now than they had been in their youth. The elder, domineering by nature, suppressed

the younger as much as she could, out of envy for the
greater love and admiration paid to the latter by most
of their acquaintances.  Unable to conceal the rude ele-
ments of her being during a period regarded by her as
unjust and unreasonable, she did not receive any offer
of marriage except such as she despised.  When Mr.
Macfarlane began to visit at her father's house and apparently with matrimonial intent, she believed that his
aim was for herself; but when it became known that
her sister, just come to womanhood, was the favorite,
she made little effort to hide her disappointment, and,
almost none, her resentment.  Marriage some years
afterward with Mr. Guthrie, a man of corresponding
wealth and social position, seemed to satisfy her ambition that had been waiting so long, although she continued to have little affection for Mrs. Macfarlane,
whom she could not cease to regard as a rival who had
surpassed her.  Their husbands were friends and co-
laborers in behalf of the general welfare of the community, and their families had always lived on decently
affectionate terms with each other.  Since the death of
Mr. Guthrie they had become yet more reserved in
their intercourse because of the widow's conviction that
some of her actions in managing the estate bequeathed
her by her husband were not approved either by Mr.
Macfarlane or her sister.  Occasionally she consulted
with the former about her business, but she neither
thanked him for any unasked counsel nor heeded it except when convinced of its importance.  Under her
management the Guthrie property had grown to be
considerably larger than his, and she rather suspected
that secretly he had repented of having gone behind

herself in his choice of a wife. If he did not she knew he ought, and that was enough. Her superior bearing was accepted without complaint by her sister. In the family it was a matter for pleasant jesting as well as felicitation that she had learned thoroughly how to prevent assaults from Mrs. Guthrie by making the latter always foresee that they would not be resisted.

The younger members had been fond of one another always, and now and then Charlotte made a visit of a day or two to Mrs. Stapleton, whom she dearly loved. An impulsive, generous girl, she had spoken several times and in honest terms to Duncan about the treatment of his sister, and said that it was his duty to see that it was different. Once when she had reported such appeal at home her mother said:

"Charlotte, interference on your part is sure to do no good to Caroline, and, if reported to sister, will set her against you. She always would reject advice from anybody unless when it coincided with her own notions and resent it whenever voluntarily offered. You see that already she looks with less affection upon Alice, and it is for that reason mainly. Your father has quit talking to either of them upon the subject, and I charge you never to allude to it again with Duncan. Of course, you don't need any warning about talking to your Aunt Hester about it."

"That I don't," answered Charlotte laughing, "but I say it is a shame."

"Of course it is, and your father has warned sister that it is hardly to be expected but that Mr. Stapleton some time or another will seek to enforce by law what he already believes to be his right; but that is his own

affair.   It is and ever was difficult to get along with
sister by the practice of constant prudence. — It will be
impossible if either you or I interfere in this or any
other of her affairs."

About a week after the visit of Alice this family
gave a party.   There was nothing unusual except that
Guthrie's deportment during the whole evening was
serious.   He did not speak once to Miss Jewell.   This
change was obliged to be noticed, especially as several
times he was quite near her.   In her manner also was
not the gayety nor even the self-possession that were
habitual.   She seemed to prefer the society of the elderly ladies, as if she was trying to recover something that
she feared she had lost or to secure what she believed
herself in some danger of losing.   When asked to play,
her pieces were such as she supposed might be most
pleasing to them, and she refused Tolly's request, made
more than once, for those of another kind, her plea being that she was not in correspondent mood.   In this
while Guthrie kept his back toward her, and what chatting he did was with Alice or other married women.
Once during the evening, while passing by Alice, she
saluted her with some hesitation.   Alice returned the
salutation with politeness and nothing more.   When
near the breaking up, Tolly asked if he might be her
escort home, she answered :

"No, thank you, Mr. Tolly.   I am going with Cousin
William."

"I haven't seen you since the picnic."

"No; I wanted to see you after you had left to tell
you something.   On reflection, I was glad you were
called away and I didn't."

All this was said in a low voice, as the following also :

" Won't you tell me now ? "

" No, nor ever. It's of no importance to you, and telling it would do more harm than good."

When all were gone some family commentings were had.

" Young Tolly looked well to-night, Louisa," said Mr. Macfarlane.

" Yes. I was much pleased with his manners. He knows well how to act toward a hostess, and to be considerate of elderly and plain women. He moves in company with the more ease because he makes no special effort, and then he talks as if what he was saying he neither expected nor wished to be regarded as of any more importance than it is in point of fact."

" I like the fellow's simple manliness. He carries a level head upon his shoulders, and looks like one who is willing to wait for fortune because he expects it with confidence. They tell me that his law practice is improving constantly, and has already gone ahead of Duncan's. Duncan won't like him for that. By the way, Charlotte, what was the matter with him and Miss Jewell to-night? If they even spoke to each other, I don't know it. Whenever I have seen them together heretofore, he seemed very devoted ; more so, I thought, than a married man ought to be. Miss Jewell also looked, not as serious as he did, but more staid than usual. Have they fallen out ? "

" It looks so, father, but I'm confident that nothing very serious has taken place. Alice seemed rather worried by Cousin Duncan's neglect of her at the picnic a week ago, and I was glad that, as I believe, Miss Jewell noticed it. I asked her to-night why she was so re-. served, and she answered that she had some reason, but could not then tell me what it was. I am a little afraid that Cousin Duncan was more pronounced in his admiration for her that day than was becoming. I never saw him so gay and so overflowing."

"You suspect, then, that she is shying off from him?"

"Indeed, I do, father."

"Good! I'm glad to hear it. I don't know all about Duncan Guthrie. Sometimes I suspect from his very audacity that he's a little cracked, and his poor mother has always acted as if she wanted him to be so; but I know enough to feel sure that no such woman as Miss Jewell can be entirely safe in accepting his gushing services. I wish she had discouraged them sooner; for there is some little talk about her and Duncan already, and that, if continued, would injure the school, and, what would be worse, hurt herself."

"Miss Jewell, father, has been used to society that, in some respects, is more free than ours or than that of any rural community. I think that she has become assured, at last, of this fact, and has made up her mind to conform to requirements to which she has not been accustomed, especially as she is among those who are comparatively strangers to her."

"I wish," said Mrs. Macfarlane, "that she had come to that decision sooner; for everybody except her knows that Duncan is imprudent to a degree that sometimes amounts to recklessness."

"The difficulty is," pleaded Charlotte, "that she

hadn't been in Clarke long enough to understand Cousin Duncan as, from what father intimates, I am afraid he is, or to know how he is regarded by people whose good opinions it is most worth her while to secure. I could not warn her, because it would have seemed not quite loyal to my own family connections, and might have looked as if I were distrustful of her ability, as I have been and now am not, to take care of herself. I think that day's experience has taught them both a lesson. She did not need it near as much as Cousin Duncan, for I do believe her to be as honorable a woman as I ever saw. She admits that she likes the society of gentlemen, and she does so in a way to convince anybody of her unsuspicious innocence."

"That's right, Charlotte. Defend whomsoever you know or believe to be guiltless. Society in this region has become more exacting than it used to be, especially in the case of women. Your mother, as well as I, remembers the greater freedom that was once allowed. Thirty years ago waltzing was as common almost as dancing, and card-playing as common as checkers. I never knew any special harm to come from such license; but the religious denominations, in their zeal each to get ahead of the rest, have induced conditions that women especially, for their own safety, are obliged to conform to. Duncan knows that as well as anybody; but he thinks that he can afford to be an outlaw strong enough to protect any who will belong to his following. Poor fellow! He is doing less for himself than I had hoped when he first went to the bar. His father's death was a grievous loss to him. There was one of the justest and most discreet men that I ever knew.

But what is to be expected of a young man so selfish as to be willing to accept the open, avowed preference of his mother over his own sister, who is worth a dozen of him?  I declare it pains me every time I think how Caroline is treated, and if not with his consent without enough of dissent to amount to anything.  I wish he was half the man that John Stapleton is.  Just here, I will say something, to go no further.  I don't believe that John Stapleton, careless, good-natured fellow that he seems, is going to submit always to injustice which there is no word so fit to describe as *shocking;* and if he ever does make an assault upon Alan Guthrie's will, both of them will see sights that will make them wish they had acted differently, whether such assault be made good or not.  At least Duncan will.  I'm not so sure about Hester.  What effect do you think, Louisa, that challenge to public investigation would have upon her?"

"None, husband, but to rouse her anger and confirm her opinions that she has been doing right.  Poor sister!  I hardly know what to think about her.  I never knew her to admit that she believed herself to be in the wrong.  She would be for fighting till the last."

"Oh, yes, indeed!  She's got the pluck of a whole army of veteran soldiers.  Well, I shall not volunteer advice to her any more, much as I think she needs it.  I did once get her to offer them a little more property, but she insisted upon settling it in a way that Stapleton would not and could not accept.  No man that is a man would consent to be made an exception which would lessen his standing among other men."

"And women too."

"Yes, and women too. If the law should ever be so modified as to secure all married women's property alike, such things would be tolerable because general. But Caroline was right in refusing to accept this offer; for she did it herself without waiting to ask her husband's views. My opinion of him, who has been growing upon me ever since he came into the family, is that he is as manly in spirit as he is a son of Anak in physical size and strength, and that if he ever makes up his mind to fight, he'll do it with a vigor and tenacity that will surprise even Hester. To think that they now have two children and have to econom— Look here, Louisa, has Hester been down there since this last baby was born?"

"No, I'm sorry to say. Alice told me to-night that she had not. I'd go there myself, but I know that my going before her would provoke her."

"It's a crying shame! But I won't talk about it any more to-night, and I'm sorry I got upon the subject. Yes, Tolly is a good fellow, I think, and Miss Jewell is certainly as good-looking a woman as I should ever wish to see. Perhaps they may make a match of it, eh, Charlotte?"

But Charlotte had risen and was lighting her candle.

"Yes," said her father, "I think it's high time to go to bed. I'm off too."

## CHAPTER XV.

### MRS. GUTHRIE GOES TO LITTLE RIVER.

ALICE went home and afterward to bed with a sense of varied uneasiness. The sight of Miss Jewell, subdued so far below her usual vivacity, touched her with compassion, and she almost wished that she had met her advance with less coldness. It imparted a genuine grief that she could have been so far led away as to conceive for a married man an unlawful feeling, and she sincerely hoped that if Guthrie was not mistaken in his suspicion his withdrawal from her society would restore her freedom of heart and lead her to a perfect sense of duty. Restless, beset with troublous dreams through the night, she was awakened before the dawn by the opening and closing of the front gate and the feet of a galloping horse. Roused by her, Guthrie rose, and as the rider called aloud from the ground below their bedroom window, raised the sash and asked :

"Who is there ?"

"Simon, sir, Marse Jack Stapleton's man. Marster sent me up in a hurry to tell Miss Alice, Miss Calline vay sick, an' him an' Miss Calline bofe un 'em, want her to come down dar quick as she can git dar."

"Alice, a messenger from Stapleton says—"

"I heard," answered Alice, rising and, dim as the light was, beginning to dress herself. "Duncan, please call to Marcus to get the carryall as soon·as possible, and tell Martha to make a pot of coffee for me and him."

"Oh, my dear, I wouldn't go there in that way, nor before I had got my breakfast. The case can't be so urgent as all that."

"I must go, Duncan; please, don't hinder me. Sister Caroline needs me, and that is the way to get there soonest. If you feel like going, you·can drive me instead of Marcus."

"Of course I shall go if it becomes necessary; but I think I'd better wait, if you insist upon starting immediately, and know of mother what she wants done."

Alice called to the messenger, and said:

"Simon, tell your master that I am coming at once."

"Yes'm, mistess, Marse Jacky told me to git de word, en den gallop to old miss en k'yar de news to her."

"That's right; go on and do so."

When Alice was gone Guthrie hastened to his mother's. He found her, although not fully dressed, striding about the house issuing orders in loud, harsh language.

"You Moses, I wish you'd come to me sooner, sir, when I send word that I want you right away."

"Yes'm, miss, at de minute Judy give me de word—"

"Stop it! You go and feed and curry the carriage horses, and while they're eating do you get out the carriage and give it a good greasing; and after you've got a bite of breakfast yourself, do you hitch up and bring out; and mind you put some corn in a bag to take under your seat and strap on behind some fodder. Off with you. You going to stand there all day like a fool looking at me? You Chloe! Come to that kitchen door. When you've got my breakfast, give Moses some coffee and wrap him up something— enough to last him all day. Give him a plenty. You know what that negro's appetite is, do you hear?"

"Yes'm. Law, miss! Mose know he ain' never gwine suffer for plenty t' eat, nor nobody else ner no nother creetur on dis place."

"And lookee here, now; I want my breakfast quick, and I don't want it burnt up. You may put a tea-spoonful more of coffee than common in the pot. You Judy!"

The girl was standing by her side.

"Ah, here you are. Get out my second-best traveling-gown, and fetch it to me. I'll put it on here, or wherever you find me, and then you lock up all my drawers and bring me the keys. Ah, here's Duncan! Come in, my son, come right along in. I'll have on my gown as soon as Judy fetches it. Here it is now, Fix it on me quick, and don't be awkward and fumbling about it. O Duncan, didn't I know trouble was going to come, and haven't I been prophesying it ever since she married that man? And to think that I had to be waked up just after I had got into a little bit of a nap of sleep by that negro bawling out, that if it was the last word I had to speak I thought the house was afire and not much chance of getting out of it alive! When I got up and got my senses, I gave him a caution for scaring me that way. He said he'd been to your house, and I was just going to send word to Alice that I'd go by there for her, and not have the trouble of two carriages."

" Alice has already gone, mother, with Marcus in the carryall.   I couldn't get her to wait."

" What ! the poor child went without her breakfast? But Alice is young.   You don't suppose the case is that bad, do you, my son ?   I declare I was that flurried and flustered I forgot to ask that negro what was the matter until he had done gone.   Did he tell you ? "

" He told Alice that the trouble began in her leg, and had gone to one of her breasts."

" Humph, humph !   I know exactly what's the matter.   She's threatened with milk fever and nothing *but* milk fever.   I'm glad John Stapleton got scared about it and sent for me—without he done it just to trouble and scare me—because I know what to do with such a case, and no doctor does.   Alice needn't have gone off in such a hurry, knowing no more what to do than a baby.   There's no danger if it's managed right. Are you going, Duncan ?   It isn't worth while without you want to.   I've ordered Moses to have the carriage ready time I get breakfast.   Everybody knows that at my time of life *I* couldn't start on such a travel as that without my breakfast, and there isn't any need of it. But if you've got business, my son, I wouldn't go. Your going wouldn't be of any earthly good."

" Alice seemed to think I ought to go, and I told her I would.   Of course I want to do what is right by Caroline."

" Everybody knows that, Duncan, not excepting Alice, if she'd stop and think about it.   Alice is headstrong, though I oughtn't to say that about any man's wife and in his presence.   But if I was in your place, I shouldn't be breaking off from my business and rushing down there when there's no need of it; for I tell you again it's nothing but milk fever the poor child's got, and I know what to do with that, and no man does, doctor or no doctor. I'll send you word if you're wanted for anything. You Judy, have you set the table, and got everything ready? Well, go out and tell Chloe that if she thinks it's going to take her all day to get one little breakfast for one lone person, I'll go out and help her. No, you needn't tell her that, as the poor thing hasn't had time enough, and I know she's doing her best; but you go and help her dish up and bring in what she's got, and tell her to fry a chicken for your Marse Duncan— Or would you rather have it broiled, Duncan?"

"Any way will suit me, mother, if you think I'd better not go."

"Tell her to fry it, Judy, and get up a nice breakfast. She needn't be in such a great hurry about that, as your Marse Duncan isn't going. Still, I reckon she has sense enough to know that nobody wants to wait too long after they are dragged out of bed of a morning before they can get something on their stomach. Poor Caroline! I declare—to think of what she could have done, instead of being cooped up away down there on Little River with the milk fever! It makes me *cry!*" She stopped, and for a while yielded to lamentation. "I don't know when I've cried before; but I feel some better now I've done it."

She ate her breakfast in haste, yet not without some heartiness; for she knew the importance of fortifying herself for any sort of undertaking by a substantial morning meal. The carriage appeared at the gate as she was giving directions about what was to be done during her absence.  These she broke away from, and when she was seated said :

"Moses, be careful driving over the rough places. The Lord knows there's many a one of them which is a shame to the very county, and a sin to boot.  If I was a man I think I could do something to regulate such things better; but you do the best you can, and when you come to a smooth stretch, let your horses move on.  There's a chance to water them between here and there, ain't there ? "

" Oh yes'm, Miss."

" Well, drive on.  To think a woman of my age, though I'm not as old as some, but to think that with all the work and responsibilities on my hands, I have to be dragged away from it in this kind of style, and all for nothing but disobedience,"

The carriage moved off.  At every jolt, even the lightest, its occupant gave a groan ; yet she said nothing to impede the coachman who, she well knew, was to be trusted entirely.  When on the levels she urged him mildly to make what haste he could consistently with due regard for the team.  Arrived at their destination, they were turned through the open gate and, trotting with decent speed, were drawn up at the opening of the simple little court.  Mrs. Guthrie descended with deliberation, her face wearing an air of lofty honorable compromise, betokening that its wearer was bestowing much and getting next to nothing.

# CHAPTER XVI.

### MRS. GUTHRIE WITH HER DEAD.

THE sun was not more than half an hour high when Alice arrived. She was just in time to get the last farewell of Caroline Stapleton. One of those maladies that are peculiar to women in her condition which medical skill can neither foresee nor hinder nor even delay, had seized upon her life. She had time to express her gratitude for another sight of one so well loved and her wishes about her newly born child, then, turning her eyes back upon her husband who was kneeling by her side, she expired, apparently without pain. One cry of anguish was made by John Stapleton; then rising, he said:

"Alice, you will know what to do. If Mrs. Guthrie should come, I would prefer not to meet her, at least to day, unless she should express a desire to see me about the funeral. In that event, I shall be within Simon's call."

Then he went out.

Two hours afterward when Mrs Guthrie had alighted, the girl Clarissy came running to her and cried:

"Law, old Miss! Miss Calline done dead!"

The old lady looked at the girl fiercely, and, reaching forth and inserting her fingers in her collar, cried:

"Nigger, do you know who you're fooling with? My strong suspicion is, you don't."

The negro, screaming, tore herself away and ran back into the house, her assailant following. At the opening of the passage the latter was met by Alice, and, looking at her with yet greater ferocity, she said, in tones that she tried in vain to lower:

"Alice, Alice Guthrie! tell me, tell me, *tell* me that that nigger has told me a lie! You know how the things love to scare people! For God Almighty's sake, say so, Alice!"

"O mother, would that I could! Poor dear Sister Caroline died at half-past eight o'clock!"

"My God!"

She sank into a chair, breathing as if she had been running for her life.

"Sit down here by me, Alice. I don't think—I *can't* think you would go that far with me; and then you called her 'sister.' May be it's so, as that fool nigger said. You're certain in your mind, Alice?"

"Indeed, yes, mother—she is already dressed and laid out in the room behind you, where she died."

"In this room, right here, behind me?"

And she knocked upon the wall several times with the back of her hand.

"Yes, mother."

"Yes? Well, I can't go in there yet. Alice, I want to ask you a question, and I tell you plain that I don't want, and I don't think it's any time for dodging and fooling. Can you tell me the reason why they didn't let me know sooner? Is that man—you know who I mean—is he in the room behind there?"

"No, mother. Mr. Stapleton is not in the house. We were notified as soon as possible after the attack was found to be serious. Nothing could have come more unexpectedly. When I was here a week ago

Sister Caroline was never more bright and cheerful, and Mr. Stapleton says she continued so until yesterday evening."

"*Sister* Caroline! Yes, I remember you always called her *sister*, and I liked it, because it looked well. Say, John Stapleton ain't in there?"

"No, mother. He went out, saying we could send for him whenever he might be wanted."

"The good Lord knows *I* don't want him, and I don't wonder at his going off and hiding himself when he knew I was coming. It's just like the whole set of such people. Who attended to the—to the—you know what I mean, Alice."

"I have done everything that was necessary, mother, with such help as was at hand."

"Everything that was necessary," she repeated, looking around vaguely, "everything that was necessary. I'm glad you done it, Alice; for it has all flustered me so, I'm afraid I couldn't. Those vines all up and along there, they look better than I was counting on when she told me she'd planted them there. What's become of the children, Alice?"

"The baby is in the room across the passage, mother; Alan is with his father."

"Well, is any chance, is anything been arranged to keep the poor little thing from perishing?"

"Oh, yes, ma'am. Our Eliza has a young baby, and gives much more nourishment than it needs. I have sent for her, and I'm sure Duncan won't object."

"Object? Of course not, not for *nobody* in such a case. I'm glad to hear it. Yes, I believe Judy did tell me a week or so ago that Eliza had another baby; but

I forgot it at the time.  That's the only good piece of news I've heard to-day.  Yes, yes, Eliza.  She's one of the negroes that come by you.  A rather nice, good, healthy, clean young woman, isn't she?"

"A very excellent woman, mother, and perfectly healthy."

"Ah, I'm thankful to hear it.  But won't somebody come and shoo away that mocking-bird in that bush out there?  Of course I know the thing don't know any better, but I declare such joyful, unconcerned singing and screaming—but I see it's nest of young ones there among the vines.  Let it alone.  I'll try to go in now if you'll help me to get up.  Will you promise to stand by me, Alice?  I don't know when I have been so flustered.  You'll stand by me, will you, Alice?"

"Certainly, mother."

Alice assisted her to rise.  As she held out her hand the piece torn from the girl's collar fell.  She looked at it and said:

"How in this world did I come by that rag?  I feel right foolish.  Ain't you sorry for anybody that's that foolish, Alice?  I know I am.  But I suppose everybody is liable to get that way sometimes."

She entered and walked with studied firmness to the table on which the body was laid.  When Alice removed the handkerchief from the face, she gave a momentary glance, then, uttering a fearful scream, turned away, and reeling, in spite of the efforts of Alice to prevent, plunged upon the bed on which her daughter had died.

"O Caroline, Caroline!  I wish I had never been born to live to this!" she moaned from the pillow on which her face was half buried. "I never *could* see how it is that people can be taken away out of this world so unexpected! O Caroline! if you had only loved me! Alice, Alice Guthrie," she cried, suddenly raising herself, supported by her two hands upon the edge of the bed, one leg beneath her and the other extended toward the floor, her clothes in sad disorder, "did Caroline leave any words for me? If she did, I want the truth, the whole truth, and nothing but the truth, so help you God! That's the way they tell me they swear them in the court house. Tell me, did she?"

"Yes, mother. She asked me to tell you and Duncan that she had always loved you both very much. That was all she said; she had no time to say any more."

"And did the child know she was going to die when she sent me that message? Come now, Alice. If there ever was a time that I didn't want to be fooled with it is now, and I beg—I *order* you—not to do it."

"Her mind, mother, was perfectly clear and perfectly calm."

"I tell you, child, or madam, or whatever you want yourself called, she *wasn't!* She *couldn't* have been in her right mind to leave such a message to me with her dying mouth!"

"O mother, mother!"

"Hush!"

Her voice and her face were terrific.

Then arose from a chair in a corner of the room where she had been sitting an elderly woman. She was clad neatly and tastefully in simple apparel. Her face, white and but little wrinkled, gave token of sweetness and piety which had enabled her to become resigned to whatever losses had befallen her. She moved softly to the table, with a hand brushed away a fly that had settled upon the face of the corpse, and, having placed back the handkerchief, was turning toward the door, when Mrs. Guthrie, in masculine tone, asked:

"What woman is that?"

"That is Mrs. Stapleton, Mr. Stapleton's mother."

"Ah ha! she's here, is she?"

"Yes, madam," answered the lady, "I am here, and have been ever since shortly after dear Caroline was taken sick."

"And *she* calls her *Caroline, dear Caroline*, and I suppose *she'd* say she was in her right mind."

"Indeed I do, madam."

"I didn't ask you for your opinion. I was only supposing. But *I* say again she *wasn't!* As you seem to be talkative, I'll ask you to tell me why your son didn't send me word sooner that that child stiffening on that table there was sick and like to die? Why didn't he? Tell me if you know, and if you don't I'd like to have your opinion. Now, just let us have it for the curiosity of the thing."

"The only reason was, madam, that not before late in the night did he believe that there was any serious danger in the case."

"I don't believe it! He didn't *want* me to know it, because he didn't want me here, and don't now. What was the matter with her? Can you tell me that?"

"Mrs. Guthrie—"

"How did you know my name was Guthrie? I never told you, nor nobody else, that I know of."

"I knew it, madam, and I answer that the doctor said that it was her heart that suddenly failed."

"Her *heart!* He said that because he knew nothing about it, no more than you do. They've always got some names to say, and the easiest when they're most ignorant, because they feel that they must say something. I say it *wasn't* her heart. If it was anything, it was milk fever; and if it was, and if I had been sent for as soon as she was taken, I'd have cured her. I say, mind me, if *it was anything.*"

Her face looked almost fiendish as she said these last words.

"Madam," said Mrs. Stapleton, unruffled as before, "I have no idea what you mean."

"I didn't suppose that you did, and I don't care if you didn't. John Stapleton might know; but he's out of the way, it seems."

"You can see him, madam, if you wish. He is not far off, and before leaving he gave orders to be called if you asked for him. I will send for him at once."

She started out, but Mrs. Guthrie rose, and, smoothing her gown, said:

"Not worth while. You needn't trouble yourself. I wouldn't speak to him if he was here."

"As you please, ma'am," replied Mrs. Stapleton, and left the room.

"Alice," said Mrs. Guthrie, "it would just kill me to stay in this house much longer. It has nearly done it now. Tell that negro girl or somebody to tell Moses to bring the carriage back, right straight."

Alice went out, returning in a few minutes. Several times during her absence the mother took a step toward the table and recoiled. When Alice returned she was again upon the bed, anguishing with piteous lamentation, although no tears were in her eyes.

"Alice," rising, she said, "when you was gone, I tried to look—to look at it. But I couldn't. I'll go home and send Duncan. I'd better go, anyhow. If I was to lay my eyes on John Stapleton I might say things that better not be said. You and that old woman will have to attend to everything. No doubt Charlotte will come down too when she hears of it. I'll try to be at the burying if I'm alive, and if I'm not, it won't make any difference. I'm glad that poor baby can be taken care of. There's that much good in all this distraction. O my Lord! I've *got* to go!"

She tottered to the door, turned, looked once more toward the table, took one step, then covering her face with both her hands, screamed:

"I can't!"

Rushing out of the house, she called loudly to her coachman, and as soon as he came, re-entered the carriage and was gone.

Painfully shocked by the news brought by his mother, Guthrie hastily repaired to the place of mourning. He had never been hostile to his sister, although he had been brought up with the idea that she had been the favorite of his father, and that nothing but the affection and tact of his mother had prevented his being cut off from a fair portion of his estate. Addicted as he was to self-indulgence, ambitious of influence and state, he was neither mean nor vindictive. He was not without some sense of shame for his mother's undisguised inordinate partiality; and although he was content, and perhaps believed himself to be entitled justly to much more than upon equal partition would have been his portion, yet he had wished, as has been seen, that Mrs. Stapleton could live more liberally, and that from some sense of justice as well as for hushing the commentings of people on the difference between her establishment and his own. John Stapleton he liked well in all respects except as a brother-in-law, and he treated him accordingly. Stapleton always had seemed as if he was satisfied with the terms on which he had been put, and he would chat with him about crops, politics, fox-hunting, and other topics whenever they happened to be thrown together, just as he did with others of his acquaintance. He would have been respected more by Guthrie if he had shown some coldness at least in the absence of resentment. As it was, Guthrie's feelings toward him were made up of indifference and contempt, some of which extended to his wife. When she died so unexpectedly after having lived in comparatively humble conditions, and with what he regarded as a poor married experience, he felt sorry for her, and was rather pleased than not when told by Alice that the baby had been consigned by its mother to her care until other arrangements could be made in that behalf. The heartiness with which he consented pleased himself much, and it enabled him to look with calmness upon his dead sister's face and offer to the surviving husband as many words of condolence as he thought he deserved to get from him.

The body, as she had requested, was buried in the Stapleton graveyard. The deceased had united herself with the Baptists, in whose faith her husband, though not a church member, believed. The funeral sermon

was postponed for a month on account of the absence
of the pastor and his engagement for similar service on
the next three Sundays.  Mrs. Guthrie was at the burial.
Clad in deep black she stood at the head of the grave,
watched with close scrutiny every action of the under-
taker and the friends who assisted; and when it was
over, without a word to any one present except her
son, left the ground and was driven home.

"Are you going down to hear Mr. Marston's sermon
on Caroline, mother?" asked Alice the evening before
the day set for its delivery.

"No, Alice; no, child.  I've been through already
more than I had any idea I could go through with, and
to have to listen to that preacher hinting his hints about
me, and be stared at by all those Baptists is more than
I think I ought, at my time of life, to be expected to
stand."

It seemed a pity she was not there.  The meeting-
house stood on the first rise from the river.  A large
congregation assembled.  The woods were already in
the full green of early summer; the air was full of
freshness.  In the shady grove the neighings of hun-
dreds of horses answered to the chatterings of as many
birds in the tree-tops.  Inside the house the smells from
gowns and other vestments modestly bedecked with
flowers, the healthful sheen upon all cheeks save the
very oldest, the peacefulness, the solemnity, the absence
both of indifference and ostentatious sympathy, all made
occasion for a fit discourse by a good man gifted with
ability to improve it.  The preacher, a portly man of
fifty, although mainly self-educated, was an acknowledged leader of his denomination throughout an exten-

10

sive surrounding region. He made no direct allusion to the Guthrie family, but dwelt at length and with much tenderness upon the simple, virtuous life led by the departed, and the fact that the summons coming to her suddenly had not found her unprepared. Once he did speak of the sweetness with which she had endured some trials of a peculiar kind which her childhood and young womanhood had been such as to prevent her from expecting; yet he was fain to believe that such endurance had added to the felicity of her earthly life instead of subtracting from it, and rendered her more fit for that to which she had risen. Many a tear was shed by those who in their hearts pitied all sufferers, even the obdurate, strange old woman whose mouth, if it had been there and had spoken, could have told of an anguish that, however resentful, was deeper and sharper than that of all the rest.

Stapleton placed Alan at his mother's and went back to his home alone.

----

## CHAPTER XVII.

### MR. BOND IS RETAINED.

If Caroline Stapleton had not died it is hardly probable that her husband ever would have concerned himself about the estate left by her father, at least, to the degree of attempting by legal process to obtain a greater portion of it than already had been received. It is true that sometimes he had been made to feel uncomfortable by the remonstrances of his friends, the most persistent of

whom was Peterson Braddy, whom he warmly loved.
That gentleman ever since the marriage, at every opportunity that was presented, and many others improvised
by himself, had counselled, urged, scolded, denounced,
and even employed several unique forms of imprecation
to induce or to drive him to such endeavors as he believed
it was due to his family if not to himself to exert. In
all this, as Stapleton well knew, he was not actuated to
any degree by resentment toward Duncan Guthrie, but
by affection toward himself and his sense of justice.

"I didn't know it was in me to cry any more," said
Peter, "but I had to let her run when Jack's wife died,
and everything went scattering exceptin' of him, poor
fellow, by his lone self, and if it hadn't been that cussin' come in so handy, thinkin' about how him and his
wife and children has been treated by that old woman,
and Dunk a-layin' around and a-lookin' on, and not a-
tryin' to hender it—fact is, I'm glad I learned how *to*
cuss, if no more than for jes' my own satisfaction, I be
dogamighty doggoned my skin, to dogamighty doggon-
ation if I ain't."

Having married out of affection alone, Stapleton
and his wife, both believing, from the warning of Mrs.
Guthrie beforehand, that they were to expect nothing
from her to whom they supposed that everything belonged, they had been content with each other, and
happy. When led to suspect that the injustice done
might be redressed, yet, averse both to notoriety and to
strife, he hardly had given a serious thought to the
subject of a resort to the courts.

But now a great change had come, one the thought
of which when not bemoaning his own loss led to self-

reproaching that during his wife's lifetime he had not,
stood firmly for what he had become convinced were
her rights.   In the behavior of Mrs. Guthrie at her
death, while he sufficiently understood the struggles of
such a spirit against accusing itself for its neglect, yet
his own resentment was kindled, both on his own account and for the insult thus put upon the memory of
his wife.   Above even these were considerations of his
children, between whom, and their grandmother there
had been never anything that savored either of affection
or relationship.   Indeed, he felt, now for the first time
with bitterness, that she hated them because of their
consanguinity with himself.   These children, so young
and helpless, seemed to appeal to him, their only defender, to do what he could in order to obtain for them
whatever, if anything, had been withheld.

One thing stood in his way, at least temporarily—
the affection had by his wife for Alice, which had led to
the consignment of the baby to her care.   Well he
knew that Alice would rejoice to see both children come
into possession of all their hereditary rights.   But he
reflected that Duncan must and would side with his
mother in any issue that might be made.   One night,
while in the midst of a conflict of many thoughts, he
decided that on the next day he would go to Clarke and
consult with Thomas Tolly.

Two weeks afterward, as Miss Jewell was sitting in
the piazza at the Wendells' just before sunset, she was surprised to see Bond driving by in his sulky.   He raised
his hat as he passed, but did not stop until arriving at
Junkin's.   Guthrie, who was closing his office just as
he entered upon the public square, guessed that he had

come to see Miss Jewell; for the sight of his deportment toward her during the time when these two were
together alone at the parties during court week, had
convinced him that Bond would like to marry her. He
was pleased with the thought now, although in a not
very sarcastic way he had ridiculed him in her hearing.
Now he really hoped that she would marry him, or in
some other manner be got away.

As is known to most persons who are at all familiar
with judicial proceedings, there are two ways of prov-
ing a last will and testament; one in common form, by
the oaths of the executor and one of the witnesses.
This is done when the ordinary has no reason to believe that the paper will be contested by any who would
have inherited had the testator died intestate, and is understood neither to prejudice their right afterward to
demand probate in solemn form (in the law named *per
testes*)—that is, by all the witnesses, after due notice
given to all the heirs at law. The will of Alan Guthrie had been probated after the first form by the oaths
of the executrix and the lawyer who had drawn it.
This man, Suttle by name, a year or two afterward had
removed to the State of Louisiana. The witness Braddy,
Peterson's father, had deceased, and the whereabout of
the other, if indeed he yet lived, was not known to
any in the community. Tolly had notified Bond of his
intention to institute legal proceedings, and requested
him to come to Clarke for the purpose of taking together a preliminary study of the bearings of the suit.

"I feel in good trim for this fight," said Bond, when,
after supper and a visit of an hour to Miss Jewell, he
had repaired to Tolly's room. "Do you know, sir, that

I was about to begin on a travel to this borough when
your letter came?"

"Aye? That looks promising. I had made up my
mind that you had an attraction here stronger than any
law matters could impart, and I am glad to believe that
it has put you in such case for our joint work. You're
going to tell me all about it?"

"Yes. What there is to tell. It is not precisely as
I see you suspect from the promptness with which you
congratulate me. However, I'll let you into a thing or
two after we've talked over our case. I was glad for
his sake, as well as yours and mine, to hear that the
man (Stapleton, I believe you said his name was) had decided to move in behalf of his rights, although I was
very sorry to hear of the death of the poor fellow's
wife. It's a pity he didn't take action during her life-
time. What sort of a man was that lawyer, Suttle, and
do you know whether or not he is still living?"

"I don't know whether he is alive or not. He was a
poor pettifogger, I've been told, and made a scant living
by undertaking such work as men of respectable standing
would refuse. He went from here to Louisiana. I've
never mentioned the subject to Mr. Jamison, but Braddy,
our client's most active friend, says that his father, who
was one of the witnesses to the will, told him that Mr.
Guthrie first applied to Mr. Jamison to write it, and
that he put him off because he did not believe that, at
the time of his application, he had disposing memory. My notion is, after seeing what effect will be produced by the citation to probate in solemn form—for
it may induce Guthrie to drive his mother to the proposal of a settlement, but if not—then to put in a bill

in equity, a resort we'll have to get to anyhow eventually."

"She'd swear it out of court; a matter of course."

"I don't think so. My opinion of the old lady is that she is as truthful as she's audacious. She has the courage of Semiramis or Catharine of Russia. What *she* did, if anything fraudulently, she is just the woman to maintain that she had a right, law or no law, to do; and I don't believe that she would deny any action of her own, at least under oath. Even if she would, Guthrie wouldn't let her. If he should suspect such a thing and foresee, as he must, that we would assail her veracity, he would try to drive her into a compromise. The citation will excite him intensely; for he well knows the feeling in the county about the way his sister was treated, and that a special jury would sift the case of every particle of chaff before they would render a verdict against these little children. Guthrie is very desirous of popular favor, and then I take him to be a man of his word. Besides, he has inherited his mother's courage."

"You think so, Tolly, do you?" the other asked, smiling. "So, so! I know nothing of the dam in the matter of such characteristics; but, judging from her whelp, I should not be surprised at any means to which she would resort to screen her evil deeds from detection. However, more of that after a while."

When they had discussed the several points in the case and those likely to arise, Bond said:

"Well, Tolly, you are leading counsel, and, as you say, we will need a bill anyhow; I suggest that the sooner we file it the better. A broadside upon these people, so courageous, may be the most fit way of opening upon them.   As to the pluck of Mr. Duncan Guthrie, it has become my duty and privilege to try if I can find out of what stuff it is made."

Tolly's look showed that he was startled by these last words.

"I spoke somewhat sooner on that subject than I had intended, though I was not going away until I did. I was led to it by what you said about the courage that had come down to Guthrie from his ancestors.  It made me speculate momentarily whether or not among them in the times of the claymore and its companion weapons of warfare it often, or occasionally, or even one time happened that one of the blood insulted a woman who had no male defender near by."

He smiled as if he had put to an antiquarian a question concerning a matter of history that may have been overlooked by others who had sought to save from oblivion a simple yet not wholly uninteresting incident of the past.

"I suppose I can guess to what you allude, although your words and the manner of their utterance surprise me much."

"How so?"

"I've been so busy with this case and others that I've not been to see Miss Jewell lately; but, meeting her a few nights ago at the Macfarlanes, I noticed that she was very serious, a thing unusual with her at such a time.  She said to me that she had thought of telling me something, but had decided not to do so.  But I did not suppose that it was a matter of grave importance."

"Yes, but it was.  I know all about it."

"Did she tell you?"

"No; I got it from Dunbar.  Miss Jewell wrote to her sister about it.  The mail that brought the letter had one for me, in which, altogether against my hope and my expectation, and even against that of Dunbar and his wife, she rejected my suit.  Dunbar, good fellow that he is, told me the reason, which was that she had been so grossly insulted by Guthrie that she didn't feel that she had the right to marry me or anybody else." '

"I suspected that Guthrie had had something to do with the matter that was on her mind; because I noticed on the occasion referred to that he had nothing to say to her.  Besides, he was more grave than I ever saw him, and, indeed, seemed not at his ease."

"And his wife behaved similarly, eh?  I know of that too.  There was where Guthrie made his biggest mistake—after his first.  Desperate as he was, I suppose he regarded it his best expedient to save himself from being spurned by that good woman forever and ever."

"Fact is, I've been rather uneasy, but not very much so, since a little party we had in Mrs. Guthrie's woods some time back, having heard that, after I had left, Guthrie's wife became so worried by his neglect of herself and his devotion to Miss Jewell that she left the place abruptly, followed by Guthrie, who seemed to have been brought back suddenly to his senses.  Still, I have not been suspecting that any insult had been offered by the fellow.  If I had, I should have looked into it.  I had no idea that he was so openly audacious."

"There's been some talk, Tolly, hasn't there, about that party—some little talk, in undertone, as it were?"

"No; that is, not much, so far as I have heard. But I've been busy at my office, and in reading up in my room, and have been out but little. My friend Braddy says he has heard some whisperings, and that he announced himself ready to fight anybody who had anything to say against Miss Jewell. But really, Bond, I've thought almost nothing about it, because I've supposed that if anything serious had been in it, Miss Jewell would have communicated with me, whom she knows to be her friend."

"The difficulty, my dear fellow, is that she couldn't communicate such a thing to a man."

"Is she aware that you know about it?"

"No. Do you think she's been much hurt by these whisperings?"

He rose and, putting his hands in his pockets, walked up and down in the room.

"Well, no, Bond, I hardly think so. It is an exacting society here; but it is not gossipy, that is, among those who lead in it, and they are, or they mean to be, entirely just. But for the attitude of Guthrie's wife, I should have felt little or no disquiet. She is as true as steel. Guthrie has always been a forward beau with first one young woman, then another, and I've known him to get a sharp rebuff more than once when he was too free in his manners. I am confident that his wife has been pained sometimes by such unbecoming manifestations; but I do not believe that she's a jealous-minded woman at all, naturally. I suspect, from what you tell me, that, in order to get excused by her, Guthrie has persuaded her that he withdraws from Miss Jewell's society voluntarily.　No, Bond, I do not believe that she has been, or will be hurt seriously."

"Seriously!　The idea that she, or any other honorable woman should be hurt at all by such a man!　But we shall see.　Miss Jewell has the same opinion of Mrs. Guthrie that you have.　I have heard her say myself, and she wrote to her sister in this connection, that she regards her as the best woman in Clarke.　At first she suspected that she might be a little jealous of her among other young women, but she had seemed to have got entirely over such a feeling if it ever had existed, and therefore she was the more cordial with Guthrie, especially when in her presence.　Until that day, and until that moment, she did not dream that Guthrie had any notions that were not entirely honorable, and nothing could have so amazed her as, prompted by the devil within him, he whispered that he loved her and was ready to make any sacrifice for her sake.　When she found that she was mistaken, she rose, and was almost in a run toward his wife, meaning, convulsed as she was with horror, to acquaint her with his audacious treachery to *her*, when right there, in that man's presence, another insult was inflicted that nobody but a dastard would not have made atonement for!　Yes, sir; that is just what he has done!　He has allowed that good woman to believe that he has suddenly discovered that Miss Jewell was not a fit associate for either of them.　My Lord!"

Tolly remained silent, as he walked excitedly about the room.　After a short while, resuming his seat, he said, as if momentarily disposed to change to a subject more agreeable:

"Tolly, I've got some good whisky in my trunk. If I go and bring it here, will you take a drink?"

"I think not now, Bond."

"No? Well, then, I won't. We Augusta fellows are in the habit of taking with us when we go into the country some of the article. Danger of coming up with bad water, you know, or indigestible food, or being snake bit, or dog bit, or cow horned, in benighted regions. I suspect you country lawyers feel that you must do the like, especially when you go south."

"We are not very particular as to how the compass points whither we are traveling when arranging our outfit."

"I would have guessed as much. Well, the thought of it just then, though not often do I imbibe, was suggested to me. I'm satisfied to go without it. Now I'll tell you a little bit of romance. You like romance, Tolly? You look as if you did. Indeed, you rustic boys in your greenness—I mean to say, innocence—you have it young, quite young, and you keep on having it, till finally you get caught, and then you settle down to business. As for me, although country born myself, I never felt any particular tendency in that way until last winter. Lookee here, if we won't take a drink, let us at least have a cigar. When I'm talking business I never think of smoking; but whenever I drop into the sentimental, or rise into it, however it may be properest to say, I feel like trying the weed. I notice that you bumpkins, when you can't smoke, are always chewing. Even the judge, though he's first rate in dispatch of business, has a spit-box by him behind the bench. Now for my romance, if you want to hear about it. Do you?"

"I'm eager; man, don't you see that I am on thorns!"

"There is where I wanted to get you before I began. It was brief, and so shall be its story."

Having got on a good headway of smoke, he laid his cigar upon the table, leaned back in his chair, clasped his hands neatly on his breast, as if to put himself in becoming romantic attitude, and began:

"Once upon a time, it was in the fall of the year and nigh unto the latter end thereof, a young person whose sex I will leave you to infer, arrived in the city of Augusta, having come from a distant State, intimating that it was the State of Massachusetts, and from the town of St. Botolph—"

"What town?"

"St. Botolph: I called it calmly, but distinctly, as I think."

"It wasn't in the geography I studied."

"Perhaps not; but am I to be made believe that here is a Bachelor of Arts, and a lawyer, eminent, however young, who didn't know that *Boston* was an abbreviation of *Botolph's Town*, so named from that excellent, devout, and illustrious saint?"

"How long have *you* known it?"

"Ever since the arrival of the emigrant hereinbefore referred to."

"I see; proceed, if you please. It has already become not only personally, but historically interesting. Proceed, proceed!"

"Oh, you put me out with questions exposing your ignorance, and I am driven to be even briefer than I intended. The truth is that the lady—for I saw from your looks that you had divined it to be a female—had been in Augusta not more than a month before I fell in love with her, and had no more discretion than to go to courting her straightway, not having more than a thousand dollars to my credit in bank, although my prospects for making more than a living seem reasonably good. After several months she admitted that she rather thought she liked me right well, but that she wouldn't marry anybody, at least for some time to come. I argued the case with her as well as I knew how, never having been instructed in the prolegomena of lovers' profession, and I had good help from her sister and her brother-in-law, who are the very best friends I have in Augusta. These two tried to persuade their sister to live with them, as both parents are deceased, but she announced her intention to work for her own living, and accepted the offer of her cousin, Mr. Wendell, to teach in his academy. At your March term she said that she would give me a definite answer to my persistent suit at her forthcoming vacation, which she expected to spend with the Dunbars, and she intimated that it would be favorable. Last week I got a letter saying she would not leave Clarke this summer, or if she did, it would be to linger at Augusta only for a few days on her way back to Boston. Then she added that she had nothing to say regarding the proposal that I had made, except to request that I would never refer to it again. So I went to Dunbar, and learned what I have told you. I was intending to make a break for this remote inland village when your letter came, and so here I am, ready both for a lawsuit and a fight. That's all. If you hadn't interrupted me, I've no doubt I could have made

it more interesting, not to say to a moderate degree
thrilling.  My sakes!  My cigar has gone clean out!"
Seizing it, he sucked as if for life.
"No, not quite out."
"What was the result of the interview to-night?"
"Rejection, out and out; but, Tolly, tears were in
her eyes when she said the words, and she admitted
that she had made up her mind shortly after leaving
Augusta to accept me, but that circumstances had forced
her to change it  When pressed to let me know the
cause, she answered that she could not.  But I know;
for she wrote to Mrs. Dunbar that when she found how
poorly qualified she was to prevent a man's making to
her a dishonorable proposal, she did not feel that she had
the right to marry me or any other true man.  Good
God, Tolly! Good God, man!  What can't a woman
do and endure!  Why, what answer do you suppose
she sent to her sister when she asked her why she had
not revealed Guthrie's villainy to his wife?  It was
partly because of the notoriety that might come of it,
but mainly because she could not bear the thought of
making an innocent woman whom she admired and respected as miserable as herself.  The dog said to her, as
preliminary to the insult, that he did not love his wife,
in which words I've not a doubt that he uttered a lie!  I
told her that I would not take her rejection after what
she admitted, and I appealed to her to deal with me
with greater candor, saying that with any trouble or
sorrow that was upon her mind, I sympathized more
deeply than anybody else could.  I could make no impression on that line; but I could see that she doubted
if what she was doing, or rather refusing to do, was en-

tirely right to either of us. But to think that things can remain in this state!"

"It is not easy to see what you *can* do, Bond, or what would be best to be done. I think Miss Jewell is wrong in the view she takes. If you and she were to marry, the whole thing would die out at once."

"And the insult, the silent slander in allowing these whisperings, as you call them, to go uncontradicted, and even to be accredited by his virtuous withdrawal of himself and his wife from her company, the distrust among good people kindly and sorrowful—all these to be passed over with humble thankfulness that they, by the mere accident of marriage with me, were scotched short of effecting the ruin of a good woman's reputation! By the ever-living God! even if I didn't love her, as I do, related as I am to her family, I should feel myself bound to see her righted! As it is, I am going to make the effort to do it speedily, and before she finds that I know anything about it."

"I don't see how you are to proceed, Bond. If Guthrie is called to account, of course he'll plead that Miss Jewell had mistaken the intent of his words. He'll feel that he owes that to the safety of his own domestic peace."

"Aye! he may lie as much as he pleases to the good woman whose happiness depends upon her trust in him, but if he lies to *me*, I'll put my brand upon him and then stand him up in the market-place for the scorn of all men and all women!"

"Such as that could not be done with a man like Guthrie without risk of fatal consequences to one of you or both."

"That is the calculation I have figured.   But, Tolly, when a man finds himself on a certain line of duty, if he is a man really, he can't step aside from it because of apparent dangers.   However, one case at a time.   I had not thought to get upon this to-night.   Let's go back to the other."

They conferred late, and not another allusion was made to Miss Jewell that night.

---

## CHAPTER XVIII.

### INQUIRIES ABOUT ALAN GUTHRIE'S WILL.

At that period applications for administration upon the estates of persons deceased, besides publication in one or more of the gazettes of the State, were required to be posted at the door of the court-house. A few days after the event narrated in the foregoing chapter, simultaneously with their appearance in The Southern Recorder, a weekly newspaper published in the town of Milledgeville, then the capital of the State, two notices signed by the clerk of the Inferior court of the county sitting as a court of Ordinary were placed upon the court-house door.  One purported to be an application by John Stapleton for letters of administration upon the estate of Caroline Stapleton, lately deceased, and the other by the same for letters of guardianship of the property of Alan and Caroline Stapleton, her minor children.  Men, knowing the law that married women could hold no property

11

separate from their husbands except by special con-
tract, or by settlement on the part of persons from
whom such property had been acquired by purchase or
testamentary paper, speculated how it was that Stapleton should apply for administration upon an estate
already his own, and for guardianship for his children
who had none. Mr. Macfarlane, happening to be on
the street, and hearing the notices discussed, went to
the court-house, and after reading them turned away
without remark and went back to his home. On the
contrary, Guthrie, when he had read them, said to two
or three men who were inspecting them at the same
time :

"It looks as if Jack Stapleton wanted to make himself more conspicuous since he has become a widower."

He turned, and, entering the clerk's office, said :

"Anderson, did Stapleton make personal application for letters of administration and guardianship,
notices of which I see out at the door, or was it made
by attorney?"

"No, Mr. Guthrie, Jack never applied. Mr. Tolly
and that other young lawyer from Augusta—Bond, I
believe they call him—they were in here looking over
the records, and this morning Mr. Tolly came back and
made the application for Jack. Look to me like, Mr.
Guthrie, Jack's going to put himself to useless expense,
though I don't know, of course, anything about—or
much about the law."

"That is just what he is doing. You say Bond was
with Tolly? I noticed he was in town, but I thought
he came in to see that woman at Wendell's, the school-
master."

"Fine-looking, handsome woman. They tell me she's very fond of gentlemen's society."

"Perhaps she is, Anderson. I know very little of her. Did Bond seem to be taking a part in Tolly's investigations?"

"Oh, yes, sir. They looked over the books and things together, and he seem to be wanting to study into 'em much as Mr. Tolly."

"What records specially—however, I won't ask that question."

Then he went out. The blow upon him was painful as it was sudden. The appearance of Bond with Tolly convinced him that they had instituted a case with expectation that it would be strongly contested. He was lawyer enough not to doubt that an assault was intended upon the will of his father, and from what his mother lately, for the first time, had told him of the circumstances of its execution, he foresaw that such an assault would be dangerous. Combative by nature, his first impulse was to proceed to Tolly's office, denounce both Stapleton and the threat thus sent out against his mother, and warn Tolly and his colleague to keep themselves carefully within the limits of what was due to their client in prosecution of the case. A little reflection convinced him of the imprudence that would be in such action. Going to his office, he remained for half an hour reflecting upon what first movement it was proper to make. Coming out again, he noticed Peterson Braddy, who, having borrowed a chair from within the court-house, was sitting and leaning back against the wall near the door. Stopping and looking in another direction, he overheard the following:

"You're in town early, Pete.  Through your business a'ready and taking a rest?  You look as comfortable as a bee on a rasher of watermelon."

"Mornin', Mr. Wicker.  Just about, if not comfortabler.  I never had any business.  I jes come to hear the racket and see the fun."

"What racket?  Everything seems to be about as quiet as common."

"Read them papers above thar," said he, pointing with his thumb backward and upward.  After reading the notices, the man said:

"Why, what do they mean?  I thought Jack's property all belonged to him, and I didn't know that his children had any."

"So it does, what they is thar; but it ain't all thar, Mr. Wicker."

"Where is it, then?"

"Now that I can't answer—that is, not egzact.  Some of it's in land, and some of it's in niggers, and some in town lots, and some's in horses and mules and stock of various kind, and nobody knows what's in money a-drawin' of interest; but my suspicion is it's a pile."

Guthrie turned away and moved across the street, Braddy the while looking at his retreating form as if pleased with the sight.

"Pete, what *does* it mean?" asked Mr. Wicker.

"Why, sir, to my opinion, it means no less, and it means no more than that man's mother you see walking so lofty yonder across the squar', that she have been keepin' one of the old man Guthrie's children out of her sheer of her lawful father's property, exception of sich driblets as she's been o' mind to allow her; and now that child's dead, and Jack Stapleton, what by good rights he ought to done long ago, he have made up his mind that him and his children sha'n't be kept out o' thar right any longer if he can help it. It's to my opinions that it's that them notices means you see up thar, Mr. Wicker, neither more nor neither less."

"But I thought the property was all left to her to do as she pleased with it."

"Yes, sir; but you see it never pleased her to do right about it. Thar's the p'int, Mr. Wicker; and more than that, they have been people and they *is* people that believes when the old man Guthrie signed that will he wer'n't strong enough in his mind to make his signin' what the law allow, and that's another p'int. You see I'm jes a-talkin' at randuoms, as the sayin' is, Mr. Wicker, and a-expressin' of my opinions, which I suppose everybody's liable to do that much."

"Well, if Jack has such rights, I, for one, will be glad to see him get them. It never seemed to me to be right for him and his family to have to live so close and managy, and his wife's brother to have everything he wanted."

"Yes, sir, yes, sir; I've heard varous make them same remarks. Well, I jus' thought I'd ride in and peruse around a while. I think I'll go back to Tom Tolly's office and jaw him a little siege before I go back home."

When, after a brief call, he had gone from Tolly's, Bond said:

"I was much impressed by that man. He's a sensible, generous, brave fellow."

"That he is; I know no one more so. He loves Stapleton with all his heart, and he'll be worth more to us than Stapleton himself in working up the case. He dislikes Guthrie, and has some reason; but that consideration, if it had any influence, would tend to make him keep silent. He is actuated only by his affection for Stapleton, whom ever since his marriage he has been urging to do what is now being done. He's an ardent admirer of Miss Jewell."

"Bless his heart for that! Oh, yes, it is plain to see that he is full of sense and spirit. You've got *Fonblanque's Equity?* Yes, I see."

Guthrie, finding on inquiry that Mr. Macfarlane had been on the street but had gone back home, decided to repair to his own.

"Alice," he said, after reaching there, "it looks as if mother were going to have some trouble with Jack Stapleton. I saw on the court-house door just now a couple of notices, in one of which he has made to the Court of Ordinary application for letters of administration on Caroline's estate, as he terms it, and in the other for guardianship of the children. Anderson, the clerk, informs me that Tolly and that man Bond, he believes, are at the head of it. I knew Bond had been in town for some days, but I supposed that he came to see that Jewell woman."

She made no answer, but looked as if she was solemnly pondering his words.

"I wonder at Tolly," he continued, "not giving me some sort of notice that such proceedings were going to be had, knowing the interest I must have in the case. I wouldn't be surprised if Charlotte has floored him, and so he feels as if he must get revenge out of some of the family."

"I hardly think, dear, that Mr. Tolly is capable of such as that. I suppose that he feels as if he ought, as his counsel, to keep his client's secret."

"That duty would not have been at all violated if he had known what was common professional courtesy. What do you think of Jack Stapleton making an underhand attack upon mother when his child is being taken care of in the house of her son ?" he said petulantly, already angry at the thought that he could not make her views accord with his own.

"My dear husband, I am as little disposed to suspect Mr. Stapleton of underhand conduct as Mr. Tolly of unprofessional. The notices you speak of, it seems, are on the court-house door, where everybody can see them who cares to. I can not imagine that he means to do any wrong, or that he does not feel grateful for the care that temporarily is bestowed upon his child by you and me. If he did, or if he thought that you would so suspect, I really believe that he'd make haste to procure a nurse and send for the child."

"You entirely mistake that creature !"

"I don't think so."

In the few domestic disputes between these two, the wife had been able to hold her own reasonably well, because of being always in the right. The results had been some subdual of arbitrariness on his part, and involuntary increase of spirit on hers. Decline, resisted as it had been, in the respect which she had for his character, had been leading her slowly toward forming and

expressing her opinions and corresponding indifference
to what he might think.  She had been led by Charlotte
Macfarlane to doubt the full verity of what he had been
saying lately about Miss Jewell; for Charlotte, observ-
ing the coldness with which Miss Jewell had been
treated by her, had mildly remonstrated and assured
her that in her judgment that young woman was entitled to the very highest respect from all, women and
men.  The bare thought that her own husband had
maltreated a woman so situated terrified her, because
there was danger of her having to postpone her own
grief and shame to those of a greater sufferer.  That
very day she had met Miss Jewell and Charlotte together in one of the stores, and had exchanged such civility as she must not neglect.  She had looked into her
eyes, and it made her sick at heart to believe that in
them she could see innocence as unspotted as that she
felt in her own being.  She had come back to her
home longing, if but for a brief time, to get away
from her surroundings and go upon a visit to her
father's house.  Such things are bound, if not ended,
to become fatal to conjugal peace and dangerous to
conjugal love.

It was on Guthrie's tongue to say something contemptuous about his wife's defense of Tolly and Stapleton, but he withheld it, and, taking a chair near the end
of the piazza, seated himself and ruminated what he
was to do in a case wherein he knew that he would not
have her support, which, if he had had it, he would not
have counted at its worth, but which it now pained and
angered him to be without.  It occurred to him again
that this woman, meek as she was, needed to be treated

with more carefulness and conciliation than he used to believe to be necessary. Shortly afterward, while he was in such a reverie, Simon, the man who had brought the news of Mrs. Stapleton's last illness, came riding a mule along the carriage-way. Arrived at the steps, he dismounted, and, holding to the bridle, gave humble salutation and said:

"I 'feared to let my mule go loose o' de bridle, Marse Dunkin, fear he tromple on Miss Alice bushes en things. Can't you please call one dem boys or gals 'bout de house, en let me give 'em dis here paper I fotch from Marse Jacky's. I be much obleeged to yer ef yer will, Marse Dunkin."

He removed his hat and took out a letter. Guthrie, descending a couple of steps, reached forth, and when he had opened and read it, said:

"All right, Simon—that's your name, isn't it?"

"Yes, sir, marster. My mammy she name me dat atter her daddy, en dee been callin' me dat ev'y sence I 'members. Yes, sir, dat so, jes like I tell yer, dough my granddaddy, big Simon dee called him, he been dead en gone dis long time. Yes, sir; dat so."

"That'll do. Take your mule behind there and tell Marcus I say to show you where to put him. I'll reflect upon your master's note, and may send an answer by you."

Calling to Alice, who had gone within the house, he said:

"Here's a note from Stapleton. Read it and say what you think."

The note read thus:

"*June* 20, 1828.

"*To Duncan Guthrie, Esq.*

"DEAR SIR: I have been advised that my children may have more interest in the estate of their grandfather Guthrie than what was received by their mother, and I am about to begin such legal proceedings as may ascertain if this be so. It may or may not be necessary to give you my assurance that the investigation will be conducted with entire fairness. I write now especially to say that, embarrassed as I am, and as you may be, by the fact that one of these children is now in your family, my intention is to send for it as soon as I can find a woman qualified to take care of it. This I have a prospect of doing very shortly.

"Respectfully yours,

"JOHN STAPLETON."

"The fellow has some more grace than I gave him credit for, eh?"

He felt that he could not say less when his judgment had been so soon set aside. Quickly, after reading the letter, Alice said:

"O Duncan, this must not be! Poor Sister Caroline an hour before her death asked me, provided you were willing, to take care of her baby until it was old enough to be put into other hands without risk. I answered her that I was sure that you would not object, as you did not. The dear little thing is doing very well, and I feel as if it would be almost a sin to let her run the risk of going to another nurse. If it is likely to be embarrassing to anybody—though I can't see how such a thing is possible—let me go up to Broad River. You promised me, you remember, that I might make a

good long visit home this summer, and I am sure that
both father and mother would be glad for me to take
the baby with me.  Surely the business will not require
a very long time to be brought to some sort of settlement, and I—"

He well knew what she would have said if she had
continued to speak, and, instead of being displeased, he
was rather gratified by it.  For he was ill at ease, and
he felt that if his wife were absent for some weeks, he
might be less embarrassed by contingencies, which, however indistinctly, he could not but expect to arise.
Therefore he answered promptly :

" Certainly, my dear Alice.  Jack Stapleton needn't
have been so very touchy and so formal, especially if it
be true, as he says, that he seeks only a fair investigation.  He shall have that as far as I can help to give it
to him.  You know I've always wanted mother to do
more for them than she has.  I shall advise her to propose such a settlement as the fellow ought to accept,
whether he will or not.  The property is mother's to do
with as she pleases, but I have always thought that she
ought to have given them more of it.  I rather think
your suggestion a good one, although I shall be deuced
lonesome here by myself.  It would not be embarrassing to me, nor—with all his talk—would it be to Stapleton ; but it might be so to you to remain here with the
baby pending his 'investigations,' as he calls them ; and
of course it would not do to separate so young a child
from a nurse that suits her as well as Lizy does.  So I
consent for you to go.  The case isn't going to take very
long, if the other party will come to a reasonable settlement, that is, if I can get mother—as I hope I can—

to the point of proposing one.  I don't want to have
her bedevilled long by Jack Stapleton, and I shall give
Tolly and his colleague—that Bond—notice that they
have a care how they refer to her in their pleadings,
and what they may have to say to a jury, if it ever
gets there."

"Duncan" she said, as if she had not been attending
to his latest words, "suppose you shut up the house and
stay with mother while I am gone.  I know she'll want
you to."

"Yes; no doubt of that.  I'll at least take my meals
there, and see how it will be as to sleeping.  I'll try it a
night or so here.  Will you write to Stapleton?  I
shall not."

"Yes, if you think it best.  Perhaps it would be.
I shall make no allusion to the first part of his letter, of
course."

"Write what you please, my dear."

She wrote a brief note, saying that she was about to
leave home in order to make a visit of some weeks
to her parents, and that she considered it decidedly best
to take the child along with her, as she was doing well
in every respect.  As for what arrangement it might
seem desirable to make hereafter, that was a matter
that he might consider during her absence.

"I think it is all right, Alice," said Guthrie, hand-
ing her back the note when he had read it.  "You
write," he added, smiling, "as if you were going right
away."

"I think I'll go day after to-morrow.  It will take
me this afternoon to put away things, and I must get
some to-morrow that the baby may need.  You'll want

to spend this evening with mother, no doubt, and I'll go with you to tell her good-by."

"Oh, no," he answered quickly. "I shall not trouble her with it until you go. I am bound to have a time of it with her, and I'll wait till you are away, unless some fool runs up there and tells her about it beforehand. I don't believe I'd go there if I were in your place. She might suspect from your sudden departure that something was wrong, and I'd have to tell her before I am ready. I shall go to Uncle Dennis's to-morrow and advise with him first."

"Then I'll go to work and get off to-morrow."

"I don't know if that isn't best, Alice. I must tell her some time to-morrow, and I'll feel thankful that you are out of hearing of the bother and the bustle."

This arrangement lifted much of his anxiety. During the rest of the day he seemed to be more as he used to be, affectionate in his words and manners, and anxious to assist wherever he could in her preparation for departure. When she was through with all that night, he asked her to play. He sat upon a sofa and looked at her with unwonted pride and fondness. Indeed, he loved her dearly, and now he wished in his heart that all his actions toward her had been such that she would know, at this very time, how fondly he did love her, and that he could feel that she would be as eager and as thankful to return to him as now she was to visit the home from which he had taken her. Feelings of apprehension and sadness fell upon his heart deeper than at any time before in all his life. Her value to him seemed inestimably higher than ever as, sitting aside and shading his eyes, he looked at her and thought how beautiful,

and pure, and true-hearted she was, and how long would
seem the separation that would begin to-morrow.  Yet
he gave no expression to his thoughts in words.  He
made no objection when at last she said she was fatigued
and would retire.  Rising, he closed the piano for
her.  After she had gone out, he sat for a few minutes
longer, and then followed her.  The next morning, after he had seen her go off so like a young child fondly returning to the bosom of her parents, he went to the
same seat in the parlor whereon he had sat the night before and shed tears.  How inconsistent and incomprehen-
sible is this human frame!  When he had dried his eyes
and looked around him and felt the solitude, the
thought came upon him that he was enduring more
than he deserved, and he accepted without resistance the
relief, poor as it was, that came from an indefinite yet
conscious sense of resentment.  It was too late for him
to unlearn the wrong teachings that he had been having
all his life.  He rose, dressed himself afresh, then
walked with vigorous, swift step into the town.

## CHAPTER XIX.

### GUTHRIE CONFERS WITH HIS UNCLE.

Wishing to have some conference with Mr. Macfarlane before acquainting his mother with the notices and their probable meaning, Guthrie looked for
him on the street.  A servant whom he happened to
meet answered his inquiry by saying that his master

had ridden out to one of his plantations and would not
return before noon.  So he decided to wait and dine at
Junkin's.  He sat nearly opposite Tolly and Bond.
Less conversation than usual was held during the meal.
Guthrie occasionally, while making or listening to some
insignificant remark, looked at these two as if he would
notify them that whatever they had to do or say at any
time about any matter in which he might feel himself
to be concerned there were limits which they would do
well to observe.  They ignored, if they noticed such
menaces, and Bond particularly spoke with a hilarity
that none of his acquaintances there had suspected to be
in his nature.  Few words were addressed between
them directly.  Before the rest had finished, Guthrie,
rising from the table, said :

"Mr. Bond, I see you are becoming quite familiar
in our village ; I am glad that, small as it is, it has
attractions to draw you at other times besides court
terms."

"Yes, Mr. Guthrie, thank you ; I like Clarke somehow, and then, through our friend Mr. Tolly, I have
been put into some little business."

"With promise of satisfactory condemnation money,
and good fees for you both, I trust."

"Yes, sir, reasonable."

"In cases of very uncertain contingencies I think
it is always well to start with a good retainer ; don't
you ?"

"Oh, yes, when a client is able to respond ; but when
not I am content to look mainly at a contingent fee, especially when I suspect that he has not been treated quite
fairly."

"The difficulty is that clients so often claim that to be their case."

"True, sir; still, occasionally one on its bare presentation has marks that seem rather distinct."

"Will you be here some days?"

"One longer, certainly; most probably but one."

Bowing generally, Guthrie then went out.

"That was about as much talk as he has ever honored me with," whispered Bond. "He has a good, clear voice, and puts his words together very well—very well, indeed. Do you think that he suspects what is up? I take it that he does."

"Oh, yes; no doubt of it. He has seen or heard of the notices. If he hadn't I doubt if he had come in here to dine, knowing that he would meet us both. He wants to give notice also."

"Yes; well, we'll admit its service."

An extended conversation was had between Guthrie and Mr. Macfarlane. The latter, as we have seen, had forborne to offer his counsel to Mrs. Guthrie except upon occasions whereat he felt that he would be inexcusable to remain silent. For she had always shown impatience at his interference, although occasionally acting in accordance with his suggestions. Mrs. Macfarlane Guthrie did not even ask for when he called at the house. She had never so much as thought of offering to her sister or her nephew remonstrance or advice, thankful to live upon terms of respectable friendship, with little show of natural affection on either side.

"Duncan," said his uncle, among other things "the case, if these young men understand how to conduct it, will seem to outsiders an ugly one, whatever are to be

the difficulties from lapse of time and the absence of
direct testimony. The public, as I told her more than
once, has always been against your mother in the esti-
mate she puts upon John Stapleton, and the treatment
that her hostility to him led her to inflict upon poor
Caroline. I doubt if in this whole county there's a
young man who is held in higher estimation, and a jury
would go as far as the rulings of the court would allow
to give weight to every species of evidence that will be
offered in support of his claim. Everybody believes
that your father, if he had been of entirely clear mind,
wouldn't have made a will by whose provisions one of
his children could be made rich and the other dependent
wholly upon accident. What sort of a man is this
Bond? Tolly, they say, is a young man of much promise. I've heard him speak two or three times. He
seems always to have studied his cases, and he is certainly eloquent. What about the other?"

"I know little about him, Uncle Dennis, and I
never saw him until our March term, when he had a
little case that was settled. I've been surmising that
his coming here was mainly to see Miss Jewell."

"It seems to me, Duncan, from what I have heard,
not here at home, but outside, that you and that young
lady some time back were a little imprudent in your
deportment toward each other. A man and a woman,
particularly when one of them is married, can't be too
guarded in their intercourse."

"Possibly we may have been, uncle; but there's
been nothing very serious. I found that Alice didn't
like the woman. She saw it too, and that ended it."

Nothing more was said about Miss Jewell. Mr.
12

Macfarlane ended as he had begun, by urging a settlement, and that it be effected as speedily as possible.

"John Stapleton is not going to be very exacting; and you see from his application for guardianship that although entitled by law to prosecute this claim in his own behalf, he intends that whatever he may recover, or at least a part, shall go to his children. He is not exacting, I repeat; but he is firm, and he is popular. I have little or no influence with your mother; and I don't know to what extent yours may lead if you decide that my suggestions are of any importance."

"I have tried several times, uncle, during Caroline's life-time, to get mother to do more for her, but always without success, except that she offered her some property for her separate use that Caroline refused to accept."

"And was right in doing it."

"I don't say she was not, uncle; still, if she had, it might have been better."

"No; it would not. It would have made it appear that Caroline was contented to see her husband regarded as a mere tenant by courtesy, which, sensible woman that she was and true-hearted wife, she was determined should never be. Duncan, acquaintance with that very fact adds to the feeling that is already in men's minds against your mother's side of the case, and it has already hurt you and will hurt you more. I am obliged to talk plainly, because I think I can foresee that if this matter ever gets to a jury there will be attendant circumstances, and there may be results more unhappy than the whole property is worth. You may or you may not, just as you think best, report to Hester what I have said. I shall stand ready to offer any further counsel or assist in any mediation with Mr. Stapleton, if I am requested. If I am not, I certainly shall not volunteer."

Guthrie spent the rest of the afternoon in his office. By this time he rather wished that the news had got to his mother, for he dreaded being witness to the excitement that would be produced at his announcement. It was after sunset when he entered through the gate and saw her walking slowly up and down on her piazza.

---

## CHAPTER XX.

### THE EXECUTRIX'S DEFENSE.

Since the death of her daughter, Mrs. Guthrie, in spite of her resistance to introspection, had been having an experience far different from any that she had ever counted upon. Her singular delusion about this daughter, conceived when the latter was an infant dependent upon her breast and resented even then, had been, as has been seen, a source of greater or less bitterness always. A temper irascible, sensitive, jealous, combative, had hindered her making friendships when young with those of either sex, and her family felt a sense of relief when, far past girlhood, Mr. Guthrie from the neighboring county, came, and, after a brief courtship, married and took her away. The suspicion that the memory of his first wife was more frequent and more fond than it ought to be, and that both he and her first child felt nearer to each other than either was to herself, had such results as we have heard her admit. From the date of this imagined discovery, she had tried not to love her daughter, and she believed that she had succeeded. Yet she prided herself that she had never been harsh in the treatment of her. She seemed to have looked upon her as an unlucky accident that had befallen her, but which, being inevitable, must be endured as she endured a slight unsightly cast in one of her eyes. Her anxiety lest her husband would prefer this favorite in the disposition of his property had been intense, and had so continued until his death. Thereafter the relations between herself and her daughter were as those between a wealthy dowager and an orphan whom accidental circumstances had devolved upon her hands, to whom she owed nothing, yet for whom without complaint she was providing already, and whom, when married, she expected to provide more generously than Caroline could have any sort of right to expect. The sense of victory and security had subdued her resentment except to the degree that was necessary to the justification of her own actions in her behalf. She was pleased that people called her beautiful and lady-like. She cordially wished her to marry a rich husband, not less for her daughter's sake than because the vast distinction she intended to make between her and the child of her affection in the distribution of her property might be less subject to public commentation and blame. The girl had more than one offer of that sort among the extensive property owners in that county and beyond Broad River. When John Stapleton offered himself, a youth with almost no property of any kind, and of a family which, although entirely respectable, was not of their set, and she saw that his suit was favored, disgusted and incensed, she declared to both that if they married they should never have a cent of her property, except what would be enough to keep Caroline from abject want. They waited until the latter was one and twenty. The mother let them be married in her house, although she would not be present at the ceremony. She even offered to give them something of a party; but they chose to be joined privately one morning, after which Stapleton took his wife to the modest home that he had prepared. His apparent indifference toward Mrs. Guthrie, both before and after the marriage, had offended her deeply and pained her more than she would have admitted. The few negroes that she gave had been sent without any message, and were received without expression of thanks except a few words returned by the daughter through the driver of the wagon that brought them. The failure of her prophecies about the misery that was bound to follow such a marriage had disgusted her with her daughter and she had grown to cordially hate the latter's husband. It has been seen how she behaved at Mrs. Stapleton's unexpected death. The fierce assault made by remorse and the wailing utterance within her breast from an affection that she had believed to have gone thereout must be resisted, because they could not be endured. It was for these that she poured her wrath against John Stapleton, and hid herself from the obsequies of his wife. Since then her consolation, such as it was, consisted in increased hatred for him and increased yearning for her son. In this while she seemed to have grown much older.  Her face, although maintaining its redness, had become more thin and worn.  She was more often silent, less stately in her gait, less autocratic in the discipline of her household.  Her snow-white gown and caps, relieved by a black ribbon here and there, made it interesting to note how her scrupulous neatness abated not amid the other changes that had come upon her.  Companionship with Duncan's wife, never cordial because of the quick detection by each of the other's want of congeniality, became less so now.  Her intercourse with the Macfarlanes, except a weekly visit from Charlotte, had become yet more infrequent.  Going out never, she eagerly craved the society of her son, to whom she poured out her feelings without restraint, and it was evident both to him and herself that she had become more than ever dependent upon him.  She had not seen the babe at his house, but had said to Duncan that the sight of it just yet, especially with the name it bore, would be more than she could bear.  It was for a double reason, therefore, that when early that morning she received a note from Duncan that Alice had gone to her father's and that he would be with herself that night, she felt a cheerfulness sweeter than for many, many months.

"Who is dat I ben hearin' a-singin' in de house?" asked Chloe, the cook, of Judy, who had just come into the kitchen.

"Ef you'll b'lieve me, Aun' Chloe, hit's mistess.  I hain't hear miss try to sing befo', not sence Marse Duncan got married en went off to live long him en Miss Alice.  I declar' it sound so quar, I wouldn't believed it, widout I lookin' at her."

"Well, I'm glad po' mistess ken have de heart to sing wid de trouble she have on top o' *her* min'."

"En hit's onlest because Marse Duncan saunt her word Miss Alice gone to her pa's en he gwine come en stay here whell she come back. She told me tell you be monsous partick'lar 'bout havin' good supper for him."

"Well, I'm thankful she takin' a intruss agin in eat'n o' some kind, for somebody. Tell her I say ' Yes'm.' "

What can it be in our destinies that lets us be wholly without preparation for distressful accidents, and which so often, just before their approach, diffuses over our hearts an unwonted sense of freedom from anxieties? Mrs. Guthrie had spent the day in almost jubilant expectation. She had been feeling herself drawn more affectionately toward Alice with something like a sense of thankfulness for going away and leaving Duncan all to herself, and she believed that kind was her own thought to persuade him to let her make her visit as long as she should desire. As soon as he came within hearing she saluted him.

"Why, bless your heart! I don't know when I had such a pleasant surprise as when I got your note this morning. Come in. Now, throw off that coat, and put on this grass linen you see I've kept for you. I know you're hot from working all this warm day in that hot down town."

When he had done as she bade, and they were seated, she said :

"I'm glad Alice went; I knew she expected to go some time before long, but I didn't know quite so soon.

Poor child! She needed some rest from this everlasting housekeeping, that a body, no matter how much they may see being done, is always seeing something else that needs it as bad. I'm glad she went; the country air will do her good—and that poor little baby too, as to that. Yes; she needn't have sent me word about her going. You know I never liked to say good-by to people, and may be I might have felt it my duty to tell her to bring and let me see one time—which I just couldn't have done, and I don't know when I've felt as calm in my mind as I have to-day. Are you right well, Duncan? You don't look so very bright. Been feeling lonesome about Alice, I reckon; but I think you *might* be satisfied for me to have you part of the time. She needed the rest, and if I was in your place I'd let her make a good long stay of it if she wants to. Has anything gone wrong that you look, seems to me, rather bothered in your mind? I've been thinking all day what a nice good time we were going to have for a while just to ourselves."

"Of course, mother, a man must feel some little lonesomeness when his wife has just gone away from him upon an extended visit. But I've not been upset much by that. Let's have supper first. I ate dinner at Junkin's to-day, and it being earlier than I'm used to, I had but little appetite. I was thinking, when I came in, about some business that may be rather troublesome before it's finished. We'll talk about it after supper. How are you this evening, mother? You are looking well."

"Oh, I'm well enough!" she answered low, showing that the cheer in which she had been had suddenly gone from her.  She called to Judy to hasten supper, but not so as to have it spoiled, and then began talking of things indifferent.  During the meal he spoke as usual, but she detected that his cheerfulness was unreal, and she made brief answers to his words.  When they had retired to the piazza he reported to her the posting of the notices and a part of their probable meaning.  He spoke with as much indifference as he could assume, fearing an outburst of her passion.  She kept entirely silent until he was through, then in a low voice, determined to restrain as much as possible excitement that she knew would add to his distress and her own, answered :

"Well, that don't scare *me !*  I'll let John Stapleton know, and I'll let those meddling lawyers know that if they think they can do that with me, they know nothing at all about me.  I had made up my mind to give them children five or six thousand dollars apiece, and may be more, and now I'll not do that unless this mean disgraceful business is put an end to.  I'm ready for any sort of fight they want."

He had hoped that the news would have caused her to have some apprehension ; so he said :

"It is not a matter of mere fight, mother, and it is not worth while for us to talk in defiance of people who are moving according to the set forms of law.  The question for us to consider first, is what defense we can make against the attack that is to be made against father's will, and next, how much we are willing to pay in order to avoid possibly a long, certainly an exasperating lawsuit, that, to say the least, will endanger your peace of mind."

"Endanger my peace of mind!" she replied, in yet lower tone, and after a bitter laugh "*my* peace of mind! As if I was ever let have any of that since I was a little child!"

She became silent, and by the starlight he could observe the heaving of her bosom. After a few moments, she took out a large white silk handkerchief, and, wiping her eyes, resumed:

"No, *I* never knew what it was nor what it meant to have peace of mind! My father, nor my mother, nor my brother, nor my sister, not one of them ever loved me as they did one another, nor cared a straw whether I loved them or not; and they were every one of them glad—as I always knew they would be, when I got married and went off clean away. My very husband didn't love me as I hoped he was going to; and even before his first child was born I had the very instinct that if *it* loved me at all it wouldn't love me like it did him; and, sure enough when it came, it didn't and never did. And when you came, and I found at last, *at* last, that I had somebody to love me as I loved them, they had me scared nearly out of my life, one way and another, that you'd get cut out of the property. And when all danger of that was over, I was scared fearing that even *you* might get so after a while when I began to get old, or got old, *you* wouldn't be to me always as you was then. Wait a little bit; don't say anything yet; I'll go on directly."

She rose from the chair, and going to the front of the piazza looked up a moment or two at the stars, then resuming her seat, proceeded:

"To go back to Caroline. Do you know the pains

I took with that child ?  I did it all the time before
your father died, and I promised him I'd keep on doing
it after he was dead, and nobody can say I ever broke
my word.  She had the best clothes of any girl in this
town.  I sent her to school and kept her at school until that John Stapleton began to follow her around, and
she had as good an education as any girl in this whole
region of country ever had, not excepting Charlotte
and Alice; and I took pride in her because everybody
praised her, and I knew she was my own child.  But, if
you believe me, I was always anxious about her, and
afraid that she'd at last do something to make me think
it wouldn't be right to do for her all your father expected of me.  And sure enough she did, and then—
I declare it seemed that it all came about just to hurt
me and keep me hurt in my very soul as long as I'm to
live—the poor child, after she'd had two children by
that man, lay down and *died*, when I was no more expecting such a thing than for one of those stars you see
up yonder to break loose and fall out of the sky!  O
my God! my God!  Talk to me about peace of mind,
Duncan ?  To-day I did think I was beginning to have
a little of it; but I thought even then it wasn't going
to last.  God knows what little of that I've had, has
come from you.  Come here ! "

As he approached her, she reached forth both her
arms, pressed his head against her bosom, and groaned
aloud.  A moment after, loosing him, and almost push-
ing him away, she said :

" That'll do, go back, and don't you say a single
word to me until I tell you; I want to think a while."

She walked heavily several times up and down the

piazza. Suddenly stopping and resuming her seat, she turned toward him and asked:

"You say there were two notices? How came that?"

"One was as Caroline's administrator, and the other as guardian of the children."

"You don't mean that John Stapleton is after any of the property for himself, his lone self, do you, Duncan?"

"His asking for guardianship would seem as if he was moving mainly in behalf of the children. Still the law, as it now stands, would give the property—if any should be recovered—to him as administrator of Caroline, which means the same as turning it over to him personally."

"Well, then, he *sha'n't have* it!"

She rose again and traversed the piazza, this time for a quarter of an hour, as if to marshal her thoughts. Then, going up and standing before him, she said:

"Duncan, you go to bed. I want to think over this thing by myself. But tell me first, have you said anything to your Uncle Dennis about it?"

"Yes, mother. I spoke to him this afternoon."

"What did he say?"

"His advice is to offer a compromise."

"Yes; his advice is always against me! But now let me tell you—I'm not going to do it! Dennis Macfarlane was always a man that didn't know what was best even for himself, let alone other people, and my suspicion is he's found it out; he ought to by this time. He sees how I've managed this property better than he's managed his own, and he—don't talk to me about

Dennis Macfarlane and his advice to me! But you go along to bed, child; I'll let you know in the morning what I'm going to do. My Lord! When I was feeling so easy in my mind about your coming and staying here a while I knew all the time that something was going to happen to spoil it. It's always been so with me, I've got something I want you to do; but I'll tell you to-morrow. Go to bed and get some rest. And don't you go to sleep thinking I'm scared; for I am not!"

IIc went off to bed.

"Judy," said his mother, when the maid had come to her call, "put your cot close to the door in the room behind mine, and go along to bed. If I want you I'll call you."

For several hours, with a black shawl around her, she walked and sat alternately on the piazza. At last she went in, locked the door, repaired to her chamber, and undressed herself. Trying to arrange her hair for the night-cap as it was done usually for her, and disgusted that she could not, she threw down the comb and brush, seated herself, and again ruminated. Late in the night, taking a candle, she went softly up-stairs to the chamber where Duncan lay. Sitting down upon the rail of the bed, she looked for some moments upon his handsome face, then, passing her hand over it, awakened him.

"Alice!" he said, startled; "what's the matter? Oh, is it you, mother?"

"Yes, I wonder you could have been so mistaken, even between sleep and awake. I come to tell you, Duncan, some of what I've made up my mind to do.

I don't suppose the case is going to come up right away; because if it is, I want you to go straight to-morrow after Seaborn Torrance. You've got to go soon any how; but I don't suppose it's necessary to break off to him quite yet, is it?"

"Of course not, mother," he answered, as he rose into a sitting position.

"That may be so, or it may not. I know, from what you say and from what Dennis Macfarlane says, though he was always a timid and—I don't know what else sort of man—yet I can see that there's some danger of the *law* of this business. There always is when it comes to the case of a woman, especially when she's a widow; and I reckon that's what makes 'em so willing to marry again when they have lost their husbands. But that's neither here nor there to me that had as much of that sort of experience as I wanted, and the very idea of marrying again has always been to me—I'm simply speaking for myself—it's been nothing else but disgusting, as the very death! As a widow I have fought my way the best I could, and I'm ready to do it again. I know you are sleepy, and don't want to talk about business this time of night; but I just *had* to tell you something before I went to bed, and it's this. Duncan, you're mistaken if you think I haven't been preparing and keeping myself prepared for such as this; and I come to tell you. Half, at least half of the money that your father left and that I have made off the property is in this house, and is in metal. I've put some of it out at interest; but I know how to shave notes and debts as well as anybody, and I'm going to gather it in and hide it along with the balance; and

I'm going to put the land into money, and do the same with that. I thought about running the negroes off to Alabama or Mississippi, but somehow I haven't the heart to do that, because it seems like the poor things feel that they're dependent upon me, and they're fond of me—I don't know what for, without it's because they think I'm rich; and then they've got wives and husbands and children scattered about everywhere, nobody knows where, and I just haven't the heart. So I reckon they'll have to stay as they are; but as for the balance, John Stapleton may take it out in whistling!"

He pitied her too much to say anything against the practicability of her proposed action. He tried to comfort by assuring her that, however the case might re-result, he himself could get much more than half of the estate.

"Go to bed, dear mother," he said, "and get some sleep, which it is plain that you need. You are already provided against the worst. We can keep them in court as long as we please, one way and another, and I doubt not that Jack Stapleton will be willing to accept, in compromise, whatever you may at last decide to offer to the children."

"To the children? Yes. But to him? Not a dollar will I compromise this side of my grave!"

A little while longer she sat and looked at him. Her only love, the sight and his words wrought a calmness which was exceeding dear. At length she said:

"And you think you can stay here contented a while, and not be longing for Alice?"

"My dearest mother," he answered, smiling, "I actually haven't thought about Alice since we began to talk about this business."

She felt like embracing him, but she did not. Such as that had always been embarrassing to her. So, without other words, she rose and went out. Descending the stairs and entering the room where her maid was asleep, she roused her with these words:

"It is actually astonishing to see how young people and niggers can sleep. If it wasn't for old people, and white at that, they'd all get burnt up whenever there's a fire in the night-time. Judy, go to the kitchen and fetch me some hot water. I told Chloe to keep a pot on the fireplace. You needn't blunder about and wake her; but go and get it, and come in my room and give my feet a good bathing."

When the tub was brought, while she lay back in her chair pointing out to Judy the parts of her limbs for special attention, she said:

"Judy, if I was to break up housekeeping and want to sell out, is there anybody particular who you'd want to buy you?"

"Law, miss, I ain' been even studdin' about you breaking up your house—fine house like dis, en got all you want in it, en more too."

"But, suppose the sheriff was to come and sell me out. Then, what?"

"Laws of mighty mercies, miss! I knowed you wa'n't well de minute I see you not eat'n no supper hardly; en I knowed it agin when you made me move my cot; en now I know it worse'n befo', you talkin' dat way; for because you 'bleeged to know in your mind dat I wants to belong to nobody exceptin' o' you, not while my life's a livin'."

"I'm not sick, nigger; I was just fooling. Stop and dry me well with the towel, and then fix my hair."

Shortly afterward she was abed, soundly sleeping.

---

## CHAPTER XXI.

### THE NEED OF COUNSEL.

THE next morning Mrs. Guthrie rose early, feeling more refreshed than she had expected. Taking a cup of coffee, she gave orders for breakfast to be delayed until Duncan should awaken. When he came down, she said:

"Good morning, my son. I wouldn't let you be called, because I wanted you to get a plenty of sleep. Let's go in and get something to eat. It's to be hoped that Chloe has got us some sort of a breakfast."

Half an hour afterward, while Guthrie, with cigar just lighted, was walking on the piazza, he observed a man about to open the front gate. Descending the steps and passing over the walk, he said:

"Well, Simmons. You come to see me?"

"No, Mr. Guthrie; I came to serve a paper on your mother."

"All right; hand it to me, and I'll give it to her."

"Shall I enter 'Left at the abode,' Mr. Guthrie, or will you acknowledge service for her?"

"Either, Simmons, it makes no difference; but I

13

may just as well acknowledge service, and if you'll call at my office an hour from now I'll do so."

The man, one of the sheriff's deputies, went on back, and Guthrie returned to the house. His mother, as he was coming up the steps, asked sternly:

"What man was that, Duncan, and what did he want?"

"It was a deputy sheriff, mother, who wanted to hand me some documents."

"Wonder why he couldn't wait till you'd had time for your breakfast to settle, and go down town. Is it anything concerning of me? because I want to know everything that happens, and when and how it happens, and I want it to come facing of me."

Tired by so long experience of her impatient, fiery energy, he answered petulantly:

"Mother, I have only run over the indorsement on the back of the paper, and noticed that it was a bill in equity—a thing I was expecting, but not quite so soon. I can study it at my office better than I can here. Besides, I have an appointment there at half-past nine, with a client. As soon as I can find time for it, I will look over the thing and report to you at dinner; or sooner if you wish. I don't see the use of talking to me as if you had no confidence in me."

"Why, Duncan," she responded, instantly softened, "confidence in *you?* The Lord knows that you are the only one that I *have* got complete confidence in. I'm just excited and worried, and I've no doubt I spoke too hasty. Go on to your business. You needn't to come up here before dinner-time, without it's necessary, as I've no idea it will be. I understand them. They

would like to scare people; but I'm older than any of·
them, and have seen folks before they were born."

Then she went back into the house. As Duncan
turned from the gate, Mr. Wendell and Miss Jewell
entered the street on the opposite side. A double pain
shot through his heart; he felt intense regret both that
his father had not died intestate and that his eye had
ever rested upon that young woman. He hastened forward, as he must have saluted this party if their eyes
had met. He could hear Miss Jewell's voice, clear, and
refined, as she chatted with her cousin, and he made
greater haste. When he reached his office, taking out
the paper which the officer had served, he read it carefully.

A bill in equity, as is known to those who are at
all familiar with judicial investigations, is a petition
wherein a complainant asks for special aid and protection from the court in cases wherein an ordinary action
according to set forms of proceeding at Common Law
is alleged or apprehended to be insufficient. The one
in this case was named A Bill for Discovery, Account,
Relief, and Injunction. It alleged:

That Alan Guthrie, owner of property of several
sorts to the amount of at least two hundred thousand
dollars, had deceased, leaving a widow and two minor
children, Caroline and Duncan.

That the wife, Hester Guthrie, after his decease pro
pounded in the Court of Ordinary of the county a paper
purporting to be his last will and testament, which, by
proof in common form, had been admitted to probate,
and letters testamentary had been issued to her as the
executrix named therein; and that the estate at the pres-

ent time was believed to amount to the value of not less
than three hundred thousand dollars.

That at the time of the signing of the paper Alan
Guthrie was so prostrated by various bodily and men-
tal infirmities that he was not of that degree of sound-
ness of memory required by law in a testator at the
execution of a last will and testament, but that the
said Hester, taking advantage of his infirm condition,
had acquired over him an influence which he was not
strong enough to resist, and thus compelled him to sign
the fraudulent paper by which his whole estate was bequeathed to herself to the exclusion of his other as
rightful heirs from any part thereof.

That the testator while in life, as was well known to
all his friends and acquaintances, had had much affection for his children, and that to some of the former
during his decline he had expressed apprehension that
injustice would be done by his wife, particularly to
his daughter Caroline, against whom she had ever indulged a prejudice without just foundation, and for
that reason he had executed a paper in which he had
deputed her to divide his estate equally among herself
and his children, which sayings of the testator were
made in the hearing of several witnesses (some now
living) after the date whereon said pretended last will
and testament purported to have been executed, all
which tended to show that he did not fully understand the provisions in that paper contained, and that
many other things done and said by the testator ante-
rior and subsequent to its date left no doubt that he
was wholly incompetent for the execution of a last will
and testament of any sort.

After alleging the marriage and death of Caroline, leaving a husband and two children, and their failure to receive their just portion of the estate, the bill prayed that the said pretended last will and testament be set aside, the testamentary letters be revoked, that an account be required from the executrix of her actings and doings in the management of the estate, and of the interest and other profits that had accrued since the death of decedent; and that respondent be required to answer under oath all the allegations in said bill contained, and that she be enjoined, under such penalty as the court should deem sufficient, from selling, removing, or otherwise disposing of any portion of the estate except under decree of the court.

The concluding prayer was for such other and further relief as the judge, sitting as a court of Chancery, might deem necessary for complainants.

The bill was in the name of John Stapleton in his own right, as administrator of Caroline Stapleton, and as guardian of the minor children left by her. It was signed by Thomas Tolly and Christopher Bond, solicitors.

Sick at heart, Guthrie, putting the document upon his table, paced about the room, pondering the blow that, so long delayed, had fallen at last suddenly and with a force that seemed to him as cruel and revengeful as it was appalling. Several times he went to the door and looked out. It was anguish to him to see men walking about doing and chatting, some of them laughing, as if nothing unwonted had happened. After some time, closing his office, he went up to his own residence. His judgment was that if the allegations in the bill could be substantiated even partially, his mother must be defeated: for it must appear that his father in executing the paper, even if proved to have been of disposing memory, intended to constitute the executrix as trustee of two thirds of the estate for the benefit of his children. How to deal with her, so passionate, so fearless, so defiant of other's opinions, so incapable of denying solemnly anything that she had done, so resolute to maintain it without avoidance or compromise, so apt to resort to desperate expedients, perplexed him sorely. He sat upon his piazza, or moved about the house and grounds the rest of the forenoon. He had never thought to feel as now the absence of his wife. It seemed as though she had been gone a long time already. Never before had he felt how necessary she was to his being, how dear to him. He put his hands upon several things which she often used—things on her bureau, on the piano, and the parlor center-table. Raising the piano lid, he discovered her handkerchief which had been left when she had closed it last. He put it to his face and smelled the delicate perfumery. Folding it carefully, he put it into his pocket, shut the piano again, and left the house. On the way to his mother's, it was some relief to remember that on the night before she had spoken of retaining in her case the lawyer Seaborn Torrance. He commended her sagacity in fixing upon such a man, and he was eager to have as soon as possible the help of his counsel.

In spite of his efforts to appear calm, she detected at a glance the anxiety upon his mind. When he had reported what was alleged and claimed by the bill in equity, she was silent for several moments, then, with a sad, bitter smile, said :

" Well, if I am to have to make another fight in my old age, I'll show those people and all the rest of them some things that will be interesting.  Now there isn't going to be one single particle of doubt about that.  As for Judge Ansley sending his sheriff to me with his paper, ordering me what to do and what not to do with what's *mine*—but come, let's have dinner.  I told them to have it ready a little before one, as I've hardly ate enough since yesterday dinner to keep a cat alive, much less a woman that's got on her hands what's on mine, and I'm hungry.  What I want to say now is that I want you—this evening or to-morrow morning early—to take your sulky, and go straight for Seaborn Torrance, and bring him right here to me.  I told him when he was here last court, that if I ever had a lawsuit that was important, I'd want him, and he promised that whenever I sent for him, he'd come right away if he wasn't too busy with something else.  I want the best lawyer that can be got, and from what I've heard about him he's that.  He knows when and how to talk, and how and when to bring on and put off, and never give up.  I'll send him by you a thousand dollars, and you tell him there's more where that came from.  That's all I've got to say now.  Come along to dinner."

He was gratified at the subsidence of her excitement, for he had feared that it might lead to indiscreet action.  She relished the good dinner that had been provided, and kept urging him to try to do the same.  Some, only a little reprehension of his distrust and timidity was in her words and manner.  During the afternoon and evening she exhibited the kind of cheerfulness that in the being of the intrepid comes with the threat of danger. Occasionally she would give way, but only briefly, to resentment, which contempt hindered from reaching exasperation.

"Poor John Stapleton! You know, Duncan, that if I didn't despise the creature so from my heart, I almost feel like I could get sorry for him? My suspicion at the time about Caroline was that she wasn't exactly in her right mind when she let herself down to marry such a thing as him, whether or no. Decent born as she was, of course she was obliged, living with him, to hold him back from some of his savage wildness, but now, here, as soon as the breath is out of her body, to come at *me* with his *notices*, and his *citations*, and his *bills of equities*, or what you mind to call 'em, and think to scare *me!*"

In the midst of such speeches her fan would fly like that of a winnowing machine, and the laugh that followed gave whatever relief was possible. It was evident to her son that she was trying to impart to him some of her own courage, both for his own comfort, and to render him more competent for his part of the work in hand and to come. To her question how long the case could be kept in court, provided she should so desire, he answered that that would depend upon circumstances. She replied:

"Well, from what I've been told about Seaborn Torrance, he's the very man to help get them up. As for those children, now their poor mother is dead, I've been intending to give them a good deal more than I ever expected to do; but to be settled so that John Stapleton was to have not one blessed thing to do with it. You know he's going to marry again, and keep on marrying as long as he keeps on killing up women that think no more of themselves than to be his wives."

"Oh, yes, he's pretty sure to marry again—but killing his wives? What do you mean by that, mother?"

"I mean nothing—that is nothing so very particular, Duncan, that you look at me so strange. I don't mean that the creature actually took up a stick and knocked her brains out, or even poisoned her, or smothered her; but he just wore the poor thing out with trying to make something of a decent man out of him and dying in the attempt. And besides all that, I wasn't satisfied and I never will be satisfied about her dropping off in that way all so sudden. From the way they told me she was first taken, she had nothing in this world but milk fever, and I can't but have my suspicions that he, or his old mother, and may be the doctor—God Almighty knows, I don't—but among 'em they got to projecking and fooling with the case, and the first thing they knew, they killed her. *If* that man had anything to do with it—and I'm not accusing him nor *excusing* him—but if he *did*, it was because he saw that he wasn't going to get any more property by her."

"Oh, dear mother, he was entirely innocent of everything like that!"

"I don't say he wasn't, Duncan. I *told* you I wasn't accusing him nor *excusing* him. That's between him and his God. I was glad I didn't see him the day I was there, and she laid out. I was mighty nigh distracted any how, and I might have used words which of course I couldn't prove. Well, well, well, don't let us talk about the thing any more. You start soon in the morning for Seaborn Torrance."

She turned away from the subject, and made no further reference to it during the remainder of the day.

Simultaneously with Guthrie's departure in search of the lawyer who was to be his colleague, Bond left for Augusta. The equity proceeding had been begun somewhat sooner than might have been had he not other business which he thought to require early attention. He had called upon Miss Jewell twice since the visit on the evening of his arrival, once in company with Tolly. His persistent suit, aided by solemn remonstrances from her sister, had impressed her perceptibly, although she still avowed her resolution to remain single. On this last visit, in which Tolly accompanied, the latter had a long conversation with her while Bond chatted apart from where they sat with Anna Wendell. After they had left, Tolly said that he felt almost sure that he would prevail.

"I try to hope so, Tolly, although I can't get her to say a word to warrant it."

"Nor I, directly; but I could see from her looks at you when I was talking about you, and her confused irregular answers to me, that her affections are entirely yours, and that she will be obliged to follow them, resist them as she is doing, most unreasonably, I think."

"No, Tolly no, sir; I've been thinking about it a great deal, and I'll be cursed if I haven't rather come to the conclusion that the woman is right, hard as it is on me. She wants the field perfectly clear, and she doesn't see how it can be made so; and I admire and love her the more for it. Why, sir, what do you suppose she said to me last night? 'Mr Bond' said she 'I could tell you something that would make you agree with me that I

ought not to marry.' By George! that scared me, because
I was afraid she was going to tell me and then ask for a
pledge to do nothing with Guthrie. I answered her
that I didn't wish to hear a single word against, but
whatever I could in favor of her marrying me. Tears
were in her eyes. I couldn't stand it; so I trumped up
some sort of lie that you were expecting me, and I got
away as soon as I could. But I'm thankful that you
think favorably of the case. Their school term ends in
about a week; but she says she's not going to Augusta,
except for a short visit toward the last of her vaca-
ation. It is plain to me that she intends to live it out,
God bless her! By the way, you ought to hear how she
praises Miss Macfarlane, and you also, confound you!
She says you two are bound to marry each other if you
both live a year or two longer. I asked her to-night,
the little time I had with her, how she thought this case
would affect your prospects. She answered, not at all, or,
if anything, would assist them. She says that the whole
family are against Guthrie's mother in the treatment of
her daughter, and Stapleton also. Put that in your pocket. And so, my dear Tolly, with such hopes and a good
law case, give me your hand. There; I feel another
sort better than I did when I first got into this town."

He waved adieu as he drove by the house on the
next morning. Mr. Wendell, who yet knew of no special difficulty in the way, said after he had passed:

"Sarah, it is plain to me that that man wants to
marry you, and if he does, I think you ought to consider
well before you reject his suit."

With her folded fan she patted his cheek playfully,
then went in for her bonnet.

## CHAPTER XXII.

### ALICE JOURNEYS TO BROAD RIVER.

In her preparation for departure Alice busied herself for the baby more than for herself. Instead of Marcus, the carriage was driven by the husband of Eliza, because the mistress was not willing to separate them from each other. Susie, another of the house servants, was taken along to assist in nursing. Marcus, as Aunt Ritter would have guessed, was well pleased secretly, because the journey would have taken him too long away from the "ladies" and "females" of Clarke, and forced him to try to be content with what society could be had among those beyond Broad River. The two babies were provided with abundant outfits, and the extremest care was observed that they should not be hurt in this their first exposure to the perils of a day's travel. It was a mild morning, the sun throughout the day not shining too hot for the comfort of the horses as they walked up the hills and trotted leisurely along the stretches of level.

The cool shades through woods, and along their edges, the liquid fragrance from myriads of leaves and wild flowers, and the gleeful music all along were enough to make a thoughtful mind have a sense of religious thankfulness. Yet Alice was sad throughout her journey, except when busy, or imagining she ought to be busy, with her charge. Even the sweet prospect of soon being at her native home was saddened by thoughts of the life that she had been leading since she had left it. It would have frightened her too much if she had felt that her heart was not loyal as ever to the husband who had taken her thence, notwithstanding the disappointments that had befallen.

The sun lacked half an hour of setting when, having crossed the river by ferry, the travelers, turning toward Dove Creek, arrived at their destination. Nearly midway in a plantation of several thousands of acres, on a high plateau surrounded by oaks and hickories, interspersed with poplars and chestnut trees, was the large mansion, its perfect white making pleasing contrast with the varying green around. Below and above was a wide piazza extending along three sides, at either end of the lower being a long one-story room, and between these another piazza whereon, when the weather suited, the family were accustomed to take their meals. Outside were signs of wealth as unostentatious as abundant; within, furniture massive and of a style which had out- lived others more ornate but less tasteful and less adapted to comfortable uses. The dining-table stood al- ways extended beyond the needs of the family for the ac- commodation of any one or more of the neighbors, rich or poor, who might drop in by invitation or chance at meal times; for already there obtained among the cult- ured and wealthy of that region the custom of dispensing a hospitality that became so important in the making of the people of middle Georgia. The family now resi- dent there was limited to the parents and two sons, one who would graduate at the State College after two years longer. Two miles away, with his own family, was the other, who already had become, like his father, a successful planter and leading citizen.

All sadness, for a time, must be driven away by the

welcome extended by all—parents, brother, slaves, the affection of the last mentioned of whom the true-hearted Georgian always prized, and wherever he is living now, cherishes with fondness its recollection.  Cordial as to her was the welcome to the baby, the getting out for whom of things that had been lying in ancient chests and drawers was to have no end.  For a time Alice felt as she used to feel in her girlhood without thought of the troubles already known and without apprehension of the greater that, already near, were to follow. Her father was tall and massive, with little diminution of vigor and activity; his countenance showed firmness and benignity.  Her mother, of about her own height and figure, seemed somewhat younger than she was indeed, and much younger than her husband, although there was a difference in their ages of less than ten years, her hair being slightly turned, while his had become nearly all white.  To see the two together for only an hour, one must observe that their domestic life had been one of affection, trust, and peace.

It is not in the nature of such a woman as Alice Guthrie to live without confiding or wishing to confide to somebody the secrets of her emotions, especially her sufferings and anxieties.  Away from her native home, at which never had been a secret that was not known to every member of the family, in the society wherein she had been living there had been but one with whom, if their separate conditions and circumstances, though nearly allied, had not been so widely different, she would have lived in the free intimacy out of which is wont to come so much consolation in distress. Many a time had she yearned to tell Caroline Staple-

ton what she must withhold about herself and the compassion she felt for her, although knowing that she
lived a far happier life than her own was or than she
ever hoped for it to become.   Even as it was, a sympathy had been between them which now it was dear
to her to recall, and she was thankful that in the care
of this infant she was rendering some compensation,
slight as it was, for the injustice that had been put upon
its mother by her family.   Yet in her experience there
was a thing which she never could have imparted to
but one, and it was she from whom, until her marriage,
not a feeling or impulse of her breast had ever been
withheld.   In the face of her daughter, Mrs. Ludwell,
despite the childlike happiness at being there again,
had detected evidences of care beyond what comes naturally along the line of married life.   Tears were in
her eyes several times as she looked into the faces of
her parents and at old familiar things in the house,
showing that her heart was too full of gratitude for
being again in that loved presence, and on that first
night, even if both had wished and tried to delay, they
would not have been able to forbear, the one from
asking and the other from answering heart to heart.
Already her parents knew, what before her marriage
they had known only in part, of the relations main-
tained by Mrs. Stapleton with her mother and, to a less
degree, with her brother, and they felt a disgust which,
though not as painful, was as decided as her own.
Then to them much more than to her had come whisperings of Duncan's deportment toward young women,
including Emily Simkins, which, had they been heard
in time, inquired into, and found or suspected to be

be upon good foundation, would have prevented their consent to the marriage. Latterly other rumors, though of not such gross kind, had reached them, and filled the mother especially with anxiety.

The evening was given up to congratulations and affectionate chattings. They sat on the piazza, so much more peaceful than the one in which during the same evening Guthrie was listening as his mother poured forth her bitterness and resentment. The night's loveliness must have been remarked by all but that it was common to the nights of the season throughout that region. Their talk was of pleasant news that every one had to give about pleasant things, or of Caroline Stapleton, her husband and children. To a question of her father about Stapleton, she answered:

"Father, he is a man among a thousand! I've not seen anywhere one whose appearance and whose deportment discover the gentleman more clearly. Sister Caroline was most dearly devoted to him, and well she might have been; for if I ever met a man more capable of winning and keeping the whole heart of such a woman as she was, I don't remember. He is extremely handsome, too—perhaps I should rather say manlike—courteous in his manners, and one to be trusted to the very last degree."

No allusion was made to the treatment which their family had received, nor to the lawsuit that seemed about to begin. This must be postponed until after a time of needed rest. Alice yielded to her mother's suggestion to retire to bed early, and when she had undressed herself, Mrs. Ludwell said:

"Now I will leave you, darling, although there are

many things I want to talk to you about. Go to bed
now and sleep well in your old own bed-chamber."

"It is so sweet to be here, mother," she said, looking around. Tears came into her eyes, and instantly
were answered by some in her mother's.

"I don't feel like going to bed quite yet, mother,
unless you insist. I'm not at all fatigued, and I am
loath to let sleep come and shut my eyes so soon from
you and the things in this room. Yet I'd better, on
your account and on father's. If we should get to talking we won't know when to stop, and father will be
kept awake."

"No, dear. If you don't feel fatigued nor sleepy
we can have a little talk. Your father won't mind it.
Indeed, he doesn't expect me quite yet, knowing we
might have something special to say to each other.
Only he cautioned me not to keep you up late, and to
let you lie in bed as late as you pleased to-morrow
morning."

"That was good of him and just like him."

They chatted until late. The mother was led soon
to regret that their conversation had not been postponed. Now the door of the heart of her daughter
once opened, all therein must come out in that dear
presence. That heart, parted from none of the loyalty
of its new allegiance, yet could not but confess—for it
seemed and felt like a confession—some of the things
that had brought so much anguish and shame. With
bitter grief she spoke of the neglect of Caroline Stapleton, a neglect which, if her own husband had not con-
nived at it, he could have mitigated, or at least com-
pensated by affectionate behavior on his own part,

14

neither of which things, as was well known to every-body, he had ever done. When she came to speak of Miss Jewell, her face reddened and her voice was low and tense, tending to frighten her mother with the suspicion that herein she had received a wound that was incurable. Several times she besought her to stop, but she would not.

"No, mother, not yet, not quite yet. I can not sleep until I have told you all. After that I am sure that I can. I must let all come out to-night, since it has begun; then I shall get some relief. May God forgive me if I have said, or if I shall say, anything inconsistent with the vows I have taken upon myself, to be followed by temptations so much more trying than I could ever have been made to expect! It is to *you* I am talking, and it seems to me now, as it always seemed, that when I am talking with you it is as though I am talking with my own heart, and with God's full permission. Now listen to me further about this young woman; for you haven't yet seen the peculiar, the deepest pain upon my heart when thinking about her. O mother! what terrifies me most is the thought, the constantly increasing thought, that she is innocent. I believed, because I was *made* to believe, that she was not. I do not mean that I was led to suspect her guilty in any very wicked, impure sense, at least so known to herself, and intended by herself; but that she had for Duncan a feeling of attachment to which, instead of resisting, she yielded with too little thought of inevitable consequences; and that Duncan, having suddenly discovered the degree of her weakness withdrew from her company abruptly, and induced me to treat her with only such civility as, without rudeness, must be observed whenever we met in the company of others. But do you know, mother, that sometimes, when I've been looking toward her, I have said to myself, if that face, beautiful as it is, be not innocent, it has been gifted with preternatural power to counterfeit. She has looked at me sometimes—indeed, she did so as late as yesterday afternoon, when I happened to meet her with Charlotte Macfarlane in one of the stores—as if she would like to draw near to me for the purpose of undeceiving, and that she is hindered mainly by *pity*, pity for the delusion under which I am, and for the worse grief I should have if she were to remove it. I declare the thought of that sometimes so frightens me that I feel as if I must die!"

Her mother, in much anxiety, watched as she rose and walked silently but rapidly in the room, feeling that she must say something, and not knowing what.

"Come, come, my child," she affectionately remonstrated, " I can not believe that things are as bad as you fear."

She stopped abruptly, moved slowly to her mother, and, getting upon her knees and taking both her hands, said :

" Mother, I could, or I think I could, have borne what many women far better than I am have had to bear in their husbands, especially when sorely tempted, as in this case—for she is faultless in face and in shape —but mother, *mother!* suppose it should be, and be made appear that—that the man whose wife I am, in his infatuation for this fair creature, so deported himself toward her as to frighten her away or as to incense her,

as all good women must be incensed by a man's audacity, and that therefore it is she, instead of me, that has
been most outraged; and yet she can afford to look down
with compassion upon me, and decline, for my sake, to
put aside a veil that would show him to whom I am so
bound to be not only a treacherous husband, but an as-
sailer and a slanderer of unprotected innocence! If
that is proved, O mother! *how* am I to continue to live
with a man who—to put my own poor self aside from
such consideration—sought to blast the name of a good
woman whom he endeavored, but failed to destroy?"

She buried her face in the lap of her mother, who
let her weep for several moments. Then, raising her
and taking her within her arms, she said:

"My daughter, I am very sorry that I let you speak
of your troubles this first night. They are more serious
than I had apprehended. But you must not say another word about them now." Then, looking around
the room, she asked:

"Is everything arranged as you wished? That was
your crib; I know you haven't forgotten it."

"That I have not!" she answered, smiling. "Yes;
all is just as I would have it. I keep the baby close by
me while she is so young. I feel better now, and I'm
going to get a good night's sleep. I'm sure I am."

The outpouring did no harm, rather good. The
feeling of home and its abounding sufficiency in love
and protection, outside sounds and fragrances, soon
brought on sleep. She did not awaken when the nurse,
twice in the course of the night, entered the chamber.
The sun was high up next morning when, opening her
eyes and contemplating curiously for a moment the

things around her, so long unwonted, she rose quickly, called to the nurse, and began to dress herself.

"Why, Liza, I'm ashamed of myself! What did you let me sleep so for? How is the baby? Did she wake in the night?"

"Yes'm, Miss Alice; twice't. I wa'n' guine wake you when no use, en I knowed you want de sleep, en your ma, en your pa, bofe un 'em say it not got to be done. De baby well as she ken be, 'pear like de trav-'lin' en de a'r up here already 'gins to 'gree wid her, de way she hold on to me when I takes her."

At that moment, after a knock at the door, a wait-ress entered with a tray, bearing a goblet overflowing with golden and green.

"Mawnin', Miss Alice; hope you res' well larse night. Marster sent you dis min' julep, en he say you got to drink it every drap, because he say you needs it. He say he don' want no foolin' wid it jes wid de spoon."

"Oh, Tempe, good morning! Tell father I say that I find he's the same good, glorious old fellow that he's always been. Breakfast is over, isn't it?"

"No'm; marster en mistess say dee ain' goin' to have breakfast tell you wake up en come down, exceptin' mistess she made marster take a cup o' coffee."

"My, my! go down and tell mother she may give orders to have breakfast brought in. I'll be down by the time it is ready."

The meal was served in the piazza at the rear, from which they could look upon the poultry of various spe-cies in the yard and over into the garden, along whose front fence were fig trees, cape jessamines, rose bushes, and lagestræmias.

"I knew you two girls would want to have some special talky-talky to yourselves," said Mr. Ludwell. "Whom did you gossip about mostly?"

"Not you for one, father," answered Alice cheerily. "You may be sure that you escaped unscathed."

"I suppose you took up those whom you regarded as the biggest sinners first; my time will come on a little later. Did you drink the julep I sent you?"

"Oh, yes, and it was delicious, especially for being made by you."

"All right; now I want to see if you can't eat something. You're rather thinner looking than I like to see, daughter. I hope Mr. Guthrie doesn't allowance you on that line."

"Oh, no," she answered, imitating his tone. "He is quite fond of good eating himself, and he wonders sometimes why I eat what he calls so little. But I'm in good health physically, father, and I mean to enjoy fully you and mother, and everybody and everything else, while I'm here."

"That's right. Nothing like a good appetite for health, supposing, of course, a reasonable conscience. I hope, as some of our good neighbors about here say, that you've tried to keep a livin' holt on the lessons your mother has taught you."

"Good lessons have been taught me by others besides mother," she answered, with a look of affection, "even if I might justly count her as at the head of my teachers. I can't say how well I've profited by the instructions."

"Well, well, I'll take it for granted that you've done as well as could be expected. But fall to, fall to—we mustn't let the breakfast get cold, what allowance your economical mother has set before us."

This joke, pleasant as habitual, put all in good frame.

---

## CHAPTER XXIII.

### MRS. BUCK.

In that region were fewer marked distinctions than in the villages between the educated and the ignorant, the wealthy and the poor. I should hardly say "the poor," for there were almost none who could not, and who usually did not, make sufficient maintenance for themselves and their dependents out of a soil so fertile and a climate so salubrious. To a frontier region, near the line of dangerous savage existence, few are accustomed to migrate who have not courage, vigor, and activity sufficient for their own essential wants. Here large estates and small—the former few, the latter numerous; the former not too large, the latter not too small—covered the country from the Savannah beyond the Ocmulgee. Remote from large towns, bordering upon an extensive space occupied by the Indians, it behooved this people within degrees to ignore personal, and even family distinctions, in view of the needs and perils that were incident to all. And so the uncultured poor man (thus to name him for want of a more accurate appellative) was led to feel a freedom as distinct as his wealthy neighbor, with whom his intercourse often was more frequent and confidential than

that held with his equal in property and intelligence
who lived half a dozen miles away. The outcome of
such relationships was benign to both classes. It is not
every man of wealth, with sincere intentions thereto,
who knows how to deport himself to his neighbors who
are of the humbler sort. There is a condescension that
means and wishes to be considered charitableness which
to the eye looks well enough to be praised, and it sometimes makes grateful recipients out of those who have
been used to nothing different. Yet between these and
the givers is a wall which, though not visible to the
eye, is felt by both to be impassable; and this feeling
tends to suppress emulation and hinder development
on the line where some might make their best achieve-
ments. On the other hand, where there is no wall except that made by the natural fitness of things, along
which is many an open gate for going in and coming
out, whatever is original and individual has opportunities for all possible growth. There was an aristocracy in rural districts as in villages, an aristocracy of
excellent type, with definite but not oppressive peculiar-
ities, effecting good results. The broad line between
the white man and the negro had the effect of hinder-
ing any other. The aristocratic element did not keep
itself aloof from the democratic, but associated with it,
elevated it, and sometimes allied itself with it. In its
very highest representatives it was least ostentatious. Its
graciousness was not misunderstood by the humble, and
they not often sought to overleap barriers to entirely
equal intercourse which, not convention, but nature and
different fortune and opportunities had raised. No
man could feel himself to be more of a freeman than

the white man of middle Georgia sixty years ago. The products of this freedom have been seen on fields of multifarious endeavor. Intermixture of classes among the whites accounts both for the racy humor among inferiors and the sturdy character that was behind it. Few sights bring laughs heartier or more kindly than that of a weak man who, imagining himself the equal of a strong who treats him as an equal, essays to do as he does. Such laughs are free from the petulance that comes from contempt when in the innocent mimic are seen qualities more easily imitated, and they are those which make the genuine freeman everywhere. Inter-marriages, not frequent, with few exceptions, lowered not as much as they exalted. They produced a race having for forms neither more nor less regard than they were believed to be entitled to, as exponents and conveyances of true manhood and true womanhood.

On a plane much lower, yet not far dissimilar, were the relations of the white people to negroes. Constant close contiguity to their owners gave rise to humanity and fidelity. In no portion of the country was domestic and community police upon a scale of less vigilance or greater security than on plantations

"Father," said Alice after breakfast. "you should have heard Susie this morning commenting upon what seemed to her carelessness in guarding these premises at night, and Eliza's answer. Susie said to me; 'Law, Miss Alice! Dee don't shet nare single door in all dis big house of a night, let 'lone winders. I speck your pa, he so rich, he don' min' what people can steal.'"

"And how answered Lizy? I'll be bound for her to undertake to clear up the mystery."

" ' Gal,' said Lizy, ' you astes dat question 'cause you ain' never lived nowhar 'cept in a big town, whar people has to lock up what dee got, or keep dey eye on it. But up here, it's differ'nt. Marster know his niggers ain' gwine steal from him, en ef anybody else niggers comes prowlin' around here of a night our dogs would make sich a racket somebody would wake up en chase 'em off befo' dee could lay day han' on anything to steal it en k'yar it off out'n dis house, en den may be come up wid 'em en git some of dey hide. Marster, warm night like dis, he ain' studdin' 'bout rogues; whut he studdin' 'bout is keepin' hisself cool."

"Good for Lizy! That's as satisfactory an answer as I could have made, and in more expressive language."

About two hours afterward, while her father was out somewhere on the plantation, Alice received her first visit. It was from an elderly lady who dwelt a couple of miles away on a small tract adjoining Mr. Ludwell's. She came riding upon a mare followed by a colt, and alighted upon a block in the grove before she was observed. Hearing the youngster whinnying, Alice looked out, and ran to assist the visitor to the house.

"Why, howdye, Mrs. Buck?" she said, putting herself within her embrace. "I knew you wouldn't be long in coming to see me after you heard I was here. How are you, and all the rest?"

"Howdye, Alice? Monstrous glad to see you, child. But now, stop now right here before we go any furder, and let me give some directions to Abom—I see him a-comin' yonder—about that mar', and special about that colt, which I do think they're the biggest fool things—colts, I mean—in this whole troublesome world. Abom," she continued, addressing herself to a negro man who had come up to take the mare, "when you put her up, you better lock the barn door, because if you don't, that animal of a colt he'll muander everywhere, all over the lot, and what he can't manage to jump over, he'll jump intoo, and if for nothin' else but for jes a-goin' everywhar whar he have no business a-goin'. 'Tweren't I made up my mind before I left home to stay to dinner, and may be toward the shank of the evenin' like, I'd a not let him come. You understand me, Abom, does you? It's to fix him whar he can't jump nother over anything ner intoo it, nor meddle with it no ways."

"Oh, yes'm, Miss Buck," he answered with the condescending respect usually paid by negroes to humble white friends of their owners, "I'll fix him so he k'yarn hurt nothin', nor git hurted hisself."

"That's right, Abom. How you been, Alice? Seem like to me you're some thinner than when I see you last time you was here, although you ain't altered so monstrous powerful much, like some girls does when they git married and go off from their parrents, and when they come back home they look like they been dragged through a bresh-heap or somethin'. The more I look at you, the more you look like yourself. How's your ma? Ah, here she is, to speak for herself."

Mrs. Ludwell met her at the foot of the steps, and with Alice assisted her to ascend.

"The good Lord help your two souls, both of you! I don't need all that to git in, nor none of it, in fact."

Yet pleased, she submitted to the escort, and when she was seated upon a large rocker, in answer to the invitation to remove her bonnet, she took off the vast

straw covering, plucked at every point of imaginary
derangement of her cap, at length suffered Alice to re-
adjust it, and the while looked at her mother and her
alternately.

" I do believe the child' will look jes like you when
she gits your age, and she's a-beginnin' to look it now."

"Oh, thank you, Mrs. Buck," Alice said.

" Well you may thank me, child ; for she was pretty
as a pink, and she hold her own, to my opinion, oncom-
mon well.  Warm, ain't it?  Yes, as you all's Ander
was drivin' the k'yart by my house on the way to mill,
I hailed him and ast how all was, and he said all was
well as common, and then he up, he did, and he told
me that his Miss Alice come last night, and I made up
my mind I wanted to see how the child look, and hear
her tell all about herself, and I told her she looked thin,
but yit she grow more like herself as I keep on a-lookin'
at her.  The good Lord know I'm proud to see her
once more and a-lookin' so nice and well.  And how you
like livin' in town, Alice, or do you think you got usen-
ed to it yit?  Look like you been thar long enough."

"Oh, right well, Mrs. Buck ; but not as well as
home."

" Ah, now, thar it is!  What made you quit it, then?
Howbeever, it's never worth anybody's while to ast sich
questions as that of young wimmens.  They'll all quit
their home when the time comes for 'em to think they
must drap thar parrents and go off a-follerin' a man.
Your own ma done the same, and me too, and my
daughter done it, and them that don't it's mostly because the man didn't come for 'em, or if he did, it
wer'n't the right one, or he didn't 'pears to them he

were the right one, and I suppose it's the natur' of people, and I've never yit decided in my own mind which is the best, and I've a mighty nigh come to the concludin' that it's mostly accordin' to people theirself and the way they act, married or single, and behave theirselves and not be too easy to find fau't or to be found fau't with."

At that moment, Susie, the baby in her arms, came out to say something to Alice. The old lady, after a prolonged stare, cried:

"Why, bless my souls alive! Why, Alice! Why, Missis Ludwell! you never told me nor sent me word that Alice had a baby! Why, I thought her baby died when it was born, and I never heard she had ary 'nother! Why, I *am* took back! Fetch it here, 'oman, and lay it right here in my lap, and let me see who o' the family it's like. My! That *is* news! I wonder *nobody* sent me no words; because common as babies is, somehow it's a ruther interestin' thing to me when another of 'em comes, and special when a body knows their mother, ef not their father. I suppose the good Lord made people so, special them of the women tribe. Fetch it along here."

Alice, blushing somewhat, told the child's brief history, and added: "But I love it very much, Mrs. Buck—it seems to me nearly as much as if it were my own."

"Well," said Mrs. Buck when the child was laid in her lap, "a sweeter-lookin' ner a good-lookiner baby I don't *know* the time! But Alice is mistakened, ain't she, Missis Ludwell, when she talk about a-lovin' it the same ef it were hern? No, child, sich as that ain't 'cordin' to natur', and it's right it ain't. Well, well, it look like a pity for sich a leetle teeny bit of a thing to have to have its mother took away from it. But the good Lord allays knows what's best for them that's took, and them that's left behind. You may take it now, 'oman—I'm thankful it fell into hands that'll try to do a mother's part by it. You didn't tell me if it was a boy or if it was a girl, for that make a great diffunce, special' in motherless children. I wonder at myself I never ast that question sooner. People gen'ly does, me among 'em. Girl, eh? Well mayby that's all for the best, too. Girls, I've often notussed, is a more comfort to their parrents and them that has the keer of 'em than boys, and when they git married, they most always is, special' to their mothers; for somehow I don't know how it is, but it's so, that a mother can git along with a son-in-law when they mayn't not so easy with a daughter-in-law, which my expeunce is, *that's* a often a case that a body might call tech-and-go. Howbeever, if when a mother that have her son's wife close by, if she'll try to be prudent, and not be too jealous in her mind, or try not show it if she can't he'p it, why, in them case they can all manage so as to keep some sort o' peace from risin' in families, as the sayin' is. Yes, you may take it now, my 'oman, and God A'mighty bless the po' innocent thing! I got to take up my knittin'; I brung that along, as I made up my mind I'd spend the day, if it was convenant, and I want you all to tell me if it ain't."

"Of course it is, my dear Mrs. Buck," answered the hostess, "it is always so. Mr. Ludwell would be much disappointed when he returns if he found that you had been here and not stayed to dinner, and so would Alice and I."

"All right, then," she said, taking from her pocket a large ball of yarn and an unfinished stocking, "now I feel satisfied in my mind. I didn't know but what Alice bein' jest come, you and her pa mout want to have her all to yourself for a day or so. I thought once't, yes, twice't, I thought I'd wait tell to-morrow; but, tell the truth, I were that anxious to see the child, and git the news she had before it got cold and her a tired o' tellin' of it, that I jes couldn't stay away. So I made 'em put the side-saddle on Rhody, and I got my ridin'-skeert, and I come along, colt and all, and I do think if they can't run up and down, *up* and down, and git over more ground to no onuseless purpose. But I give directions to Abom to put 'em whar he couldn't romp over inter every place whar he had no business a-goin', nor break his naik ner skin his laigs ner cripple hisself a-tryin'. Horses is convenant things to have, but it's troublesome and résky, jes like childern, to raise 'em from colts."

Having disposed herself comfortably for her work and for listening, she asked Alice to begin and tell her, if not all she knew, such portions as would not tire her too much.

"I hain't never see your town, ner I never expect to; but they tell me it's laid off reg'lar, same as g'yarden beds, and everybody thar have to shinny on his own side, as the sayin' is. Don't it 'pears like to you that things down thar is crowded and jammed in agin one 'nother ruther much for comfort, so to speak, raised, as you been, whar thar's plenty of a'r for every-

body—man and beast? I do jes wonder what that colt
o' Rhody's would think if he was turned a loose down
thar one time.  I wouldn't be 'tall surprised ef it
wouldn't jes fling him into fits, if the things could have
'em."

She laughed heartily at this pleasant conceit.

Alice, with as much accuracy as possible, answered
her many questions about Clarke, its crowded thorough-
fares, its five stores, its three churches, its two schools,
its three physicians, its four lawyers, its court-house,
its jail, its two blacksmith shops, its two shoemaker
shops, its carpenter shop, its wheel and wagon shop, its
tan-yard.  The main difficulty was how to make the
listener comprehend how it was that so many people,
none or but a few of them of kin, could live and keep
peace from rising all huddled together in that way,
everybody seeing into everybody's business, hearing
everything they said, jostling one another everywhere
up and down, by and large, not able to eat, have a little
chatting in desired tones, or even doing a necessary bit
of domestic scolding, which, in her opinion, was just as
important as bread and meat, without people's hearing
and going off laughing and talking about it, and may be
some of them having no more manners than to be doing
such as that right before a body's face, all of which, besides others that might be, and that were mentioned by
her, had made her decide in her mind that some people
might get their consent to live in that way, but, as for
herself, nobody might ever expect such a thing of
Charity Buck, because, to go no further, she did not
believe all such as that to be healthy.  Yet she was
thankful to be relieved of some of the most painfully

compassionate of the cogitations that her mind had been used to indulge regarding so abnormal an existence. Her mind reverting to the child that had just been lying upon her lap, she said:

"And you hain't never had a child o' your own, Alice—that is leastways nare livin' child. Well, in the times I ain't been at work—which is mons'ous sildom—and sometimes even when I has, my mind, a all onbeknowin' to myself, it have run on childern, and on them that has a many one of 'em and them that has less and some few that although if so be they're married ever so long they has none, not nare one; for I'm not talkin' about them that the law and the good book don't allow sich a thing ef they can hender—which sometimes they can't—but which that's neither here nor thar, only I kin but be always sorry in my mind when I hear uv sich a acs'dent; but what I *am* talkin' about, if I can make myself plain, is that it seem like and it 'pear like to me that them the good Lord *do* send, he send 'em accordin' to *his* notion, and not people's—not even them that has 'em, be they rich or be they po'. And it's the same with niggers and other kind o' prop'ty, and that I've notussed in my time they sildom and not always goes together, childern and niggers, but a most always sip'rate, them with the moest childern havin' the fewest niggers, and them with a houseful o' childern sometimes havin' nare nigger to their name. And, to my opinion, it's accordin' to the lots of people, and they got no right to complain, as some does. Now here's Alice, and thar's my Sallann, that you both got married in a munt o' one 'nother, which your ma give her and had made for her every stitch o' weddin' close, same as she

done for you, that she's already got two childern, and
you nare one—that is, of your own,   Yit nare one of you
got rights to find fau't, which 'twern't for my warnin',
Sallann mout of done it, they crowdin' in on her so
rapid.   For I told Sallann, and she knowed it without
my tellin' of her, that I got married when I were fifteen
year old, and I had fourteen childern right straight
along until my husband died, and of course after that I
quit; but if are one o' em ever wanted somethin' to eat
and couldn't git it, I never 'membered the times.   I
know you ain't forgot Sallann Buck, though they moved
clear 'cross the Oconee River."

"Of course, we couldn't forget her, Mrs. Buck.
She was of the same age as our little Ellen, you know,"
Mrs. Ludwell said.

"Yes, yes ; and how well I 'members that child !
that both them childern was took with the measles
when they was ten year old apiece, and they was o'
them kind all a body *and* the doctor could do, the
things *wouldn't* come out.   And Mr. Ludwell, he rid
over to my house every single day, and he never told
me, but the doctor told me Mr. Ludwell told *him* not to
spar pains with Sallann, no more than he spar'd 'em
with *his* child, and he'd see all about it, and shore
enough, Sallann she scuffled through, but poor little
Ellen, she had to go, and it look like a pity, because
you didn't have but four children, and me—but you
knowed it was the good Lord, and you didn't find fau't
with him."

Tears came in all eyes.   After drying hers, Mrs.
Buck said :

"But, Alice, you hain't told me about the old lady

Guthrie. I reckon she'd put on her dignitied if she was to hear I called her *old*, though they ain't five year diffunce in me and her age. She was always active, I tell you, and she wer'n't afeard o' nobody, male nor female, people nor Injun. She never married tell she were a old girl, but, of course, that were because her time hadn't come. But she was active; I tell you she was active, and everybody said she married suitable and well. Her son that got you was a beautiful young man, the onlest time I ever see him, the night you and him was married. But tell me, how is all her healths? I hope, if she ain't as active as she wus yit she's reason'ble peert. Our people all knowed her younger sister some the best. She never hilt her head away up high like Hester."

She enjoyed well her visit, and so did all, including Mr. Ludwell, with whom at dinner she had many a merry jest. She knew herself to be an ever-welcome guest at that long table where a hospitality was dispensed that never led to abuse, and was good for both the receiver and the giver. When it was time to go, she got a promise from Alice of a visit as soon as she had rested well, and she acknowledged to a feeling of pride when assured by Abram that the colt had behaved as well as could be expected in one of his age.

## CHAPTER XXIV.

### MR. LUDWELL INTERPOSES.

THE visit of Mrs. Buck Alice felt to have done her some good service. The witness of contentment in a condition that had been so limited always, of a trust in Divine Providence that made sorrow more endurable and cheerfulness, even humor, more cordial, living near by and to a degree intimate with abundant prosperity with never a sigh of envy or painful sense of inferiority, these, she felt, ought to subdue some of the bitterness and the apprehension that were upon her own heart. No allusion was made during all that day to her own peculiar case; but on the next morning when her father had again ridden out, her mother said:

"Alice, I've been thinking much about what you told me the night you came. I haven't said anything to your father; you must talk with him yourself after a while, if you don't feel better. He will know what to say and how to advise. I do not. What you've been going through has been so far away from my own experience that really I am at a loss to know what to say, except one thing. You spoke of not being able to endure this affliction if certain things about Mr. Guthrie and Miss Jewell were as you fear. Why, my dear child, you ought to try to nerve yourself to bear anything that may come that can not be avoided. Mr. Guthrie is a young man used to gay society, and may have been tempted in a way that some men, right in other respects, are weak enough to yield to, although in their hearts they feel themselves to be and are true to all other obligations. I think I know of a case or two where women have tried to ignore that weakness in their husbands and thus have seemed to be losing comparatively little of married happiness. They endure because they have to endure or undergo the disgrace of a divorce, which you know nobody, husband or wife, has ever sued for in this whole region, and a man and his wife living separate doesn't look very much different."

"I feel better, mother, since I've been here—that is, I'm not so prostrate in heart since I've disclosed everything to you, and I mean to try to follow the counsel that you and father give. I had made up my mind to endure any degree of faithlessness to myself; but if that other be true—that an innocent woman has been maligned—the question will be, how can an honorable woman endure to live with a man without honor and without pity, and take the risk—"

She covered her face with her hands, as if she would hide even from her mother the blushes that burned like fire.

"You, dear mother," she resumed, turning again, "can not put yourself in my case, having such a husband as father."

"No, perhaps not; still, my child, our Lord never subjects those who trust in him to burdens that—but oh, I know not what to say. Talk to your father."

"No, mother, I want you to do that for me. I can not. I *can not* look up into that clear, good, manful face, and make an admission so full of deadly shame. You do it for me, mother, and then tell me what he says. I will follow his advice if it is to lead me to death or madness."

"Well, well; I'll do so to-night."

After supper, Alice said : "I think I'll go to bed early to-night, feeling a little fatigued."

"Now," said her father, "that's what I call sensible, and I'm glad to hear you say so. You and your mother kept yourselves up too long the first night you reached here, and perhaps you got rather tired of poor old Mrs. Buck's long visit, though I would hope not, as it did her a deal of good to come to see you."

"By no means, father; I was very glad that she came and spent the whole day with us. I like her very much, and she knows it I am sure. I am only a little jaded from going about so much lately and going through scenes, some unhappy and others rather trying. I'll be all right to-morrow."

"I hope so; indeed, I know so, as soon as you get needed rest. The baby is all right, and looks as if she felt as much at home as anybody."

She retired early as she said. After she had gone, her father, drawing his chair close to his wife, said :

"Ellen, something is the matter with Alice, I feel sure. She may have told you what it is, but she has not me. Now, if it is anything that she prefers I shouldn't know, of course I won't ask to be told. I am afraid, what I have suspected all along, that Guthrie is not acting toward her as he ought. A man that is capable of maltreating his own sister, or seeing it done, if he takes a notion, is apt to maltreat his wife; and if this is so, I think I ought to know it. I do hope in my soul it isn't, but I am very much concerned. The poor child tries to be cheerful; it is positively pitiful to see the struggle she makes."

"Now, husband, I've been intending to have a talk with you about Alice, and I do hope that you'll try to keep calm. As it is, I've been so excited by what she's told me of her troubles that I've hardly enjoyed her visit at all, and if you get excited too—"

"Never mind about that, my dear. Let me have the facts, and then if I can't take care of any excitement that may come, the excitement will have to take care of itself, that's all. Give me the facts."

When she had made her report, which had much, but not too much of detail, her husband, in an apparently indifferent tone, answered:

"Yes; at his old tricks, I see, from which it is always hard to break a dog, whether he has four legs or only two."

Then he rose and walked the circuit of the piazza several times, occasionally pausing near the edge and contemplating the stars, as if among them he would search for a solution that would be wise and prudent. After some time he stopped before his wife, and, raising his arm on high, said in a tone that, striving to be not loud, made up in tremor and in depth:

"Ellen! By God! Do you think Alice is asleep? No, no; I'd better not wake her. What I'd say would be too painful for her to hear. Poor, poor child!"

Again he turned and took a brief walk, slower than before, and afterward said:

"May be she would rather I wouldn't say anything about this matter to *her*. The loyalty of her true heart might be too sorely wounded. But I'll tell *you* what I have decided upon. You say she has permission from her gracious lord and master to remain here three or four weeks. My prediction is that it will be longer than that, and if she will follow my advice, as I expect to offer it after I've looked into matters somewhat, she'll never consent for him to put his eyes upon her again; and if she does not, and he comes here, I'll run him off with the dogs. I haven't a doubt that her suspicions are well founded. If they are, he is worse than an assassin! From what you tell me about Macfarlane's daughter holding to the young woman, I feel as sure of her innocence as I could be of any fact of whose truth I had not positive assurance from personal witness. As soon as I can get through with work here, that for a week or so longer will need my special supervision, I am going down to Clarke, and I'll find out the whole truth. Duncan Guthrie may believe that he can fool that unsuspicious child, but, by the God of heaven, he shall not deceive me! If he had only done what some men with half-and-half wives, and even occasionally one with a wife a great deal better than himself, are tempted to do, I wouldn't say one word, except to advise her to go on back to him and submit and bear. *But*, if he has sought to ruin a friendless woman, and then, in order to shield himself from odium and other punishment that such outrage deserves, undertaken to blast her reputation, I say, let him go his way down alone! You may let her know my opinion. I shall not even hint the subject to her; and perhaps, for the present at least, she'd better not mention it to me. But tell her this, my dear, that she owes to you and me, and she owes more to herself, to try to cast away all her troubled thoughts, and, taking care of herself, wait for deliverance—and expect it, by the living God!"

Taking his hat and his cane, he went out and did not return until the night was half spent.

---

## CHAPTER XXV.

### SEABORN TORRANCE.

PEOPLE used to say that if ever a man had been born a lawyer, it was Seaborn Torrance. All during the period of his childhood, in the issues of domestic and school life, wherein sweetmeats and playthings were prizes to be striven for, and the hickory or peach tree switch the penalties to be shunned, he had an adroitness both in attack and defense which with parents and schoolmasters often prevailed, contrary to the evidence, not only before the rendition of judgment, but after it.

"It won't ever do," his mother used to say, "to let Seaborn go to talking when you've made up your mind that he's got to be whipped for something that you know he's either done or neglected; for if you do, he'll either convince you or he'll manage to persuade you that you are mistaken in your very own eyes or ears, or he'll make you feel ashamed of yourself for making such a great ado about such a little thing; or he'll actually quote you against yourself, so to speak, by reminding you that you let somebody else off from punishment for the same thing, or something that's no worse than that. And then positively when you've had to shut your eyes in order to give him what you know he deserves, after you are through with him, he'll look at you so that you feel sorry you've done it, and in such way he'll get off many and many a time afterward. I do think, on my soul, that's he's got the pleadingest mouth I ever heard in all my days."

With a fair common education, such as he could obtain at a neighborhood old-field school, at seventeen he went to work on his widowed mother's small farm, and having purchased, with the first cotton money he had made, a copy of Blackstone's Commentaries, he read it in the times of leisure, which seldom came except of nights and Sundays. By the time he was one and twenty, he was admitted to the bar in his native county. The successes gained in trials before the courts of justices of the peace and in petty trials in the inferior court of the county, which at that time had jurisdiction co-ordinate with the superior court except as to appeals, equity, land titles, and criminal trials, were not long in attracting attention. The fluency of his speech, his vigilance during the progress of a case, his aptitude in the direct and cross questioning of witnesses, his adroitness in getting continuances of weak or insufficiently prepared issues, the quickness with which he seized upon a point made favorable to his client by a word or omission of a witness or an admission of his adversary, the promptness and vigor with which he assailed a weak point in the latter, his imperturbability while standing before the judge and the old great lawyers, seeming not even to notice their smiles at any crudeness in his conduct of a case, a natural eloquence that knew how to be nervous or persuasive or pathetic, these soon brought him into good practice. By the

time he was forty, nobody would say that in the Northern circuit, or in any one of the three adjacent, they
knew his superior, especially in defense of suits involv-
ing complicated accounts and inaccurate, conflicting
testimony. He was now forty-five, in full practice that
for some years past had been occupied mainly in suits
where important moneys were involved. These took
him often out of his circuit. It had got to be said that
it must be a desperate case indeed wherein, if Seaborn
Torrance could not gain or save the condemnation
money to his client, he could not at least put off its pay-
ment until time or other such auxiliary could subdue
the triumph of the adversary and mitigate the discomfiture of his client.

Among the profession his standing as a man of
honor had never been impeached seriously. His word
of promise was regarded as trustworthy as his written
obligation, and all knew his courage to be unquestion-
able. When rallied pleasantly, or perchance with some
seriousness, by an intimate personal friend, or one whom
he recognized as an entirely honorable opponent, for
what seemed too severe a straining of the law or the
evidence, he replied with coolness and sincerity that
his client, like any other man, was entitled to every
benefit and advantage that the law had provided, as
well as to the exertion of the best powers of his counsel.
He often said :

"People that complain of lawyers who avail themselves of the law's opportunities are after the wrong
quarry. If anything deserves reprobation it is the law
itself, which *they* made and provided, and with which
they don't find fault when it is employed in their own

behalf. It is a very easy and sometimes a very convenient and pleasant thing to condemn others; but introspection, close introspection, in my time I have found not often."

Yet he would have driven out of his office one who would even have intimated a wish for him to do or attempt anything that he regarded dishonorable, and perhaps with a kick accelerated his exit, and he would have fought any man who would have insinuated an aspersion upon his professional integrity. There were those—a few—who were regarded superior to him in legal learning. He knew this, yet he never indulged a thought of envy; for in the conduct of complicated cases through all their intricacies he well knew himself to be without a peer.

"No, Guthrie," he said after Duncan had stated the case and given his mother's message, " I doubt if it's the thing for me to go to Clarke right away, unless you think I might have more influence than yourself with those fellows regarding the status on which to put the case, and unless we ought to see how they feel about a continuance of it until both sides can manœuvre and find out what chances there are for a compromise, provided such a thing is thought well of by your mother. A continuance is important for her, as you can easily see, being in the defense. Besides, I expect I know more than you do of the opinion of people in your county about the way your father's estate has been managed. It might hurt to have the case brought on while people will be talking. It's better to wait until that slackens or gives place to something else which they'll think it's their business, instead of the courts, to decide.

Meanwhile we will be getting the case better and better in hand. We may want to get Suttle's testimony. At all events, it must seem so. I don't doubt that they'll wish to have it, supposing that he'd of course do what he could to bolster up his own action. So about Butcher. We must find him if possible. Some time, not very far off, you and I must get out some interrogatories for him, if you know, or can find out if he's alive, and where he lives. If not, so much the better for us, at least for a while. I'm rather glad, as your mother's counsel, that the fellow has moved away. There was a good deal of prejudice, I remember, among some people against Suttle. It may be no particular disadvantage to us that he has not become so known to fame that his domicile can be easily ascertained. Yes, yes, that's all so, it seems to me, looking at the case at this stage."

"I'd much rather you would go, Mr. Torrance," answered Guthrie earnestly. "Mother would be better satisfied. Then, I feel so outraged with these men, Tolly and Bond, Tolly especially, for giving me not a word of notice of intention to bring this suit, and for the harsh terms which needlessly they have put in some of the allegations of their bill, that I do not feel like saying a word to either of them, especially one that would sound as if I had apprehension or would desire at their hands any sort of indulgence."

"I see, I see. Then I will go. Perhaps it may be as well any how to have an early conference with your mother. Her mind, woman as she is, and not as young as she used to be, is naturally bothered, and may be a little fretted, and a good solid talk, all of us together,

might tend to relieve it somewhat.  Yes, I'll go along
with you to-morrow morning."                  .

He knew all the time that he was going; but he
meant for his doing so to be admitted urgent, and therefore insisted upon.  Noticing the satisfaction of Guthrie from this announcement, he continued:

"Yes, I've no doubt that your mother is considerably harrassed.  Do you know, my young friend, that
I always preferred to defend such cases to prosecut-
ing them?  Of course, I speak without reference to
their particular merits.  Somehow I always feel easier
in mind and stouter when I'm on the defense.  Who
was that old English fellow?  Walpole?  Yes, it was
old Walpole.  You remember what he said about dis-
turbing things that are quiet?  *Quieta non movere* is
the way he put it.  Those English lawyers are always
better up in their classics than we are over here.  But
it's a good maxim.  It always went rather against the
grain with me to begin the stirring up of litigation
against people, especially old people, and more especially old women (begging your mother's pardon), years
and years after the transactions have passed, and people
have been seeming to acquiesce in their results, until
most of those who knew about them have gone away,
either to the grave or somewhere else where it's about
as hard to find them.  I've seen so much distress from
such things that I've got about where I will not appear
for a plaintiff in one of them unless I can see that his
case is perfectly clear, and that either from ignorance
or some other sufficient cause he has not instituted
proceedings before.  Even then my advice invariably
is to accept a compromise that seems to me fair, or

nearly fair. Many people don't believe that about me. But what do I care? It is my business to get for my client—if I can—all his legal rights; the generosity part and the charity part and all such as that are his own. I counsel compromise, but it's neither my duty nor my right to undertake to enforce it. In defense, I fight every assault, and there, if needed, I hang my client's banner on the outward wall. There, too, as I am going to do in this case of your mother's, I can and I do counsel compromise. How would she feel like acting on that line, eh, Guthrie? You, too? Peace, sometimes—like other things of value—has to be purchased, and there are occasions when it is at a higher price and, indeed, is worth more than at others. Don't you think so?"

"Certainly. I should be more than willing for a compromise, Mr. Torrance, that was at all fair. I have always desired—that is, since I have been grown—that my sister should have more of the estate, and she would have got it but for her unequal marriage—"

"I see, I see," interrupted Mr. Torrance, looking another way.

"At least what my mother considered unequal. Indeed, she offered other property to her, but upon conditions that made her refuse to accept it."

"I see, I see," and he nodded his head up and down two or three times.

"I have not suggested to her any proposal, because she is not in a state of mind to consider it, at least when coming from me. My mother believes herself to have been wholly in the right in all she has done, Mr. Torrance, and—"

"No doubt about that, Guthrie," he interposed quickly, spreading forth his hands, "not a shadow of a doubt about that. *That*, my opinion is, nobody will ever doubt. I am speaking in entire sincerity. The only question is how much, if anything at all, how much she can be made to consent to lay down to the end of buying her peace."

"So I regard it, and I trust that you will be able to convince her of its importance."

"Well, Guthrie," he said, going to a file of papers and withdrawing a bundle, "as you think it is best, I'll go with you in the morning, and *pe*-ruse around, as country people say, and feel of Tolly, and that other young chap, if he's there still. Tom isn't a bad fellow, Guthrie, and he's very far from being a bad lawyer. I'm glad he isn't either one of them; for you can always deal more satisfactorily with such a lawyer as him than one that has neither sense nor principle. Bond, I never saw but twice, at your last court and, before that, at Washington Court, in the Middle Circuit. The Augusta lawyers that I meet down there tell me he's promising, quite so. I don't remember now who it was that said that he suspected Bond of being at Clarke more for the sake of that fine-looking Miss Jewell than the little business he had there. I saw her at your mother's, at the party she gave that week. My! but what a magnificent creature! By the way, I haven't told you what an impression your mother made on me then. Grand woman, sir! I'm not flattering her at all, nor you, either; but she looked like a queen, and her head is full of sense. I just now remember that she told me that same night that if she should ever have an important law case, she wanted me for counsel. I did not dream of it's coming, especially so soon. But it shows the head she's got for looking forward. Well," resuming his seat, and beginning to untie the bundle, "if we can't get out of them terms such as your mother will be satisfied with, all I've got to say is that we'll keep those young lawyers waiting longer for their fees than they have been counting on. To-morrow morning, Guthrie, to-morrow morning, as soon after breakfast as I can get off."

## CHAPTER XXVI.

### MR. TORRANCE GOES TO CLARKE.

MR. TORRANCE spent an hour at his office the next morning in writing some letters which he said could not be delayed, and then they set out upon their journey of forty miles. Conversation in this mode of travel was more practicable than persons nowadays might suppose. Often the light two-wheel vehicles could get side by side, especially in that season when the red roads, though frequently ascending and descending, were almost as hard as if they had been macadamized. Law, politics, agriculture, incidents in the lives of common acquaintances, whatever was suggested by accident or otherwise, they discussed at intervals. Not often was reference made to the business on which they were going. Occasionally the elder, who traveled behind, getting alongside, put an inquiry about

one or another matter touching the value and items of
the Guthrie estate and the several investments that
had been made by the executrix, and suggested a point
of the law that was likely to rise during the litigation.
But this last required too constant nearness to make it
satisfactory, and so they chose to chat at random.  At
about noon they halted for their luncheon.  It was a
good one; for Mrs. Torrance knew how to provide for
her husband's taste.  While he was cutting his favorite
meat, he said:

"Guthrie, have you noticed that very few women
know how to prepare ham for a lunch?  They either
broil it, or fry it, or sandwich it boiled, and it gets to
be so dry that I won't eat it if I can do any better.
Now my wife, whenever she has timely notice that I'm
going away from home, has boiled for me a piece of
the hough end of a ham, with the skin on; hear me?
with the skin on.  Now that chicken, and that pigeon,
and that cake and preserves she put in for you."

"I thank her very much.  They are delightful.
I'm quite content to leave to you all of your favorite
morsel."

"Ah, ha, that's because you are not old enough, and
haven't traveled enough and have been too little out of
town life to know any better.  If it had been that I
was going by myself, my wife wouldn't have thought
of putting that stuff in the sulky box, knowing that I'd
give them to the first negro I met."

Guthrie admired his simplicity less than the heartiness with which in his one item he made up fully for
his abstinence from the others.

"There, now," he said to the remains, wrapping

them in the cloth, "you'll do for to-morrow, and I'll get some fresh biscuits and corn bread from my friend Mrs. Junkin."

Once during the afternoon, after getting closer, he called out:

"I say, Guthrie, that Miss Jewell; blamed if I don't think about her often, old as I am, and married, to boot.   I never saw a finer-looking woman.   She made me almost wish I'd had on finer clothes; I'll swear she did.   They tell me she's accomplished, too. That don't look fair on other young women.   However, she hasn't got money nor negroes, and that takes off something.   It seems like a pity for her to have to keep school for a living.   If Bond wants her and has business enough for both of them to live on, I'm not sure but that she'd do well to take him.   It don't require so very much to begin such as that with.   Two can live together cheaper than they can apart, and then these Northern women know better than ours how to economize and manage generally.   Eh?"

"I incline to think that perhaps she would be doing well enough, Mr. Torrance."

"If the fellow is in dead earnest, and you think his chances are rather slim and we find that he's too well posted in our case, how would it do to—well, to try and give him as good a lift as you can with a friendly word of compliment to his princess?   If I knew her well blamed if I wouldn't!   No harm in it.   Might turn out the very thing for her, and such things do a cause good one way and another.   What do you say, Guthrie?"

"I know too little of either of them, sir, to take or to feel any interest in their affairs."

"Hoo, hoo!" ejaculated the other softly, falling back and soliloquizing. "Screw loose somewhere, certain, and that only lately; for I saw you that night at your mammy's looking at Bond and her as a falcon watches a hawk after a partridge. Screw loose."

Then he suggested another topic as remote as possible. They reached Clarke a little before sunset. Guthrie invited his senior to sojourn at his mother's, apologizing for not being able to take him to his own house.

"No, oh, no, Guthrie. I never talk to a woman on business at night if I can help it, and I advise you to adopt the same rule. Women are more nervous than men, because they can't take in every side of a subject that troubles, and every danger that threatens, and when they are thrown out of their accustomed sleep it hurts them. I'll fall in at Junkin's. Junkin, or rather his wife, knows how to make a fellow quite comfortable, considering what a lumbering establishment they've got of it. Yes, I'll hold up there, thank you, Guthrie. Tolly boards there, you know, and if he's at home and don't propose to go out sparking among the girls, I'll tackle him in a friendly way and find out if I can how much confidence he's got in the range of his gun. Tell your mother, after my best respects and thanks, that I'll call up at her house to-morrow morning at nine o'clock, or, if she'll send me word, at any hour that will better suit her convenience. And tell her I say not to let herself be made too uneasy. It does no sort of good, but it does several sorts of harm to worry over a matter like this, which may take a long time to settle and which, I tell you again, *will* take a long time unless it's settled to her satisfaction."

He halted when he arrived at the hotel, and Guthrie, turning his horse, drove on to his mother's. She was looking out in evident anxious expectation, her cap and her cape and the ruffles around her wrist showing that she wished to appear as well as possible to her distinguished guest.

"Where is Seaborn Torrance, Duncan?" she called by the time he was half-way from the gate. He did not answer until he had reached the steps. It was a way he had—the only one even partially effective—of curbing her impetuosity. A remonstrance such as that, coming from him sometimes, as now, softened her.

"How have you been, mother, these two days? I'd like to know that first, if only from courtesy."

She put out her straight hand, saying:

"I've been well, my son; how have you been? I didn't mean to be impolite."

"I've been quite well, I thank you. Mr. Torrance stopped at the tavern. He sent you his regards, and said that he would call upon you to-morrow morning at nine o'clock, if the time suited you."

"Ah, well, then. I was afraid when I saw you by yourself that he hadn't.come, and it flustered me some. Yes; that'll suit well enough; but I'd a heap rather he had come .to-night. How would it do for you to go down after supper and invite him to breakfast, so we can begin on the business that much sooner. I can give him another sort of breakfast to what he'll get there. Suppose you do it, Duncan."

"It would be a mistake, mother, I am confident. We've had a great deal of talk about the case during our all-day ride. He's tired, I am sure, just as I am, and would prefer to remain there until the time he has appointed.”

“ Very well, then, if you think so.  I feel easier, anyhow, since I know he’s here.  What does he say ? Does he think they can get anything out of me more than I’m willing to allow to the children ? ”

“ He expressed no definite opinion, mother, but said what I knew he would, that he could not form any reliable judgment until he had conferred fully with you and learned all your doings, feelings, and wishes ; but he seemed hopeful that the case could be so managed that it would result nearly, if not entirely, to your reasonable satisfaction ; and he bade me to say to you, that he hoped that you would not take on any undue anxiety.”

“ That’s good !  I knew it !  *Juday* ! ” she called loudly, looking back ; “ bring in supper as soon as Chloe has it ready.  Your Marse Duncan is hungry. I know he hasn’t had anything fit to eat since he’s been gone, and I feel like I’ve got something of an appetite coming back to me.  The Lord knows I think it’s about time for it.”

After supper, when, at their accustomed seats, she had been chatting in a more cheerful tone than for quite a long time, she said suddenly, the thought evidently having just come to her mind :

“ Duncan, what is this talk about Miss Jewell ? Judy brings me what news I get, as I don’t go out to gather it, and don’t want to.  But Judy says that some people are wondering what it is that makes her so pale here lately and have so little to say, when she used to be so chatty.  And they say that since that frolic you all had in my woods, you and Alice both have little or nothing to do with her, and she says they told her that Peterson Braddy said on the street one day, when people were insinuating something about her with which your name was connected in some way, that she was as fine a woman as was in this whole town, or anywhere else, and that whoever said to the contrary was a liar, and that he was ready and willing any time to make good his words. Is anything the matter?"

"No, ma'am; not that I know of. Alice got into a pet that day because I showed Miss Jewell more attention than she thought I had any right to, and perhaps the woman herself may have been rather indiscreet. But there's nothing in it, and old Pete would do well to keep his mouth shut, because talking only magnifies the thing. I wish myself that the woman would get married or go away."

"I'm sorry, on her account and Alice's too, that your name has been connected with her's in any way that is not entirely honorable. Charlotte was here yesterday. Louisa sends her to see me sometimes, I suppose to keep up appearances, though I believe the girl herself likes me right well, and *she* says that Miss Jewell is as good a woman as any other, and that what talk has been is certain to die out. I was right glad to hear it. As for the woman's being fond of dancing and running on with young men, in my day all girls did it that felt like it whenever they pleased, and no harm ever came of it. It's only for just a few years back, when the Old Virginia Church for want of a bishop in the State has dwindled out to about nothing, that so many denominations and meeting-houses have started up, and all trying to run down one another, that some of them have come to be too good, and they've got to calling fiddling, dancing, and playing cards, and even taking a walk on Sunday sinful, when they're not half as dangerous as when twos and twos get off into corners and go to whispering. I am sorry about it all. It's bad enough for a man that has a decent, respectable wife, as Alice is, but it's worse, because it's death, or equal to it, to a woman in Miss Jewell's position. Well, I'm glad it's stopped between you and her. Alice ought to know better about the ways of men, married or not married, when they're with pretty women that will let them take little liberties, and often without thinking even of the slightest thing wrong. And she might know, Alice might, that no harm could come to her, as in her style—which, true, it's different from Miss Jewell's—she's every bit as good looking. If anybody asks me about it, I'll tell them that it's nothing but that you and the young woman were having a little mischievous flirtation, and having found out that Alice didn't like it, you, both of you, concluded to break it off, and that in short."

"Oh, no, mother! I'd much rather you wouldn't mention the name of Alice. Just say you know nothing about it, but that you believe there's nothing in it."

"But, Duncan, there *is* something in it, you acknowledge yourself."

"But in a delicate matter like that people must use some policy, mother."

"Ah, well! I never was one that could make any headway with that. I'll tell you what I'll answer if anybody ever mentions the thing to me, which I don't expect they'll do, and hope they won't; but if they do, I'll tell them that it takes me all my time to attend to my own business without bothering myself to find out about other people's. How will that do?"

"I think that would be the very best answer you could make."

"All right. That's very easily said, and it would be every bit the truth. I reckon you're getting sleepy. I am."

He went to his room, glad to be by himself. The honorable, compassionate words which his mother had spoken of Miss Jewell had cut him deeply and put out all thoughts of the pending lawsuit. He felt that in his efforts to save himself a wrong had been done much more serious than he had foreseen. The words of Peterson Braddy brought painfully to his remembrance those other from the same lips which he had not dared to resent, and it pained but it angered him more to reflect that in this new issue there was no chance to redeem whatever he might appear to others or feel in his own breast to have lost by a conflict with one whom he could meet on equal terms.

## CHAPTER XXVII.

### MR. TORRANCE BECOMES LEADING COUNSEL.

Mr. Torrance, as usual, was the life of the supper table. Mrs. Junkin had always a place for him near

the head; for what he said habitually about the housekeeping and other subjects interesting among her class
were put in such phrase that indeed she never had any
hesitation in saying that of all transient people that
came to that tavern and to her table lawyer Torrance
was the pleasantest in his speeches and the least fault-
finding in his behaviors.  She often reported with
much pride that over and over again he had said that if
there was any place where he felt as he did at home,
it was at the Clarke tavern.  On this particular occasion his speeches and behaviors were uncommonly felici-
tous, and they came very near bringing water into the
eyes of the hostess.  She felt some moisture there, as
she confessed afterward, but she wasn't going to forget
herself and go to blubbering right at the table before
everybody.

"Guthrie," he said, "Duncan Guthrie, Mrs. Junkin
—you know him, and a bright, smart, intelligent fellow
he is too, in his way, and going to make a good lawyer
if he lives and keeps on being steady—he and I came
together from my town to-day.  He invited me to go
with him and put up at his mother's, where he told me
he was staying while his wife was on a visit to her
father's t'other side of Broad River.  He married a
Ludwell up there, you remember, Mrs. Junkin, fine
people, rich too, and all that.  It was very kind of him,
of course, for he's a very polite young man in his manners,
and I've been told that the old lady—a most remarkable,
sensible, excellent woman—that she lives well, and has
everything nice about her house.  But I had to tell
Guthrie that no, I'd stop with Mrs. Junkin.  I don't remember that I ever mentioned the name of *Mister*

Lawyer Torrance and Mrs. Junkin.

Junkin. There he is down yonder, looking as well and as good-providing a fellow as anybody ought ever want to see at the foot of a tavern table. No; the one I named was *Missis* Junkin; for it's her at last that has made this house what it is and given to it the name it's got. The fact is, that when I come to this town of Clarke, and a nice, stylish, clean-looking town it is with fine people living in it, I never even think about stopping anywhere else but here, right here, where, if anywhere I know I'm going to feel as I do at home. And I think I was right."

Mrs. Junkin merely called to one of the waitresses and said to her: "Go out and tell Mimy to send the hot waffles in fast as she can."

"Now, there's my young friend Tom Tolly over there. I call him *Tom* because I've been knowing his father before he was born, another good man. I'm glad to see, from the way Tom throws his knife and fork and handles cups and tumblers, that he knows and appreciates good things when he can get them. I've been having my hopes about that young man, Mrs. Junkin."

Now the lady could exhibit her feelings without embarrassment, and so she smiled right out aloud.

"That is, provided, madam, he don't get wild and undertake to go too fast; there's the danger with these talented young fellows. I'm thankful he's with you, madam, for if there's anybody in this whole town that will have the opportunity and will have the knack at such charitable, and, I may say, missionary work, it is you, who, when you see him rushing into extravagance of any sort, can call him to come right straight to you and then lay your hand on his shoulder and say: 'See here, young Mr. Tolly, thus far, sir, thus far!' Eh, Tolly?"

"She does already as you say, Mr. Torrance," answered Tolly heartily. "Mrs. Junkin takes first-rate care of me, and scolds me sometimes."

"*Sometimes!* I think I hear him say 'sometimes.' Mrs. Junkin, I beg you, madam, if not for his sake at least for the sake of his old father and mother, excellent people that they are, both of them, and, I may add, for the sake of any family which, accidentally as it were, he may stumble on of his own sometime, do, my dear madam, try your best, what time you can leave more important business, try to hold back that rash young man from rushing too fast and spoiling every good prospect before him."

It was such a good joke that the whole table, regular boarders and transient, all the way down to Mr. Junkin, laughed out with great heartiness, and both Mr. Torrance and Tolly took another hot waffle apiece and spread their butter on it in high glee. Yet, somehow, in Tolly the feeling of courageous exaltation that came over him at the moment of the arrival of the great lawyer, knowing well on what errand he had come, had lessened somewhat while he had been listening as he indulged in language in which he almost suspected that he could detect a grain of compassionate satire. Mr. Torrance saw into his thoughts, and immediately began to address him with remarks that indicated all proper respect for his opinions. After supper, and after all except those two had gone from the piazza, the elder said:

"Tom, move your chair closer here and give me some account of yourself. Don't light that cigar I see in your mouth unless, from mere patriotic principles, you hold it a duty to smoke such as your town affords. But now try one that *is* a cigar. I don't know how it is, but it's so, that I never can find in this borough, respectable as it is and rich as you all are and proud according, a cigar that's fit to smoke. We don't set up for being very great people in our town, although there's a few that can hold their heads as high as anybody—I don't mean me and my folks, of course, but a very good fair sprinkling of others who can trace as far back as the best in the land. Yet we would be ashamed to offer to any decent stranger such cigars as you have here. That's right; only I'd rather have seen you—except for economy's sake—throw away the one you had, instead of putting it back into your pocket. And now, my illustrious and learned young barrister and affectionate friend, what is all this ado about that most respectable and somewhat aged fellow-citizen of yours whose repose you are seeking to molest? She sent me word to come up and talk with her about the defense. I haven't seen her yet, but, knowing you as I do, and judging from what I know myself of her and from what Guthrie has told me about her, I don't suppose but what we can settle in a short time what there is in it, unless you fellows want to make a long years-and-years' thing of it. Do you know where that fellow Suttle is, if it's a fair question, and whether or not the other witness besides him and Braddy is living or not?"

It had occurred to Tolly and Bond that it might be well, in order to lay a supplemental foundation for their equity proceeding, to apply for a citation to the executrix to prove the will of Alan Guthrie in solemn form. This must have been done at the next sitting of the Court of Ordinary, which would come in thirty days. Both sides were desirous of postponing this issue, and they knew, of course, that a motion for continuance on account of inability to get in full testimony must prevail. Yet each was unwilling for the other to know of such desire, and Tolly could not but be amused when Mr. Torrance succeeded in getting from him a proposition to appeal the whole case by consent to the Superior Court, which would not convene until October.

"Oh, yes, yes, Tom, if you and Mr. Bond want it done. I am going to fight the case fairly, and, though I haven't seen her yet, I've no doubt but that the old lady will abide by my counsel and that it will coincide fully with her views and feelings to meet the issue fairly, entirely so. As far as I can see, Tom, I must say to you that I don't think you've got what I should call very much of a case, to say nothing of the Statute of Limitations and what the law calls Lapse of time. Still, it may be best for both sides not to rush together in hot haste, but wait a little and study how to arrange and play their cards."

Tolly changed the subject several times, but afterward he had to admit to himself and to Bond that, despite all his caution, he had let out several things which he thought that he might as well have kept to himself. They talked to a late hour, and during a greater part of the time Mr. Torrance seemed as if he had forgotten the errand on which he had come. Occasionally he indulged in partially commendatory terms of the need young lawyers had not to turn away from cases wherein was little prospect of obtaining anything beyond the notoriety that was essential. He retired satisfied of the results of what, not without some humor, he had termed "feeling" of Tom Tolly.

The next morning he was much impressed by the mingled cordiality, grace, and dignity with which he was received by Mrs. Guthrie. In the conference that followed were to be seen his calm wisdom and sagacious comprehending of possibilities dependent, not only upon the law of the case, but the temper, courage, power of endurance, and prudence of the client. He listened with attention, not always fixed, to her long, circumstantial narration. He looked admiringly into her eyes as, always lighted, they flashed occasionally with a resentment which she did not care to repress. Not an item in her conduct, from the first till now, did she seem disposed even to gloss. More than once Duncan felt his cheek burn as she made admissions that he knew to be surprising to Mr. Torrance. Before she was through, the latter had decided to withhold most of the opinion he had to give. When she ceased and looked at him with earnest interrogation, he said :

"Yes, madam. I see, I see. I think I understand the business, and I am glad to say that it has less difficulties than I had apprehended. I am glad, very glad indeed, that you had intended to give your daughter property, although stipulating, as was your perfect right to do, that it should be held for her separate use. It ought to make for your interest that your offer was declined. I am *more* than glad that you have had it on your mind, since her death, to make over something

(I am sure it would have been a liberal and just allowance) to her children. Such as that is bound to help
in the defense of this suit."

After other conversation upon the general aspect of
the case, he said:

"We'll all think about it, madam, and, of course,
we must keep our counsel to ourselves. That is important. Nobody must look over our hands or get a
glimpse of them. Your son, my young friend here,
will advise me of anything to occur that may make it
seem advisable for me to come again soon. I don't expect it, however. There will be nothing needed for
some time yet, as I have agreed with Tolly to appeal
the whole case to the Superior Court. I know you
and your son will say that was right, as we shall want
all the delay we can get. I will come again some time
before the court meets, when he and I will prepare your
answer and have an extended conference about the line
of defense."

"I shall follow your advice implicitly, Mr. Torrance," said Mrs. Guthrie; "I want to assure you of
that at the outset."

"Ah, my dear madam, I could see that as soon as
we began to speak about the case. You are a lady that
understands business, and therefore will readily judge.
of our counsel. My opinion is that we can get terms,
if not right away, after a time that will be reasonably
liberal, and that it will be at least worth our while to
consider. These men, like the common run of young
lawyers, will want, and they'll need their fees, and
they are not going to forget that if it is to depend
on fighting in a case like this, your son and I know

what that means, and how long it can be made to last. I don't know," he continued, smiling, "that Tolly meant for me to find it out, but I did, and I was glad of it. Indeed, I rather thought so from his client having made application for guardianship; but he is suing really in behalf of the children, not of his own. That, I've no doubt, will make a difference in your feelings."

"Why, certainly, certainly."

"I knew it; and now I must take my leave, as I am to meet an appointment in Milledgeville to-morrow night, and it will be as much as I can do to make it. It was hardly necessary for me to come at this time, except for your own satisfaction and for having the case appealed. I am delighted to find you so self-possessed and resolute. I was afraid you might be over-anxious. Some time shortly I will return; then we will confer about defense. The first thing we shall do will be to file a demurrer. You don't understand that term, I suppose; but your son will tell you that in law it signifies to *delay*. That is our hand for the present, and it may continue to be longer than these young chaps have been counting upon. Good-by, madam. I commend your pluck—I hardly know how better to style it—and I haven't a doubt that it will serve you to the end. Good-by, Mr. Guthrie. It strengthens me much that I have you for my colleague."

"That's the sort of lawyer for me!" said Mrs. Guthrie almost loud enough for his hearing. When he had passed through the gate, he turned, took off his hat, and waved a final adieu, which she answered with a low respectful courtesy.

17

"By blood!" said he to himself, as he moved away. "Grandest woman I ever saw; but crazy! Crazy as a bed-bug!"

Half an hour afterward, having ordered his horse to be brought out, he made a parting visit to Tolly at his office.

"Well, Tom, my son," he said, "I just stepped in to tell you good-by. I've just come from the presence of the very head citizen of this town, whom, I'm simply amazed that none of you people understand well enough to appreciate at her just worth. I want to say to you at parting, Thomas, my boy, that—where was it the Ghost notified Brutus of his intention to meet him?"

"At Philippi, according to my remembrance.

"I believe you are right. Well, sir, there expect me, and when you've suffered a more signal defeat than he got, don't make an ass of yourself, and go to falling upon your own sword. Hear, Tom?"

"Good-by, Mr. Torrance. You will find me there in force sufficient, I trust, to avoid the fate of that illustrious patriot."

Tolly had hoped that he had come to propose a compromise. But such was not that lawyer's policy. It was, while supposed to be ignorant of all the bearings in the case, to raise expectations which acquaintance with them had led him to disappoint. As he was riding out of town, he turned his head toward the high grove wherein was his client's mansion, and thus soliloquized:

"A woman fit to be a queen! A good one, too; worth forty of that Dunk; I see now where some of his ways started from. He knows no more about her than the rest of them. Wonderful! I had suspicion of it that night at her party. I was expecting it to be a long case; but it won't. Get up, John! We've got to make time to-day."

---

## CHAPTER XXVIII.

### BOND UNDERTAKES ANOTHER CASE.

FOUR days afterward everybody except Tolly was surprised at the reappearance of Bond, accompanied by Julius Holt, a slight, bright-eyed, dressy young lawyer of Augusta.

"Well, Tolly," said Bond, after shaking hands and introducing his companion, "here I am. Anything new in our case? But you can tell me of that afterward. I brought my friend Holt along in order to show him that Augusta and Savannah were not the only places wherein nice people abode. But it is stipulated between us that he is not to lay eyes on Miss Macfarlane while in this town he stays."

"How do you suppose Miss Macfarlane will regard such treatment?"

"Oh, if she complains, tell her that he was extremely busy (a thing not habitual), or that you hesitated to take him to her except by her permission, which you had not time to ask, or that he was bashful and you couldn't get him to go, or that he was already engaged and was afraid to go near a young woman of whose perfections he had heard so many speeches, or frame any other reason that may occur to your mind so fertile in resources and expedients.

"The safest thing for me to do, Mr. Holt, I suspect, is to take you to see the young lady and trust to your generosity."

"Thank you, Mr. Tolly. From what Bond has told me about yourself, I should be the last to engage in any sort of contest with you, with hope of success."

"There!" said Bond. "Now everybody can feel easy. You may see this paragon, Holt, if we find that we have time and Tolly don't take back his words."

After supper, Bond left the party and went to see Miss Jewell.

"Why, you back here, and so soon?" she said. "Yours and Mr. Tolly's case must be pressing."

"Yes; but you must remember that I have one of my own that is much more so."

"Which I have told you several times that you must give up."

Yet she could not conceal the pleasure she felt at his coming. She was dressed with unusual care, and the color returning to her cheek showed that the frame of her mind was beginning to be happy again.

"Yes," he said with seriousness, "and you know well that that is what I can not do. After what you admitted to me, I can not comprehend that you should be willing that I should. To me, it seems simple injustice to put upon a man who loves you with all his heart punishment—only punishment—when you admit that your preference would be to reward."

"Punishment! punishment, Mr. Bond? Why I love *you* also. I love you very much. I love *you* more and more.   No, no, keep your seat, or I will leave you."

The deep blush that overspread her face soon sub·sided.

"Since I have found that my feelings are more enlisted than I had known of, I have felt that I ought to go back to Boston.   After the term of Cousin William's school ends, my intention is to go to Augusta for a week's sojourn with sister.   While I am there, under certain conditions, I will tell you frankly and fully why I can not marry you.   At least," she added, with a yet deeper blush, "why I think so.   Please do not ask me for anything more—now."

"I will not; but you will at least let me take your hand ?"

She looked at him.   His face was as full of respect as affection.   She gave no answer; then he rose, advanced, took her hand, and, as she turned her face away, kissed her cheek.

"Perhaps I ought not to have allowed that, Mr. Bond; but the thought of leaving you—" then she covered her face with her hands.   To help her embarrassment, he said quickly as if he had forgotten to tell her sooner :

"Oh! I forgot to tell you something.   Holt is with me, Julius Holt."

"Julius Holt! Why what could have brought him here ?   Why didn't he come with you to see me ? "

"Well, now, to tell the truth, Miss Jewell, I didn't care about his company, this evening."

"It would have been better for both our sakes if you had brought him.   What is he here for ?   Have you and Mr. Tolly taken him into your case? I didn't know he was so much of a lawyer as that."

"No. When he heard that I was coming, he said that he had a little business here, and besides that he would like to take something of a jaunt, and so he came along. He'll be sure to call before he leaves."

"Tell him he must. I like Julius Holt, though I didn't suppose that he had much law business, even in Augusta. When are *you* going back?"

"In a day or two; just as soon as I can get away."

He returned to the tavern in triumph.

"I feel like a new man, my good boys." After receiving their congratulations, he continued:

"Let's fire up, and, although as they say in the cracker region, it's mighty sildom I teches it, yet on the strength of the occasion, I'll take a drink if I can git it. Bring out what you've got in that hair trunk of yours, Holt. I knew you well enough to feel sure you would bring some of the article along, and so I didn't.

> But pledge me the cup, since existence would cloy,
> With hearts ever happy, and heads ever wise;
> Be ours the light grief that is sister to joy,
> And the short brilliant folly that sparkles and dies!

But we shall be moderate. What saith the jolly yet temperate bard of Venusium:

> Tribus aut novem
> Miscentur cyathis pocula commodis—
> Tres prohibet supra
> Rixarum metuens tangere Gratia,
> Nudis juncta sororibus.

Did you hear me, Holt?"

"Bond, I did; but never since I was born—I'll swear—I never did hear whisky called by so many names. He does want it badly; don't he, Mr. Tolly?"

"He wants something, evidently, Mr. Holt. I didn't exactly follow him throughout the words of his request."

"No, Tolly?" asked the principal speaker. "Then I'll inflict upon both of you the rest of that glorious Ode to Telephus:

"*Insanire juvat*, which means it is delightful to play the fool: so hear, ye ignoramuses, or as, with proper respect for the analogies of language, I should say, *ignorami*.

"*Insanire juvat—*"

"Stop it!" cried Holt. "Just look at him, throwing about his arms as if he understood what he was trying to repeat! I'll bet five dollars that's all he knows of Horace!"

"And in the event of your losing who is to pay your bill at this tavern, Mr. Holt? But, Tolly," he continued as he poured from the bottle, "let's come down to contemporary times; you haven't told me anything yet about our law case, except that Torrance has been here. What did the old fellow do, and what did he say?"

"He came here, I think, for the purpose mainly of getting us to consent to an appeal, what, as you know, we wanted. Still, he managed to make me propose it. I found that I had to do it, and I did. What a wonderful man!"

"That he is! We have not a lawyer in our circuit to compare with him. I saw him in a case at the last term of Washington Court, and it almost demoralized my hopes of making myself what I aspire to be when I noticed his consummate power and art. Yet I have no fears of him in this case. Indeed, I thought once that I saw a chance during that trial when, if I had been on the other side, I could have given him a stab under the fifth rib. Still, I dare say he might have parried it, as Barrington, who was against him, said he would have done."

"How did the case go?"

"They stopped it before it got to the jury. Somehow, *somebody* had mislaid *some* paper, which couldn't be found, and Torrance, what he had asked for at the call, claimed and got a continuance. I heard that they compromised afterward, as the adversary declared that he couldn't afford to wait forever for the whole of his money."

"He talked about a compromise on the night he got here, but after he saw Mrs. Guthrie, he said nothing at all tending that way, but looked intensely confident, and was quite boastful."

"He had his reasons for both, we may be sure."

When Holt had retired to his room, Bond remained.

"Tolly," he said, "I thought a good deal whether or not I should call upon you to help me in this business, and I decided that I ought not. In the first place, I suspected that you are opposed conscientiously to such manner of adjustment. Then, you reside in the town, in which I am almost an entire stranger, and are on terms of friendship with this man's family and family connections. They, or the most of them in such a serious issue must, at least, appear to side with him."

"If you had called upon me, Bond, I might have

agreed to stand with you, especially with intent to try to adjust the matter without resort to a hostile meeting, though, of course, much as I would have regretted, I should have had to go with you to whatever end might result from failure of discussion, and I beg of you again to consider calmly whether or not you may let it re-adjust itself as it has almost done already. Does Miss Jewell suspect anything?"

"No, indeed. That is why I went without Holt to-night. I told her Holt had come up on a little business and would call to see her before he went away. He can mislead her easily. If she knew what we had come for, she would do whatever she could to prevent it. That is what is making her keep her secret. She said to-night that while she lingered in Augusta on her way North she'd tell it to me upon conditions. I knew what *they* would be, and that is the reason that I have been in such haste. But, Tolly, the idea of waiting for the mere lapse of time to set up a good woman's name from it's fall, or even it's decline, by the tongue of such a man as Duncan Guthrie! If she and I both continue to live Miss Jewell is to become my wife. I could never hold up my head in that man's presence afterward, knowing that he remembered how she, unmarried, without a male protector, had been made to suffer first from his ruffian insult, and afterward more keenly, if possible, from his slandering tongue or his slandering silence. The law and religious people, as they ought, discourage duel-ing. I myself am a man of more profound religious feeling than I appear to be. I admit that endurance is a higher virtue than even the justest resentment, measured by the standard of religion, if indeed any degree of re-

sentiment may be called just.   But such virtue pertains
to saints, of whom I am not and I never could hope to
be one, and I could not be made to believe that *he* could
be made contributory to the sanctification of anybody.
The difficulty is that the satisfaction proposed by the
law and religious people is sometimes inadequate or impracticable.   The latter say suffer, endure, forgive, and
be thankful; the other commends to mulct by a suit before the courts in pecuniary damages.   These point to
what to a million of endeavors is unattainable;  the
other offers what in sensitive minds exacerbates instead
of mitigating injuries.   Miss Jewell, a young woman,
a stranger in a strange land, without means, indeed, except the little wage that she earns by laborious employ-
ment of her gifts, seeking to recover from Duncan
Guthrie compensation for wounds to her honor and her
happiness- in mere money!   The dear girl *has* been
saved from utter prostration by the consciousness of
her innocence, and the support of that brave girl, Miss
Macfarlane.   My God!   It nearly made me cry to-
night when I saw upon her face the humble thankfulness that was in her heart!   No, Mr. Tolly!   That
man, however costly it may be to himself, must put
matters where they were on the first day when she came
into this town of Clarke and began her work with all
people's fair opinions and friendly encouragement.   If
he refuses so to do, I shall try to find and let this public
know the reason why.   Good-night, dear friend."

Without another word from either he went out.

## CHAPTER XXIX.

### THE CORRESPONDENCE OF BOND AND GUTHRIE.

About nine o'clock on the following morning as Bond and Holt were sitting on the piazza looking out upon the court-house square, Guthrie, having come down the street from his mother's residence, turned and proceeded to his office. Thither Holt at once repaired.

"Why, Mr. Holt! This is a surprise. I hardly recognized you at first, so far out of your beat; I am really glad to see you. When did you come? Are you just from Augusta?"

"Thank you, Mr. Guthrie, I came in last night with Mr. Bond."

"Yes!" said Guthrie, his cordiality subsiding instantly.

"I have called in order to hand you this note. I will be at the tavern where I shall be pleased to receive and convey to Mr. Bond your answer."

A subdued smile came upon Guthrie's face as he read the note which ran as follows:

"Clarke, June 26, 1828.

"*To Duncan Guthrie, Esq.*

"Sir: On Saturday, the 2nd of last month, you addressed to Miss Sarah Jewell language grossly insulting. This is meant to indicate to you the duty of making in writing distinct recognition of the truth of this complaint, and as distinct admission that nothing in her deportment then or theretofore had authorized you to expect any result other than impunity, because of the remoteness of her family and the absence of any friend to protect her from the outrage or chastise its infliction.

"This will be handed you by my friend Julius Holt, Esq. Yours, etc.,

"CHRISTOPHER BOND."

When he had read the note he threw it upon the table as if it was not of much importance, and said:

"The circumstances give me plenty of time to answer, Mr. Holt; but as I can see no reason for delay, I will do so as soon as I can communicate with a friend who resides just beyond the Savannah River. I will send a message to him forthwith, and I shall hope that he will get here by to-morrow night. If he does, or as soon as he does, I will communicate with Mr. Bond further."

"That will be entirely satisfactory, Mr. Guthrie. We shall await at the tavern the answer that, after advising with your friend, it may please you to make."

"And now, have you time to tell me any news from your fair city?"

"There is nothing to tell, Mr. Guthrie, even if both of us had leisure. I think I must now return to Mr. Bond."

"Then I won't endeavor to detain you longer, Mr. Holt. Good-day."

Holt returned to the tavern, and, having entered the room where Bond sat reading a law book, said:

"Such coolness is commendable, Bond. I hope I shall not disturb it by repeating that I am confident of our not being able to force your man to a challenge."

"Be it so; I only wanted, if I could, to get him away from pistols, at which I've been told that he is quite expert. I'm not much in that way; but if I could have a rifle, I think I would make the gentleman

limp for the balance of his life; for I should only aim
at his legs. He will be so exasperated that I suppose
he will be for doing his work effectually. Still, what I
can do at all with a pistol I can do quickly, if not with
accuracy to boast of, and I'll try to if I can't at least
give him a lame leg before he fires."

That night Holt accompanied Bond to the Wendells; Miss Jewell came down looking almost as radiant
as ever in color and cheer.

"Well, Mr. Holt, I never expected to see *you*
here! What could have brought you so far away from
Augusta, your beloved? It must have been some ex-
ceedingly important law business. I didn't know before
that you practiced in the counties."

"Most persons, Miss Jewell, pretend not to know
that I practice even in Augusta. Yet I must do myself
the justice to say that now and then I receive for col-
lection a promissory note on which the holder knows
that the maker must confess judgment. My practice
outside, except in cases of importance, has not been extensive. Hearing that our common friend Bond—you
will mark the use. of the word ' common ' instead of
' mutual '—yes, Miss Jewell, to go back behind that ex-
planatory clause, hearing that Bond, common as he is
*and* mutual, after one visit to this town, avowedly to
attend court, but, as is well known, for another purpose, had got into a fat case, when he told me that
he was coming to look after it, I fished up a little business myself, and I said to him: ' Bond,' said I, as distinctly and fairly as it is in me to speak, I said, ' Bond, if
you think I won't be too much of a burden, a bore, or
a hindrance, I will go with you.' He said nothing,

and I acted upon his silence.   You don't know it, Miss
Jewell, and with all my adjurations, prayers, and tears
I could never get you to know it, and you never did
know it, and perhaps you will never care about knowing
it, but I was always as devoted to you as Bond, every
bit and grain.   Now!"

"I see, Mr. Bond," she said, "that he's the same de-
ceiver."

"Yes, Miss Jewell, I am forced to admit.   Holt is
a young man who, but for some mistakes, perhaps, in
his early education, I rather think would mean well.
In his speeches to ladies, like that he has just now made
to you, I have sometimes believed that I noticed that,
for the time being, he felt some inspiration of eloquence,
and, indeed, so far as you are concerned, I have often
heard him speak in terms of high, unmixed praise."

"My! praise, honest praise from such a source is
something to be proud of!"

"Not at all, my dear Miss Jewell, not at all," Holt
said.   "Miss Jewell, you see that man there before you,
so cool, so calm, so self-possessed in the midst of successes that he knows he never merited as I would have
done had Fortune vouchsafed for one time to change
the rags with which she has always shown herself to
me, so fortified in his sense of superiority to all mankind, not excepting—and particularly and offensively—
not excepting me?   Well, madam, if you will pardon
the address which the solemnity of the occasion seems
to me to warrant and anticipate, I assure you that I
have often argued with that man and tried my level
best to convince him that you were the finest woman
that he and I ever saw or that we might ever hope to

see again. In time, as if to make another instance of the ingratitude of individuals as well as of republics, he turned upon me, appropriated all my arguments, and you now behold the ruined, desperate person he has made of me, madam!"

With such badinage he occupied most of the time during this visit. Before taking their leave they pleaded that stress of business would prevent their making another call, and that, if they could not get away during the morrow, they must do so early on the following morning.

After Holt had left Guthrie, the latter immediately went home, and, writing a note, dispatched it by Marcus to his friend Charles Leslie, who resided in South Carolina. A man of courage, even pugnacious, he felt a sense of relief at the prospect of settling thus with an equal adversary a matter that had disturbed him considerably. Before nightfall on the next day his friend arrived, and, after a brief conference, a note was sent to Bond running thus:

"CLARKE, *June 27, 1828.*

"*To Christopher Bond, Esq.:*

"SIR: The real or pretended ignorance manifested in your note of yesterday of the courtesy usual among gentlemen shall not obtain for you any imagined advantage that you seek. I decline to hold with you further discussion upon the matter of your complaint.

"This will be handed you by my friend Charles Leslie, Esq. Yours, etc.,

"DUNCAN GUTHRIE."

Early the next morning Bond sent a peremptory challenge, which was promptly accepted, and a meeting was agreed upon to take place on the morning of the fourth day afterward on the Carolina side of the Savannah, near a place known as Sister's Ferry. To avert suspicion from the public, the principals with their seconds left the village, Bond and Holt at once, Guthrie and his friend next morning. Guthrie late that afternoon repaired to his own home, where he spent an hour as before. Opening the piano, he struck softly some of the keys, and seemed as if he were listening to sounds from afar. Letting down the lid, he took into his hands, one by one, the vases that stood upon the center-table of the parlor and the bureau in their bedroom. Taking from his pocket his wife's handkerchief that he yet carried, he moistened it from one of the phials. He walked through the flower garden several times, lingering before shrubs that he knew to be her favorites. He felt that he loved her more and that she was more needful to him than he had ever supposed. He heartily wished that she could see him as he was and know his thoughts of her, and he hoped that if he should survive the dangerous combat in which he was about to engage she might be as happy in the possession of his single love and confidence as he knew she always had yearned and deserved to be.

His mother had been put by Mr. Torrance into a frame so comparatively comfortable that she was little disturbed by his announcement that he must go to Augusta; besides, always averse to having her own affairs known to others, she did not inquire as to the business on which he was going. During the evening they conversed upon indifferent themes. When near bedtime she said :

"You look serious, Duncan, and have been almost ever since Alice has been away. I don't see why you can't be contented and cheerful for a while with me like you used to be."

"Why, mother, I am not thinking of Alice every time you see me looking thoughtful. I do miss her, of course, but my thoughts are mainly of other things."

"Well, my son, the only way I know in order to get along with things that trouble *me* is to try to give up to what I can't help and couldn't have prevented, and to fight and keep on fighting against the rest. I've lived a fighting life, and had to do it to keep myself from being put under people's feet. What you see me now and what I've got around me have all come from fighting  If you once begin to give way to bad feelings they'll grow and grow until they'll actually become a disease, and people will see it and it will make them run over you."

"Mother," he answered, but not with apparent petulance, "when have I ever suffered people to run over me, as you style it? I think I've been able, in what few conflicts I've had with the world thus far, to take care of myself, and I trust to so continue."

"Why, my dear child, I didn't mean to make any insinuations against your bravery. I've never been afraid that anybody that has my blood in his veins could ever be lacking in that. I only meant to convey my idea that resistance is the surest defense to put against trouble—that is, those that are brought by other people. But resistance can become as calm as it is resolute. I learned that for the first time in the talk I had with Seaborn Torrance. What a man he is! I've been feeling of another sort ever since he was here. Well, child, as you've got a journey before you to-morrow, may be you had better go to bed. I shall not sit up much longer."

He was willing to be thus excused. As was her wont sometimes when there was moonlight, she took a walk under the trees. When she had re-entered the house and her maid was making her ready for bed, she said:

"Judy, do you think your Marse Duncan cares as much for me as he did before he was married?"

"Oh, yes'm, mistess. Marse Duncan love you same as befo'. Course he love Miss Alice too, bein' she his wife. He bound do dat, Marse Duncan is; but he ain' forgot his ma, nor he ain' guine to forgit her, nother."

"Don't you tell anybody I asked you that question, hear? If you do, it won't be good for you."

"Law, miss! I never opens my mouf 'bout what you says to me dat way. Ev'ybody on dis place know dat about me."

"I don't, for one; but you be careful. I tell you that for your own good."

---

## CHAPTER XXX.

### SISTER'S FERRY.

WE have heard it said that there is greater courage in declining than in accepting a challenge to fight a duel. This is one of those sayings which, out of respect for religious sentiment, goes without contradiction. At best, however, that seems to be a negative courage

which declines to give special satisfaction in cases wherein any other sort seems inadequate, except that (ulti-
mately the very highest, of course) which comes from
humble, even thankful submission to injustice. The
law provides pecuniary compensation for defamation
and kindred wrongs ; but, as was argued by Bond, the
more cultured and sensitive an innocent person is, the
more revolting is the idea of such compensation, and
the suffering would only be intensified by public judicial investigation. Then, to kill a man whose injury to
another has been most atrocious, without giving him
notice to defend himself, the law calls murder, although
juries, who in the trial of such cases are made judges
of the law as well as of facts, generally, if not always,
acquit. Yet no really brave man, except when im-
pelled by sudden uncontrollable passion, will shoot or
stab deliberately, whatever be the injury received.
Therefore, it may happen that one who suffers most pain
from injury will feel that he most sorely needs satisfaction, and not of that highest sort with which there
can be no doubt that he ought to strive to be content.
It seems a doubtful courage, however, that refuses to
give satisfaction which endangers life when it is the
only one that the injured cares to accept for a wrong
done that he feels to be worthy of death. These words
are not meant as an argument in favor of dueling,
which is justly named barbaric and is plainly forbidden
under the divine law, but merely as remarks on what is
said so often about that higher courage which consists
in keeping away, after wrong done, from the muzzle of
a pistol or the point of a rapier. I am considering the
mere question of courage—a courage that in the times

in which the things in this story took place, in the
absence of more condign penalties imposed by the laws,
municipal and social, kept shut the mouth of many a
defamer and many a defamer's wife, and let the innocent live in peace and security. To those submissive
under persecution our Lord promised extraordinary be-
atitude. Happy, happiest of all are they who, having
opportunities thereto, become entitled to receive it;
but we may depend upon it there are not many occasions wherein clearer instances of physical courage are
manifested than upon a field where each expects either
his adversary or himself to fall.

Both parties succeeded in avoiding suspicion. A
case of critical sickness hindered Dr. Poythress from
accompanying the party, and Guthrie was content with
the attendance of an Augusta physician, Dr. Holly; Dr.
Anton attended Bond. The parties spent the night
previous at farmers' houses not far from the ferry.
The combatants, covered with loose flowing gowns extending to their feet, bowed respectfully to each other,
while the rest exchanged greetings all around. Ten
paces were measured; Guthrie's second won the word.
At its call, Bond fired, instantly followed by his adversary. Both stood entirely still, something of a flush
coming over Guthrie's cheek.

"Aren't you struck, Guthrie?" asked Leslie, in a
low voice, as he went to receive his pistol.

"Hush! I felt my pants tear a little. I miscalcu-
lated where he stood under his gown, and aimed too far
front. I'll avoid that the next shot."

"You look sound, Bond," whispered Holt, "but I
see he made a hole in your gown."

"Stop!" cried Dr. Anton, "Mr. Bond has been wounded."

"Quick! reload quick, Holt!"

But when the pistol was handed to him again and he reached forth to take it, his hand trembled.

"Stop!" cried Dr. Anton, advancing hurriedly, "Mr. Bond has been wounded."

Bond grew pale and would have fallen. Being laid upon the ground, his gown and waistcoat were opened, when it was ascertained that one of his ribs had been broken. The bullet had glanced, and, after perforating the fleshy part of the breast, passed on. He was bleeding freely; but after the fainting spell was over, smiling, he said:

"I suppose I'll have to let Mr. Guthrie go this time, but I'm not quite through with him."

All except Guthrie expressed gratification that the wound was not more serious. He had aimed to kill, and he did not try to hide his disappointment. With his second he re-entered his carriage and drove away. When well off the ground, he said:

"The fellow drew a little blood from me."

"What!"

"Oh, a spoonful. I wouldn't have known it but for the warmth." Unbuttoning his trousers, his under-garments were found to be stained considerably.

"I didn't dream that he was so quick on the trigger; his bullet stung like fire as it grazed my thigh, and the smart may have made mine vary an inch or so from where I aimed."

"You ought to be scolded well, Guthrie, for not letting me know this; I could have got a liniment from Holly. Let me see what it is. Not much, but I should have known it sooner."

"I didn't want Bond to know that he had drawn a drop of my blood. We can get a piece of cloth at the next house, and at the first stream we get to, I'll change my clothes and let you bandage it, if you think it's worth while."

"It's evident, I think, Guthrie, that Bond didn't aim to kill you; for I've been told that he's a fine shot."

"Possibly, he didn't; but I thank him not. I'd rather be killed than lamed."

It was thought best for Bond to lie at the farmer's house for a day, after which, Mr. Dunbar came and had him removed to his own.

Such news always is borne rapidly, and at first is almost always inaccurate. A report reached Clarke just before noon the next day that Bond had been mortally wounded. The arrival of Guthrie and Leslie not long afterward corrected it.

The effect of the sudden announcement and its quick denial affected Miss Jewell, as was to be expected. As soon as she recovered from the shock she sent a servant to Tolly with a note, begging him to come to her at once. He was already on his way there.

"O Mr. Tolly, is it true—I think I can see in your face that it is—that Mr. Bond is not fatally hurt?"

"Not fatally, Miss Jewell, nor very dangerously, I am delighted to say. Mr. Leslie, who was Mr. Guthrie's friend, is at the tavern, and says that one of Bond's ribs was shattered, but that good medical attention and good nursing will set him up in a little while."

"Thank God! Blessed be his holy name! O Mr. Tolly! I didn't dream that that was what Mr. Bond

came here for the last time, bringing Julius Holt with
him, and I didn't suspect that he knew of any reason
why he should fight with Mr. Guthrie; but I've now no
doubt that Mr. Dunbar informed him of what I had requested sister to keep secret. If I had foreseen any
such thing, I would have run away from this town, and
never stopped till I got to Boston. I don't see how
Mr. Bond can ever look me in the face again, after—
after—"

"After having vindicated your good name against
the insult and aspersion of a bad man. That is the
proper ending to your sentence, Miss Jewell."

Looking at him thankfully, she laid one hand upon
his lips, and said :

"There, kiss, if you don't object."

"Oh, me !" he said, when the hand was withdrawn,
" with such pay, a kiss on the hand for a rib, but for my
need of Bond's help, I'd wish that five had been broken
instead of one."

"That speech was a right good one, too," she replied, becoming momentarily hilarious, in the revulsion
of her feelings. "If you had been talking all this time
to Charlotte on that key—but you are all right there, I
think, Cousin Tom. Now, do you want to know for
what specially I sent for you ?"

"No, because I know already."

"But you don't. It was to say that *somebody* has
got to take me to Augusta right away."

"That, my dear cousin, my mind had forecast.
Junkin has my orders to have ready at my call a carriage, horses, and driver for a three-days' journey."

"Tom Tolly !" her outpouring joy giving full expression to her wonderful beauty. " You are a blessed cousin, the best that any poor girl ever had, even by blood! Now, let me tell you. I want that carriage and those horses and that driver, and, last in mention but first in importance, this cousin to be at that gate yonder there not outside of two hours from this time, and as much within as may consist with my said cousin's arrangings for a temporary absence from his important engrossments."

" I am to understand, I suppose, by this haste that your purpose is to assist the surgical treatment of Mr. Bond by the substitution of another and an invulnerable rib."

With a playful push she expedited his departure, and about the time set they were on their journey, which was to require a day and a half. Miss Jewell was delighted to find how well her escort, by varied, cheerful, often bantering chat, could beguile her anxiety. When it was near sunset and they were approaching Wrightsborough, a village in the adjoining county, he said :

" My fair cousin, if it were not for prudential suggestions, wholly concerning yourself, I would get a relay of beasts if they can be had in the village lying so still and unexpectant of us two on yonder rising ground, and rush forward amid the darkness to the place where our knight lies temporarily exhausted by the strife of battle. But I am thinking that one of us, not at all alluding to myself, may grow fatigued after some longer duration of travel, and as the most interesting phase of the case must be delayed till you get there, and it is desirable for you, when there arrived, to be as fresh as

possible, in view of the important scientific operations
intended for his relief, I rather think that we should
take what rest may be got in the unpretentious hostlery,
of which I have had from several travelers a reasonably
good account; but, as it is yours to speak and command, and mine to listen and obey, if you say go, why
we—we just go on, that's all."

"My brave, generous defender and guide, words
could be only fain to express my gratitude for your
readiness to undertake the impossible. For both sakes
we will tarry the night at this inn. I must have regard
not alone for your gallant unselfishness, but for your
somnolence, whose advance is already beginning to appear."

They halted at the tavern, where cleanness, good
cooking, obligingness, and small charge more than
made amends for lack of fineness and variety. Almost
immediately after supper, Miss Jewell asked to be
shown to her chamber. Her escort must have his cigar.
As he sat in a split-bottom chair on the unpaved sidewalk, several of the villagers, some with cigars, most
with pipes, strolled to the tavern door, and as the chat
between the landlord and guests warmed, moved, but
not disrespectfully, nearer.

"Driver tell me you from Clarke, sir."

"Yes."

"And you're the lady's cousin, so she told my wife,
and I don't remember as I ever went anywheres to
find a handsomer, fine-lookiner, nice-behaveder young
woman; she say you takin' her to Agusty to see her
sister."

"Yes. This is a good cigar, and after a good supper, I believe I'll try a couple of them—cigars, I mean, and then, landlord, if my room is ready, I'll go to bed."

"Certainly, sir, whenever you say so. Glad you like. Fact of the business," he continued, with compassionate backward glance to previous administrations, "they was complainin's a'most a constant all the time about the way this tavern was kept, and it come to that, I told my wife—I got her over thar in your county—I told her that me and her, to my opinion, we owed it, not only to the bo'ders, but to the transient people, to take holt of things on these premerses, and show the civilized world that Wrightsborough, when you come to know her, they was stuff in her for a respectable tavern, if nothin' else. My wife, she see the sitooation, and she j'ined in with me, and she rolled up her sleeves, and the consequence is as people sees. But, Mr. Tolly—the lady said that were your name—"

"Yes, sir; yes, sir, and my father's before me."

"That's what people might suppose—onlest there was somethin' wrong somewhere."

Tolly laughed heartily at this merited rebuke for the remark caused by his needless wish, for Miss Jewell's sake, to avoid the man's questionings. The latter saw the advantage he had gained, and said:

"I thought I'd ask you before you went, if it ain't a onfa'r question, if you heerd of the juel that was fit day fo' yisterday mornin' about a female person betwix' two lawyers. I been thinking you must have heerd about it, as one of 'em, lawyer Guthrie, was from Clarke."

"Yes, I had heard of it. Have you any recent news as to how the other party is getting on?"

"Oh, they say he's a-gittin' on lively, but the first news come that he was slew. Everybody here was glad when that was contradicted. They are all on his side, every one of 'em, women worse than men, because the tale is that he was a-fightin' for a poor young schoolmistress that didn' have nobody else to take up for her, bein' so fur away from her people. Yes, sir, that's the sentiment o' these people in this here town, old and young, male and female, special female. They say they don't see how him come to be hit and the t'other skipped."

At that moment a gentleman, while passing, paused, looked through the dusk a moment, then, seizing the guest's hand, cried:

"Why, Tolly, you here? Bless me, but you're about the last man I expected to see."

It was Charles Hawley, a young lawyer, who had come from the county-seat for a visit to his parents, who dwelt in this village.

These had for an hour or more a conversation about the duel and other things, the landlord and some of the villagers taking part. The next morning, when Miss Jewell had risen from breakfast, the landlady, who had put on some of her best things, rose and, approaching her with a small bundle of roses, said:

"Lady, me and mine don't set up for much; but I want you to take these roses and give 'em to the young man you're going to—"

"I thank you, madam," and she turned a reproachful glance of inquiry at Tolly. He hurried away. When she came forth to enter the carriage a scene was there which she never was to forget. A dozen or so girls, from fifteen down to six, clad in their very best, simple, clean, bashful, stepped forward, beginning with the oldest, and, without words, presented her, every one, with flowers.

"What does it mean?" she asked, looking at Tolly with amazement.

"Lady, my most fair and most gracious relative," answered Tolly with high courtesy, "it means that these young ladies, having heard that two warriors have lately clashed arms on account of your ladyship, wished thus to signalize that they were unanimously on the side of him who fought and suffered in your cause; and having heard, further, that if not actually on your way to him, at least you might be in his presence before these sweet but frail memorials shall have withered, they modestly but earnestly desire that you will present them to him in testimony of their exalted admiration and their profound gratitude for his gallantry in your behalf. This manifestation, I beg to assure you, though deemed by myself eminently becoming, was, until a few moments ago, as unexpected to me as to yourself."

Her hand had already lifted her gown, preparing to step into the carriage. She let it go and said:

"Well, Mr. Tolly, you may hide your emotion beneath those courtly words, but my tears must flow, because—because my heart has never been so full!"

She stood and, putting her handkerchief to her eyes, wept freely for several moments. Then she called to her the children, one by one, and embraced and kissed them. When the last came, bare-headed and without shoes, lifting her in her arms, she took from her bosom a pretty phial of essence, and said:

"Take this, darling. It is sweet and precious, but
1 ot nearly as much so as you and your dear companions.
I can never forget you. Now one more kiss from
every one, and may the blessing of God be and abide
with you always!" Then, entering the carriage, followed by Tolly, they continued their journey.

Near by was standing a tall, red-haired, loosely-con-
structed boy, having an uncertain grasp upon the stem
of a huge sunflower. He stared at Miss Jewell during
the whole scene and at the carriage while it was rolling
away.

"Why didn't you give the lady your sunflower,
Andy?" asked one of the gentlemen.

"Well, now, Mr. Avery, you see, I forgot it tell it
was too late. When she hilt up her frock to git in the
carriage my eye got stuck on her foot, and it look so
temptin', and then that lawyer clinched the nail on me
with his speeches so I never understood nare word he
said; and time I could git my idees back, she were in
her carriage and gone. Is that the way they pleads in
court, them lawyers, Mr. Avery?"

"Something like that, Andy, when they've got
nothing to say. You see he was speaking for the girls,
and he had to put up his best."

"Well, he done it."

When the travelers were out of town, Miss Jewell,
drying her eyes, looked at her companion, and said:

"O Mr. Tolly, Mr. Tolly! Such an ovation no princess ever had! No Roman consul triumphing with
chariot and white horses ever felt happier than I did at
the manifestations of those children! 'Happy,' as the
Psalmist says, 'is that people that is in such a case;

yea, happy is that people! ' " Then, almost shouting with laughter, she said: "And oh, that speech! My dear cousin, your greatness, your varied 'greatness, grows upon me every day and every hour!"

She was indeed very, very happy.

They reached the Sand Hills by night-fall.  Learning that Bond was in the house, without taking off her bonnet she went up-stairs and knocked gently at his door.

"Come in," he answered from within.  She entered and stood looking upon his face as he lay upon a couch.

"Why, Sarah Jewell!  That you?"

She went to his side, and kneeling, said:

"Yes; it is I."

---

## CHAPTER XXXI.

### THE RETURN OF GUTHRIE.

THE cry uttered by Miss Jewell at the first report from Sister's Ferry served to make it known to Mrs. Guthrie.  She was walking beneath the trees in her front yard in meditative mood, when, startled, she called to her maid:

"Judy, did you hear that noise over at Mr. Wendell's?"

"Yes'm, mistess.  Sound to me like somebody hurted over dare."

At that moment Mr. Wendell came out through his gate and commenced walking rapidly toward the

heart of the village. Mrs. Guthrie said to her servant:

"You go around to the kitchen and find out what's
the matter. Don't you dare to tell anybody that I sent
you. You're friendly with those negroes over there,
aren't you?"

"Oh, yes'm. I friendly with 'em, dee ain' got nothin' gin me, dem folks ain'."

"I thought so; all niggers are friendly with one another when it comes to finding out all about white folks'
business; but you better not even hint about me wanting to bother myself with anything that concerns them.
Go along, and be quick about it, and don't you stop to
go to palavering with those people; but find out what's
the trouble and come back straight to me."

Judy walked rapidly to the gate, and as rapidly along
the street leading out of town until she had passed beyond view from the Wendell mansion. Then crossing,
she climbed the fence, and shied along that of the yard.
Returning in a few minutes her mistress said:

"You've been gone twice as long as there was any
need for, seems to me. I could have done it myself in
less time. What's to do over there?"

"O miss, bad news; man come dar en tole Miss
Wendell dat Marse Duncan have fit a jule wid dat
young man what been payin' 'tention to Miss Jule en
Agusty, en kilt him."

"Who killed who?"

"Marse Duncan kilt dat ter man."

"The Lord help my soul! Did the man say that
your Marse Duncan got hurt?"

"No, ma'am, de word wus Marse Duncan kilt dat

ter man, en den got in his cayidge en come away from
dar. It wer' Miss Jule dat done de hollerin', for 'cause
dee said de man en her was promussed to git married,
en now she dis'p'inted in her min' bout it. I sorry
for her, dat I is, but I thankful 'twarn't Marse Duncan."

"Did you see Miss Jewell, or hear her?"

"No'm. Dee say she hollered des one lone time,
en den she run up-sta'rs, en Miss Wend'le en Miss Anna dee went long atter her en de swaged her down.
Seem to me I mout a heerd some kind o' moanin' up-
sta'rs dar, but I didn't have no time, 'cause I run to tell
you Marse Duncan safe."

"Oh, my Lord!"

Several times she uttered these words as she walked
toward the house.

"Judy," she said, suddenly turning to her, "put on
a better frock, quick as you can, and go down town,
and see what you can gather up. Ask Mr. Junkin, the
tavern-keeper. He'll be as apt to know as much about
it as anybody else. Get along with you, and don't be so
poke easy."

In a space that to any one else than her mistress
would have seemed marvelously brief Judy reappeared
in satisfactory condition, and she was about to start
with other orders, when her mistress said:

"Stop. Isn't that your Marse Duncan's carriage I
see rising the hill?"

"Yes'm," answered the girl, casting a quick glance
down the street, "dat's Marse Duncan's cayidge, sho';
en de way Markis playin' wid his whip, I jes know he
fetchin' good news!"

With open arms she met her son at the gate, and was greatly relieved for the sake of both to hear that he had not killed his adversary.

"It would have been always on your mind, Duncan, and mine, too. And then somehow it went to my heart when I heard that young woman scream when the report first got to Mr. Wendell's half an hour ago, although I didn't know what was the matter till Judy ran over there and found out. God knows I'm thankful you didn't kill the man! The poor girl is so far away from her home, you know. Come in and sit down. Have anything in particular? You know there's plenty of wine and spirits in the house, and I'll order dinner at once, if you want it."

After dinner she said:

"Duncan, you never did anything to Miss Jewell, I hope, to have to fight a duel about her. I never dreamed that it was as serious as all that. What *was* the matter? My Lord, the fusses and fights that can be raised among men about women!"

"Mother, you know how some people have been hinting about the woman ever since that affair in the woods behind there the first of May. I've said nothing about what occurred there to anybody except Alice. We both concluded to drop her. I suppose she felt insulted, and told Bond, and he sent me a challenge. I know you wouldn't have wished me to decline that."

"No; of course not; unless it could have been settled honorably without going out and shooting at each other. I don't understand it at all. Did you say anything to insult her that day?"

19

"I'd rather not talk about that, mother. I didn't say anything beyond what I felt authorized to say. She seemed to think I did. A man can't always understand such women."

"No, indeed; nor himself either, as to that. I'm deeply sorry. Still, I wouldn't have had you back out if it couldn't be settled. It's obliged to hurt Alice. A married man owes to his wife to be particular, very particular, indeed. Your father used to say, it isn't every game that's worth the candle. He said he saw that somewhere, I forgot where. May be it was some French book. But, my Lord! if you had been killed! It makes me shudder to think about it! Or that other man either, enemy to me as he is, the same as to you; and God knows I never did him any harm. I'm glad I didn't know anything about it before it was all over. I think I should have gone distracted. I feel mightily shaken up anyhow, sometimes, thinking about all I've been through, and have to go through more of one kind and another. Still Seaborn Torrance told me I needn't fret myself about John Stapleton. Hadn't I better let Judy slip around there and tell 'em the man isn't dead, nor isn't going to die? They won't know I sent her. Somehow I hate for the poor thing to suffer when it can be helped. You Judy!"

"It's not worth while, mother; go back, Judy—unless mother wants you for something else. Uncle Dennis stopped the carriage as I came away from Junkin's, where I left Charles Leslie; I told him about it, and I saw him go to Mr. Wendell, who was standing near. There he is now, entering his gate."

The words of his mother cut him deeply, but the

sword's other edge wounded yet more sorely when he heard a shout of joy answering Mr. Wendell's announcement of his news.

"There it is!" said Mrs. Guthrie heartily. "I declare, it does my heart good to hear her! Yes, the fusses that can be raised about women! Let a little talk start about a woman, and men must go to fighting about it, and that, instead of stopping the talk, sets everybody's mouth going. Women ought to know better how to take care of themselves, their own selves. I never wanted anybody to help me take care of myself. The way for a woman to do when people are talking about her—I mean in a way that's scandalous, for nobody can stop all sorts of fault-finding, no more than they can stop the setting of the sun or the rising of the moon—but when its scandalous talk, the best way to do is to hunt up the one that started and demand proof or authority, and brand every soul that can't or won't give it as a liar. I've never had it to do, but that would have been my way of doing it. Instead of that, women get scared and go to crying, and then men get sorry and go to shooting. But that poor girl! Somehow I wish that Alice hadn't turned her back on her, and so started people to wanting to know the reason why, although Charlotte sticks to her and says she's as good as anybody. If so, it's a great pity. It's a pity as it is. It sounds badly for the town that the woman—whatever reason she might have had for a defender—had to send all the way to Augusta before she could get one. But I'm done now. I've said more than I expected to say, and more than I ought, may be, and I'm thankful the thing is no worse than it is. You are going to see

Alice, I suppose. She'll want to hear all about the fra-
cas, of course."

"Not for several days, mother. She'll hear in time
all she needs to know. I shall not be in a hurry to go
up there."

"Well, let's go in. You ought to have something
after all you've been through. Come along in."

## CHAPTER XXXII.

### ANOTHER HOSTILE MEETING.

Peterson Braddy was as well pleased at the institution of the suit in behalf of his friend as if he had
been expecting the whole condemnation money for himself. He was a person who never had tried to conceal
his sentiments or his feelings, and who, if he had so
tried, would never have succeeded. In public he spoke
freely about what he called the big case, not with the
remotest notion of affecting public opinion in advance
of the trial, but because he could not keep silent.
Honorable to every degree, he would have spoken the
same as if he had no special affection for Stapleton, nor
cause of personal resentment against Duncan Guthrie,
although he doubtless took pleasure in the prospect of
the discomfiture that was to befall one whom he cordially disliked. It happened several times upon the
street that when some one had expressed a doubt as to
the result of the attempt to set aside a will that had

been acted upon and acquiesced in so long, he proposed to wager in the proportion of ten to one.

"Gent'men, I'm a poor man ; not *dead* poor, I don't mean, not poor enough to be not able to raise ten dollars on a pinch, and I'm willing to stake it along with any other man's—*one* dollar, by the eternal—that that will is going to git kicked out of court."

People knew that this was meant merely as an emphatic way of expressing confidence in his own judgment and foresight, without any notion of forestalling the opinions of others. Despising him as Guthrie did, yet it fretted him to know that whenever his own name was mentioned by Braddy, it was with language hostile and meant to be regarded as contemptuous. Still he remembered to have tried to put upon the Braddy family a thing that was hard to bear, the full extent of which had not been made known to Peterson. Therefore, when not too inconvenient, he avoided being where he was. Latterly, however, he had been angered several times when some of Braddy's talk about the suit had been reported to him, and he had nearly decided to take some notice of it. He did not appear on the street until the morning after his arrival. After supper his mother made no allusion to the duel. She seemed to feel that he had already suffered enough for what she believed to be only an imprudence, and, therefore, with as much cheer as she could ever get up, she had talked and listened until bedtime. Never, as she thought, had she felt so proud as the next morning when he came down dressed with unusual care. He had decided to do no work that day, but go among the villagers to get the congratulations of his friends and be looked at by all for the danger he had passed with courage and safety. Braddy, only late the last night having heard of the duel, had come into town to get all the news about it. He was sitting with a knot of men in a chair on the sidewalk before the door of one of the stores. Guthrie, in the act of passing, paused and saluted generally, and when he noticed Braddy, took a step onward as if he thought well to avoid him as usual; but noticing that he had not returned his salutation, and suspecting that he could read in his face increased hostility, contempt, and defiance, he waited a short while, as if reluctant and undecided what to do, then said:

"Pete, I hear that you have been proposing to bet some of your superabundant cash on the results of certain lawsuits?"

"Lie, sir," answered Braddy, leaning his chair against the wall, smiling, and putting into his looks as much as possible of the pleasant contempt that he felt. "I've been offering to bet on but one single *one*; and as I can't git my bet took, I don't know but what I'll make another, doublin' the odds."

"You are a foul-mouthed whelp of an intermeddler," replied Guthrie, red with anger.

"That's a lie of your own make, sir," retorted Braddy, his color unchanged and his eyes opening wider. "It's a lie, like a hundred you've told, mostly about women; and for your last before the one you've just let out of your mouth I can't understand for my life how the bullet that man shot at you a' Thursday didn't go plum' through your mean heart!"

Guthrie stooped and slapped him upon the face, and as he rose, struck him with his cane and thrust him against the wall. Braddy drew from his pocket the small pistol he sometimes carried, cocking it with the hand that held it. Guthrie, seizing his wrist, pressed it downward; the weapon was discharged, the ball entering his groin.

Relaxing his hold, he said:

"That ends it, ends it all; gentlemen, he has killed me!"

They took him into the store and laid him upon the counter, letting his head rest upon a pile of blankets. Of Dr. Poythress, who ran thither from his office on hearing the report, he asked:

"How long have I got, Poythress?"

"A very short while, I am afraid, Guthrie. Gentlemen, please send for his mother at once."

"No, no, no! please, don't! O Alice! Oh, poor mother! Tell them not to prosecute Braddy. He was not to blame. He ought to have done it before. Beg Mr. Bond— O my God!"

These were all the words he said.

A boy ran up the street loudly crying the tragedy. Mrs. Guthrie was sitting on her piazza. In her hands was some delicate needle-work, for she was never willing to be idle. She had looked at her son as he left her house until he had disappeared from her sight, and never had she felt greater admiration, pride, and fondness as he went forth among the towns-people. Hearing the tumult, she dropped her work, rose, and listened eagerly. Getting down the steps, she was making for the gate when she distinguished the words of the cry as it was borne along. Uttering a fearful shriek, she rushed forward. The clergyman whose church she mostly attended met her just outside the gate, and, taking her arm, besought her to let him carry her back.

"Loose me, sir!" she screamed, "and get out of my way, or I'll call to Moses to unchain the dog and set him on you! . You think I want your pitiful, deceitful, peddling *prayers?* I don't *believe* it! It isn't an hour since he went from my sight, the handsomest, bravest, best man among you all! It's a *lie!* I *know* it's a lie! It *shall* be a lie!"

Breaking away, she ran on with all her might for a hundred yards, when suddenly she fell, striking her forehead against the root of a tree that stood upon the sidewalk. When they assisted her to rise she made no resistance to their leading her back, and, speaking not a word, looked pleasantly from one to another while they undressed and put her to bed. The body of her son was brought to the house; but of this she was never made aware, and, for the remaining weeks of her life, all recollection of his being seemed to have been obliterated from her mind.

---

## CHAPTER XXXIII.

### REGRETS: A LATE REVIVAL OF AFFECTION.

IT seems to be of the economy of life that much of the expiation of guilt is done by the innocent. These sometimes are beset more than evil doers by regret and remorse. Indeed, I am not sure that those who have had profoundest insight into the interior being of mankind, if asked what emotion in its just reality was most rare, would answer—remorse. From a man's own odiousness he must try to turn his eyes in order to get a glimpse of what is, or what he believes to be, good in his individual being; and so he represses as much as he can of the recollection of his evil deeds, or pleads extenuation that would avail little before any other tribunal than that of his own mind. Contrariwise, the innocent, whose lives have been mixed—in degrees of confidence, fondness, and love—with those persons who, if not grossly evil, are unscrupulous regarding some subjects of vital morality, when retribution has come sudden and in awful form, are apt to reproach themselves for their own imagined neglect of the means which might have prevented what has befallen. The first shock upon Alice Guthrie was perhaps more appalling than it would have been if her married life had been happier. It was impossible for her to remain in such a frame for a very long time; but the thought that the man whom she had loved so dearly, her grief for whose infirmities had been the more imbittered because they had been indulged in almost open disregard of the feeling she had for him, was now dead, wrung her heart with an agony more painful than if he had been what she had trusted that he was when she gave herself to him. Perhaps if she had submitted without complaint to the rule to which, as her husband, he was entitled; perhaps if she had taken into account on what a wider, ruder, more varied, more undefined, and more willful scale are a man's wants than a woman's; perhaps, admitted that she had any right or duty to counsel at all, if she had counseled with more meekness and humble fear; perhaps if she had not come away from him when she did, and, as it were, left him deserted in the midst of sudden great trials when he had most need of sympathy and counsel; perhaps if she had decided to accept and endure all that had come and all that was to come from merging her own lesser being into his greater; perhaps—perhaps, oh, perhaps! he might have been saved from such an end and led a life her own part of which, if not happiness, might have had content.

Fortunately she was with her parents, especially her father, just and judicious, as he was faithful and fond. He let her fall prostrate at the coming of the dreadful news, and did not lift her up; he counseled her mother to let her lie where she was, and wait until her self-accusings had exhausted themselves and her own heart would cry out for others to answer them as she could not. Not waiting too long for that time to come, in brief words fitly chosen he pleaded her cause. If it gave an added pain to know that it was a relief to him that she had been taken out from a connection that ought not to have been made, and that in some other way must have been rent asunder by a force that might have been yet more unhappy, yet she could not but listen to his wise, affectionate comfortings and appeals to her own instincts to self-preservation against remorse for things for which she in no wise was culpable, but which, as a true woman and a true wife, she had labored to prevent.

Her father accompanied her to the funeral. They sojourned at her own house until it was over. She would have returned with him but for the condition of Mrs. Guthrie. To Mr. Macfarlane, who mentioned administration on the estate, Mr. Ludwell answered, without consulting with his daughter, that neither he nor she would undertake it; and he added that she would decline to receive any of the property except what had been given by himself. After that, Tolly, at the suggestion of Mr. Macfarlane, who foresaw that Mrs. Guthrie's incompetency would be perpetual, took that trust upon himself.

It was touching to see how all these things wrought upon Peterson Braddy. Horrified at the result of his encounter with Guthrie, his anger yielded immediately to remorse and compassion. Weeping aloud, he went to the sheriff and said that he was ready to be taken to jail.

"Go on home, Peter," answered the officer. "I'm not afraid of your being out of the way when I call for you."

Returning home, when his mother was told what he had done she wept sorely, but said:

"Well, my son, I'm sorry from the bottom of my heart; but that man had tried to hurt you and this family more than you knew of. We would not let Emily tell you all for fear you'd do what you've just done. I'm thankful that we did not, and that at the last you were acting in self-defense."

"What, ma!" he said, momentarily ignoring his own misfortune. "My God! did Billy Pruitt take Emily not knowin' how——"

"O Peterson, my dear son," she quickly interrupted, "it was not anigh as bad as you seem to think. Duncan Guthrie had flattered the child into believing that he was in love with her, and, if it had not been found out in time, he might have ruined her; but when her mother and me told her what he meant by some of the words he spoke to her she was scared nearly out of her life, and she made her mother go straight to William and tell him all about it. William saw how it was, and he said he wanted her the same as before; and well he might, for she was as innocent as a baby of anything wrong more than such little vanity as most girls have that's as pretty as she was. William wanted to go to the young man and have a fight with him; but we wouldn't let him, and we made him promise not to mention the matter to you."

He bit his lips to repress another pang of resentment. It passed away, and afterward he was never heard to mention Guthrie's name.

Mrs. Guthrie lay upon her bed, and did nothing except in meek obedience to those around her. She seldom spoke, and when she did it was as if she was trying to conciliate and lull an infant. One day Alice laid by her the little Caroline. She looked at it fondly, and, for a moment or two, fumbled with the button on the neck of her gown. Then releasing it, she said in a whisper:

"No, Ritter, no; she is not hungry, she is asleep already. Lay her in her crib, and be careful not to wake her."

One morning, after a long sleep, she awoke and seemed to be troubled.

"Where *is* Caroline?" she asked piteously. "I let her go to her Aunt Louisa's to show little Charlotte how to play with her doll. Ritter ought to have brought her back before now. Won't some of you please go and hurry them on home? I'll be much obliged to you."

In a few moments her face cleared, and she said:

"Ah! here she is! Thank you. Pretty child, isn't she? That'll do. The rest of you may go now." Then she expired.

---

## CHAPTER XXXIV.

### DISMISSAL OF THE SUIT.

At the October term of the court, when the case of *John Stapleton,* etc., vs. *Hester Guthrie* was sounded, Tolly answered, requesting the judge to enter upon the docket "Dismissed." Then Mr. Torrance rose, and said:

"May it please the Court: As counsel for the respondent in the case which my brother Tolly has just prayed your Honor to dismiss, I feel it my duty to say a few words in explanation of some of her actions which were not well understood. For several years, as your Honor may have heard, the general mind of this community, when it has been rather pointedly condemning her deportment toward some members of her family, has speculated with more or less interest upon the causes which induced a discrimination so unreasonable, apparently so unnatural. It is known, however, that during her wedded life she mingled little in other society than that of her own home, and in almost none since the death of her husband. I need not argue that such seclusion from human intercourse must make few

the chances of cure from any infirmity—to be both
candid and just, I should rather say malady—of understanding, and even keep from nearest neighbors the
knowledge of its existence. Almost at the beginning
of the confidential relations between her and myself as
her counsel, I detected that her intellect had been mis-
led by delusions which of all seem most unhappy, and
therefore most to be compassionated. Ardently, intensely, passionately affectionate by nature, persuaded
that from some members of her family the returns received were inadequate to what she lavished upon them,
she had not strength to resist the impulsion which such
a delusion imparts toward resentment that, with beings
like hers, is perhaps the most grievous of misfortunes.
It is the more grievous when the sufferer exaggerates
both her own and the corresponding affections of others
to whom she turns through the instinct of forefending
absolute, abject despair. Of like origin was her unrea-
soning adherence to those, so named, class distinctions
whose inevitable disappearance in the changing conditions of our social system thoughtful minds must foresee and her passionate hostility to a union which during its brief career was signally blessed. To this infirmity it was easy for one admitted within her confidence to discover were attributable her strange neglect
on one side, on the other her inordinate favoritism and
the eager energy with which, in hope of holding on to
the only love which she believed to be hers, she strove
for the continued accumulation of what, estimating by
a standard too often true, she regarded most contributory to that end. In the case wherein to outsiders her
natural affection seemed to have been obtunded, its very

intensity was the source of its disappointment. These
words of mine have abundant proof in the fact that on
her bed of death the Divine Being mercifully let her last
infatuation take a happy form, when, in her imagination, the one whom she seemed to have discarded, became again a little child and was fondled upon her
breast.

"I am free to say, may it please your Honor, that
among my clients, even among all my acquaintances, I
have never known a person in whom the sense of truth
and general uprightness was more pronounced. Had
she lived to make answer to this complainant's bill, not
only would she not have contradicted or sought to
avoid a single allegation that she believed to be true,
but she would have insisted upon discovering other
facts unknown to the complainant, even if assured that
such discovery would have rendered vain all resistance
to the case. She solemnly believed that everything
done by her was honorable and just. But there never
would have been protracted litigation. A proposal
would have been made at this term of the court for a
settlement which, from my knowledge of complainant's
counsel and himself, I am sure would have been accepted. I thank the Court for its indulgence."

When he ceased, Bond, who a month before had
married Miss Jewell, rose, and, with much feeling,
said :

"May it please your Honor, the words just spoken
by my brother Torrance can not but impart much relief
to all minds, to none more gratefully than my own; for
there can be no doubt that to necessary degrees they
are applicable to the respondent's unhappy son. To

me, what time I held his acquaintance, it became a matter of much surprise that one so variously gifted, so fortunate in possession inherited and achieved, in hope and in prospect, diverged into ways which an understanding well balanced must foresee can lead only to misfortune. I am profoundly gratified to believe that such eccentricities were moved by influences which the very strongest and most valiant can never wholly overcome. Therefore I feel all the regret, and my mind and my heart pay all the honor that belong to the memory of Duncan Guthrie."

Mrs. Macfarlane, when these speeches were reported to her, wept many, but they were thankful tears. She remembered that in the girlhood of her sister their mother had suffered much anxiety regarding the former's sanity, and once had spoken of it to their father, but he had ignored it with much anger, and so allusion to it was never made again.

---

## CHAPTER XXXV.

### ALICE RETURNS TO BROAD RIVER.

TAKEN again to the bosom of her parents, Alice did not try to forget, unhappy as most of it had been, the experience of her married life. She would not deny to her heart that she had loved dearly the husband so gifted to win an ardent, trustful young woman's love. The singleness of her devotion had intensified the pain that had come with the discovery of selfishness that amounted to dereliction in the sense of honor. These her mind must remember along with the fond things; but mingled with a sense of deliverance from a union which had fallen so soon into disaster were a sorrow, at times profound, almost passionate, that such had been its destiny, and a pity often overflowing in tears for him who, with such recklessness, had ruined himself.

Yet the innocent can not always go bowed down, and their resilience from self-reproach, although not marked by outward sign, must be gladsome. In time the freshness and some of the cheerfulness of girlhood came back. Thankful to know that Mrs. Guthrie's understanding was proved to have been so much impaired, more painful must have been the recollection of her són's infirmities if her heart had not pleaded condonement of what inheritance and misdirected indulgence had made inevitable.

Some months after her return, Stapleton, with his son, made a two days' visit. Her parents were impressed by him much and wondered that such a man could have been ever an object of dislike. They did not see him again for more than a year. He then proposed to take back his daughter, but was gratified when Alice answered, no, not yet. In this while he continued to live at his home, trying, without much success, to make it look as during the time of his wife. Braddy often rode down, and, in his old-fashioned way, sometimes jested at his crude attempts to prune the shrubbery and train the vines. He would have chided him, perhaps, for not making more personal showing of the large estate that had devolved to his children, but that such chiding would have induced thoughts that he must not indulge.

20

On his next visit to the Ludwells, he was dressed with careful regard to prevailing fashion, and wore the air of a serious but undisturbed man of the world.

"I'm very glad you came, Mr. Stapleton, but why didn't you bring Alan?"

He looked at her on whose face was a sheen like that of maidenhood, and answered:

"Not this time, Alice. I decided not to bring him this time."

Grief and solitude soften the manners of a good man. On him comes not the wearing that often oldens women. Manful always, living in memory of a great loss had enhanced a dignity and courteousness that were very attractive. He was to remain two nights and a day.

A few rods in the rear of the mansion the ground declined abruptly about a hundred feet to a bold spring of water. Around this was a dense growth of trees and various shrubbery, among whose thickets, thrushes, cat-birds, fly-catchers, and other songsters, flitted and chirruped. Several rustic seats were around. Hither Alice often retired, mornings and afternoons, to spend an hour in reading and meditation. Stapleton accompanied her there the evening before he was to leave. Sunset came on while they were talking about the engagement of Tolly and Charlotte Macfarlane.

"Well," said Stapleton, "the visit has done me good, and I have put off till now to tell you what was my chief purpose."

She looked up, her eyelids trembled, and she turned her face away.

"That was to ask you to marry me, Alice."

Some tremor was in his voice, but the brief directness of his words showed the feeling of a right to say them, even if without a thought of anything upon which he could lay a hope.

"O Mr. Stapleton!" she said, as if overwhelmed with confusion, "*how* could you ask such an impossible thing!"

Covering her face with her hands, she wept almost aloud.

"Alice, I foresaw that the announcement of such a wish would be painful to you, although I can not but believe that you must have suspected that it was to come at some time or other. I have studied my heart, and tried to discipline its feelings. The result is, I have decided to follow what I can not, and am not willing to resist. I expected a refusal; but I beg you not to make it positive and perpetual, unless you feel that it is not possible for your regard for me ever to become different from what it has been. I know you will answer me candidly, as you have always done with everybody. I am going to put to you a question which I have, I think, a right to ask, If I have, I think you ought to answer it. If the thought, or the apprehension that I might address you as I have done just now, ever entered your mind, among the reasons that made you turn away from it was there the feeling that in no circumstances could my suit ever have prevailed?"

The paleness disappeared from her cheek, and a distinctive blush took its place.

"Mr. Stapleton—if I were to answer that question —but I can not! I—O Mr. Stapleton!"

She rose, her face suffused with scarlet, and said:

"Come, let us return to the house. Not another word must I hear upon that subject, now or ever again." And she started to move away.

"Alice!" the call, low as it was, sounded as coming from one in authority. Still seated, as she turned her face back, he continued:

"I will say no more upon that subject now; but there are one or two things which I want you to hear. I loved Caroline with a love as entire as any man could feel for a woman so richly worthy of it. As I felt toward her before my marriage with her, so now I feel toward you. There is no mystery in that, and no dereliction of loyalty. I should never seek another wife if I did not believe that I should love again as I loved her. And now one more. I am going back home to-morrow, to be away six months. Then I shall return. During that while I shall not write to you, and I solemnly ask that you do not write to me, unless it be about my child or upon a subject other than that which I have just named. I make another request, the motive of which I am not afraid of your misunderstanding. That is, that before that period expires you will let your parents know all that I have now said. But to these requests I ask no promise. Now I will return with you to the house."

Never had he shown to such advantage as during this visit. Alice was glad to get from the light of the supper table to the piazza. During the evening, sitting in the shadow of one of the pillars, she listened as, unconstrained, respectful, clear, he chatted mainly with her father. At breakfast, next morning, she showed that she was embarrassed by the unusual glow that she felt to be upon her face.   When the baby was taken from her to be kissed good-by she put out her lips but for a moment, then extended her arms back to Alice.

Smiling, he said :

"She feels that she-belongs to you, Alice."

"So she does ; but I will see that she does not forget you."

On a fine morning before the tavern door a carriage stood, the horses' heads turned toward Broad River.

"Good-by, Jack!" said Peterson Braddy.   "God A'mighty bless you, Jack!"

He turned away, and tears were in his eyes.   Immediately Stapleton entered, and upon his mind was no shadow.

**THE END.**